For my Auntie Lizzie. *Iechyd da!*

Where there is no wine there is no love.

Euripides

the West Country Winery

Lizzie Lovell

ALLEN&UNWIN

First published in Great Britain and Australia
in 2019 by Allen & Unwin

Allen & Unwin
c/o Atlantic Books
Ormond House
26–27 Boswell Street
London WC1N 3JZ
Phone: 020 7269 1610
Fax: 020 7430 0916
Email: UK@allenandunwin.com
Web: www.allenandunwin.com/uk

A CIP catalogue record for this book is available from the British Library.

Paperback ISBN 978 1 78649 837 3
Ebook ISBN 978 1 78649 836 6

Printed in Great Britain

10 9 8 7 6 5 4 3 2 1

Autumn

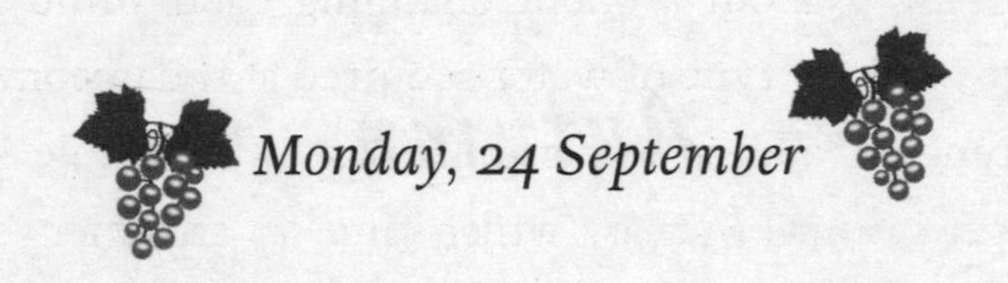

Monday, 24 September

It was supposed to be a normal Monday family supper. Sausage casserole and green beans. Quick. Easy. Fairly nutritious. But mainly quick.

We have a routine. A plan.

Every Monday, Rob does the school run both ways – seeing as it's band practice and impossible for Ruby to lug a harp around on the bus. Scarlet either goes along for the ride or makes her own way depending on which mood she's in: hormonal or murderous. My job, first thing, is to take the casserole out of the freezer and pop it in the pre-set oven so that when the four of us are reconvened back here, the one night we can all manage to be under the same roof at the same time, it will be bubbling away nicely.

It's not a lot to ask. You would think.

Unfortunately, stuff happens and I don't particularly like it if I'm not prepared, though I'm usually adaptable. At least, I reckon so – my colleagues and family might say otherwise.

Tonight has not gone according to plan.

I am cornered by Declan on my way out of the office – something about a client changing their mind last minute over the type of water required at the upcoming conference – adding ten minutes to my schedule so I don't get in until 6.30, by which time an argument's in full flow.

'You are not going to be a bloody vegan!' Rob's face is puce and marbled like an old boozer, his wiry frame jutting at awkward angles. A slightly charred sausage casserole sits between them on the dining table, its aroma filling the room.

'I haven't had an animal product or by-product for five days and you haven't even noticed, so what's the problem?' Scarlet's standing in her usual pose, hands on hips, defiant, deadly.

'It's bloody inconvenient, that's the problem.'

'It's more inconvenient for the animals.'

'Don't be a smart-arse. Nobody likes a smart-arse.'

'I don't care about being liked. I just don't want to eat dead things. We could swap the rotting flesh for Linda McCartney sausages.'

'I don't want Linda McCartney sausages,' Rob whines. 'How am I supposed to survive on Linda McCartney sausages? My hair's falling out as it is and my muscle's turning to fat.' He points at his stomach area. There might be just the smallest bulge, but he's not doing badly for a forty-two-year-old – although a forty-two-year-old who sounds more like a teenager, and we already have two of those in the house. One of whom is right now as bright red as her name suggests, the high colour of her father.

'What's Chrissie going to say?'

'I don't know, what *is* Chrissie going to say?' Then, catching sight of me, 'In fact, why don't you ask her?' Scarlet points a finger in my direction.

Rob spins round, finally noticing me standing in the kitchen doorway, briefcase still clasped in my clenched hand, heels still clamped on my tired feet. 'Oh, I didn't see you there.' He checks his Fitbit. 'You're late, aren't you?'

As if I need to be reminded. I'm about to open my mouth and respond but in that moment, seeing father and daughter reflecting each other's stubbornness, I realize I don't have the energy. So I make a sharp exit, retreat down the hallway, take off my shoes, and head upstairs to get changed.

Our bedroom used to be a sanctuary of calm and serenity but recently that doesn't seem to be working out so well. Rob has implanted an exercise bike in the corner – cycling being his latest obsession – and Ruby is currently ensconced on my favourite piece of furniture, my grandmother's cocktail chair, plucking away at her harp.

'Hi, Mum. You look terrible. Do you like this?'

I do feel terrible so I perch on the bed to gather myself and listen to her play. The relaxing, whimsical notes of Joanna Newsom fill the air.

'Actually, I really do like it,' I confirm after a trance-like few minutes.

Ruby's cupid lips turn into a big smile. She's very good and the harp is very soothing. The harp is also very big. Too big to fit in the bedroom shared with her stepsister, so she comes into my room – our room – to practise.

'I *really* like it, Ruby, but haven't you played enough for one day?'

'I want to get this piece right,' she says, brow furrowed in concentration. 'And it means I don't have to listen to those two shouting at each other.' She continues to run her fingers across the strings and I remember the first time she had a go on a harp, her hands so small I never thought she'd be able to make a tune.

'You all right, Mum?' She stops for a moment, turns her serious eyes upon me. Deep brown eyes, sometimes murky, other times bright, like amber. In fact, my mother suggested I call her Amber, but Ruby was the only name Nathan and I could agree on. Actually, that was the only thing that Nathan and I could agree on. '*Mum?*'

'Oh, yeah, sorry, Ruby. I'm just a bit frazzled, but I'll be OK after a glass of wine and some dinner.' I start to take off my work clothes and decide it's already pyjama time. 'Did you know Scarlet's gone vegan?'

'Yeah,' she says, as if it's old news. 'She'll get bored.'

'You reckon?'

'Last month it was raw food. It'll be something else next month.'

'I dread to think.'

'Don't worry, Mum,' she says. 'Let's go downstairs and eat. Scarlet can have beans on toast. That's vegan, right?'

'Yes, definitely vegan.'

We share a smile.

'OK, then. Just let me get changed.'

Ruby slips out, quiet as anything. Only her harp remains, a reminder that my daughter is an angel. And my stepdaughter... Not so much. But I love them the same. I've known Scarlet since she was a tantrumming toddler. I know her moods will pass, her emotions are changeable. I almost wish some of that passion would rub off on Ruby – quiet, shy, self-contained Ruby – but that really would be asking for trouble.

AN HOUR LATER and we've eaten. Ruby joined her sister in the baked-bean feast and put forward the idea that she might like to be a vegetarian – not a *vegan* because she could never give up cheese – so there's plenty of rotting-flesh casserole left over for Rob to consume at work tomorrow after his Friday-lunchtime spin class. Now he's disappeared and I can hear the whirr of him above, in our bedroom, pedalling away on the exercise bike, giving himself indigestion. The girls are doing homework – they're pretty good at getting on with it, I'll give them that, even Scarlet who finds concentrating much harder than focused Ruby. This gives me the chance to catch up on some work of my own at the cleared kitchen table; there are a few loose ends to tie up ahead of Saturday's conference.

I'm just contemplating a second glass of Merlot when the phone goes. The landline. There's only one person who uses this number – apart from the occasional stray nuisance caller who has escaped my eradication – and this person uses the landline because, where she lives, there isn't a single bar of signal unless you climb up the steep hill behind the house.

Mother. Or 'Eve', as she likes to be known.

'Hello, Christabel.'

My mother is the only person allowed to use my official, ridiculous name. I don't remember my father as he was gone before my memory was even a thing, though I sometimes wonder when I catch a whiff of old-man tobacco... But really I hardly ever think of him because there's been no need – not when I have my glorious hippy Eve and my larger-than-life stepdad, Des, exasperating and infuriating as they are.

'We've got a bit of a problem.'

'Oh? What's happened?'

'Calm down, my darling. It's nothing too serious.'

'Serious? Oh my God. Serious?'

'I said it's *not* serious. It's my wrist. I tripped over a vine and fell awkwardly. I'm in plaster. It'll be fine. Though the lovely doctor thinks I could have osteoporosis but that's not what I'm worried about.'

'Osteo... Wait, *what*?'

'It'll be fine. I'll eat extra yoghurt. The problem is the wine.'

'Should you be drinking?'

'Of course I should be drinking! But it's the vineyard I'm worried about. We're going to harvest this weekend.'

My mother, the winemaker. The very unsuccessful, terrible winemaker.

'Bit early, isn't it?'

'The grapes are ready. Never seen them so plump and juicy. And there's just so many of them this year.'

'I've been telling you for ages to get some contract pickers in. You can't always depend on the neighbours.'

'The neighbours love it, you know they do.' She's using that tone of voice and I know what she'll say next. 'It brings us all together as a community.'

Eve's all about the community. Ever since she lived on a commune back in the day when I was just a bun in her oven.

'You can't rely on their goodwill.'

'Of course I can rely on their goodwill. Besides, they get paid well.'

'In wine.'

'What's wrong with that?'

I want to ask my mother if she's actually got any taste buds but I can't deflate her. This is her latest passion. One that's lasted longer than Jimi Hendrix or LSD or hot yoga. I want to ask her if that's perhaps *why* the business is failing, because they're giving the wine away, but she's yabbering about the difficulty of recruiting extra volunteers, Des's gout and inability to bend down, the uncommonly harsh winter, wet spring and long hot summer which have meant a bumper crop, and it's hard to inform her that enthusiasm – and hers is as strong as ever – isn't enough to succeed in business.

'Are you managing, you know, financially?'

'Christabel, really, don't be vulgar. Of course we're managing. We don't need much.'

They live off Des's dwindling capital accrued when he was a trendy painter back in the sixties, producing vast kitschy canvases of buxom, big-eyed Tretchikoff-style women. Including one of my mother, who was his model for a time. It takes pride of place in their living room, above the inglenook fireplace, so that when you're trying to watch the telly of an evening, you're distracted by my mother's youthful nudity. Now she's sixty-nine with a broken wrist, possible osteo-whatsit and no cash in the attic.

'Des isn't exactly known for his sobriety or moderation. If you want to continue living the good life, then maybe you should consider giving up on the—'

'Absolutely not.'

'But—'

'It's our livelihood.'

A pause – while I tick off in my mind all the ways they've tried to eke out a living over the years, all those schemes that never quite paid off, never allowed them to put in double glazing or central heating. 'It's not really your livelihood though, is it, Eve?'

'Well, maybe not our livelihood exactly, but it is our *passion*.'

Passion. There's that word again.

'You could... er... get another passion?'

A humongous sigh. 'Sometimes, I wonder if I actually pushed you out of my birth canal. You don't understand the very concept of passion.'

Maybe I don't. Which is just as well because some of us have to keep our feet on the ground. I take a deep breath, blurt it out. 'You could consider... downsizing? Maybe getting a... bungalow?'

'What?! Christabel, really, no.' Eve makes an unfathomable noise – somewhere between a snort and a curse. 'This is our home. *Your* home.'

Home.

This word has emotional meaning, I know that. And I do love it, Home Farm. That big old sprawling heap set in its few acres, nestled in the bosomy Devon hills, once part of the great Chudston Estate with its woodland, farmland, pasture, gardens and a whopper of a country pile, otherwise known as 'next door'. It was my home too, where Dad's mother took us in after he'd gone. My grandmother of the cocktail chair on which Ruby plays her harp. And then when Grandma died, the house was left to Eve. I was eight years old and I'd lost both my dad and my gran. But by the time I was nine, Des had moved in and we were a family. Unfortunately, he also moved in his plethora of paintings; they'd plummeted in price as fashions changed (which is why there's still a stack of canvases in the studio). Des took on commercial work to help pay the bills, enabling Eve to continue doing her stuff – stuff which included running a smallholding, steering a women's consciousness-raising group, and keeping me in knitted ponchos and patched flares. Oh, those schemes of theirs...

'Christabel? Are you still there?'

'Yes. I'm still here.'

'This is your inheritance we're talking about. Home Farm will be yours one day. And then, in turn, the girls'. How can you suggest we sell it?'

'Because I want you to be safe and secure *now.* Des is nearly eighty, for goodness' sake. And besides, I won't ever move back to Devon. I love living in London. I love my job. I love my two-bedroomed terrace. It's all we need. We have a cleaner and she can give it a going-through in a couple of hours. And there's no grass to cut in the courtyard.'

Eve sighs, desperately holding in a whole list of reasons why I should get my family out of London, but she knows better than to reel them off. 'We'll manage,' she says. 'We always do.' A pause. 'Though it would be good if you could help out. To get the harvest in? As I said, it's a bumper crop this year. Can you make it down this weekend?'

'It's definitely going to be this weekend?'

'Yes. We need to beat the rain that's forecast from next Monday onwards. And the grapes will be perfect.'

And here's the thing. In the five years since they planted the vines, the last two have produced some fine grapes. They should make fine wine. But... something always goes wrong.

'It's rather short notice. I've got a conference on Saturday and the girls have only just gone back to school.'

'They needn't miss any school. Come down Friday night and leave Sunday evening. Four of you picking for two days will be such a—'

'But the conference...'

'You really need to be there?'

'Of course I need to be there!'

'But Christabel. Do you *really* need to be there? If I know you, you'll have it planned military style and Declan will be able to take the reins for once. Give the poor bloke a chance. He's perfectly capable.'

Eve knows how to grind me down. She knows me better than anyone and it is incredibly annoying.

'All right, *Mother*. Let me ask Rob.'

Eve chooses to let the word 'Mother' slip by; she has something bigger in her sights. 'You don't always have to ask Rob,' she says.

And there we have it.

'I *don't* always ask Rob.'

Another pause, another space where both of us contemplate whether it's worth pursuing this old thing.

As I thought, the grapes take precedence and she leaves it. For another time, no doubt. 'All right, well, see what you can do and we'll speak tomorrow.'

'All right, *Eve*,' I say sweetly, my own peace offering.

'Des sends his love. He's blowing you a kiss.'

I'm putting the phone down when I hear Des making squelchy noises. If I didn't know he was such a lovely bloke, I'd worry.

IT'S ONE OF those sticky London nights. You'd think after all these years I'd be used to them. There's something to be said for those cool Devon breezes.

It's not that I don't like Devon. There are things I miss about it. Cream teas. Rolling hills. Secret coves. But we visit several times a year for high days and holidays so it's not like I don't get my fix. We probably *should* go down and help Eve. That's what a good daughter would do. And I am a good daughter. I think. On the whole. So maybe we *could* go down for the weekend...?

I grab my phone from the top of the bedside cabinet and text Declan to ask if he'd be prepared, in theory, to do without me on Saturday. It's late so he probably won't see it until morning. Only I'm wrong. He texts me right back with *No problem. We'll manage.* I tell him he's a star but then of course I worry about the girls. They might need some persuading. A weekend without fibre-optic broadband might not fill them with unbounded joy. And Rob. What will Rob think?

'Rob? Are you awake?'

'No.'

'I reckon we should go to Devon for the weekend – you know, to help Eve and Des with the harvest.'

Silence.

'Rob?'

'Ow. What? Can't we talk about this in the morning?'

'We're both awake so we might as well talk about it now and then we can get to sleep.'

'I was asleep.'

'No, you weren't.' I flick on the light. We need to have

this out now. I rearrange my nightie as it's caught up in my legs and I'm all hot and sweaty. Rob has lost his earlier colour and, if anything, is a little pasty. 'What's going on? You've been weird for days.'

'No, I haven't.'

'Yes, you have. You were ready to burst earlier.'

Rob makes as if he's about to protest but checks himself. He's usually pretty good at this parenting malarkey, which is why I was surprised at his outburst. I mean, Scarlet and he have an emotional relationship – always have done. When we met I wasn't long single and Rob wasn't long widowed. It was the first day of preschool and Rob was watery-eyed as he dropped Scarlet off at the fusty church hall. She, on the other hand, didn't shed a tear, striding confidently away from him towards the sandpit, plunging in her little hands and ordering the boys about. I noticed the put-out expression on Rob's face. Much like the one he has now.

'I suppose I did get a bit annoyed,' he concedes.

'A bit? You were apocalyptic.'

'Don't you mean apoplectic?'

'That as well.'

He sits up, moves the pillow behind his head and shuts his eyes. I watch them flicker. He has grey stubble. 'I'm feeling frustrated right now,' he admits with a sigh.

'Scarlet's always frustrated you to some extent.'

'Not just Scarlet.'

‘What, Ruby?’

‘No, not *Ruby*.’

There’s something about his tone I’m not very keen on. ‘What do you mean by that?’

‘Only that she’s always, well, so... biddable. So compliant.’

‘I sense a criticism in there.’ I get out of bed, stretch my legs. Cramp.

‘Not a criticism as such,’ he says. ‘You know I love Ruby to bits. It’s just that Scarlet can never live up to her. And maybe that’s why Scarlet’s always pushing the boundaries.’

I know I should listen to him, but really, comparing our girls, that seems wrong. We’ve parented them together. I flop onto the cocktail chair, near the window so what little breeze there is can help me breathe deeper, think straighter, get this right. ‘Being a vegan is hardly pushing the boundaries. Every other Londoner is going through that fad right now. It’ll be something else next week.’

‘You see!’ He sounds exultant, proved right.

But I don’t see. ‘What?’

‘You and Ruby are just the same. You think the same. You act the same. You’re both sorted. And Scarlet... isn’t. Nor am I. We flounder around. We get muddled. We never have it all together like you two.’

‘Where’s all this suddenly coming from?’

'It's not sudden.'

'Oh?'

'It's been a long time coming.'

'Right.' I turn towards the window, pull back the curtains and peer out. Despite the street lights, there's a harvest moon, big and silver like you get in children's picture books. 'You didn't think to mention it?'

'I've been working things through in my mind.'

'What things?' I turn back to him, examine his face for clues. That face I know so well. 'Should I be worried?'

'Not exactly.'

'Well, I really *am* worried now, so you'd better tell me.'

I can actually see him working those things through in his mind.

Do-I-tell-her-or-don't-I?

'OK,' he says. 'But hear me out.'

My heart speeds up a little, beats a tad harder. 'All right, I'm listening.'

'I want to do something,' he says, possibly the vaguest response ever. 'It might sound disloyal but it's important to me.'

A moth has slipped through the open window and is currently battering itself against the tasselled shade of my Chianti lamp on the bedside table, one of Eve's cast-offs I've never got around to replacing.

Focus, Christabel. Focus.

Disloyal. But important to him. This can only mean one thing and that's a thing I never thought would be a thing for Rob. 'Are you on Tinder?'

'No, of course I'm not on Tinder. Why would you think I'm on Tinder?'

'Mid-life crisis?'

'I don't have crises.'

'Not much.'

'The odd flare-up. But this is something else.'

'What?'

He takes a deep breath, looks at me with the sombre eyes of that twelve-year-old boy who stares disconcertingly out of a silver frame on his mother's piano. 'I want to go on an adventure.'

'An adventure? What do you mean, an adventure?' I was right about the twelve-year-old-boy thing. 'What are you? A member of the Famous Five?'

'This is a solo project.'

'Solo?'

'Pretty much.'

'Pretty much? What are you talking about?'

'I want to take my bike.'

'Your bike?'

'Yes. My bike.'

'Right. And where exactly do you want to take your bike? Dulwich Park? The London Orbital? Cheam?'

'Slightly further afield.'

'Staines?'

He looks away, fiddles with the duvet with his oil-stained fingers. He's sodding obsessed with that bike. All that Lycra. All that kit. All that expense. Now he probably wants to go to France or somewhere abroad. The Pyrenees or Paris.

He mutters a word. A place name. Something that sounds very much like—

'AFRICA?'

'Africa,' he confirms, very quietly but I can hear him loud and clear.

'What, all of it?'

'A lot of it.'

'How much of it?'

He reaches down to the pile of books beside the bed, picks up the *Times Atlas* – the one I gave him for our first Christmas together, thinking of all the places we'd go as a family, all the world out there for us to explore. We've never got any further than Devon. He opens it up and points to that massive continent. Africa. 'From the south to the north,' he says. 'South Africa to Egypt, to be more precise.'

He's pencilled in a route and there are scribbled notes.

'How long's that going to take?'

'A while.'

'How long?'

'A year.'

'A year?'

'Give or take a few weeks.'

So many thoughts flash and beep and collide. Work. Kids. Me.

'And what about work?'

'They've given me a sabbatical. In theory. Nothing's definite. Obviously, I wanted to talk to you first.'

'Obviously.' Not obviously at all. 'And will this sabbatical be unpaid?'

'Yes, but I've got enough to cover the bills, if you can cover the mortgage.'

'You've saved all that?' I'm trying not to think of that longed-for holiday to Tenerife I wanted us to go on this summer, the one that Rob said we couldn't afford.

'Not exactly saved.'

'Borrowed?'

'Not exactly borrowed either.'

'Stolen? A win on the horses?' I see the blush on his little-boy cheeks and realization dawns. 'Your mother. You asked your mother.'

'I didn't ask her,' he says, all defensive now when he should be more placatory in tone. 'I told her what I was thinking and she said I deserved to have this time.'

'You deserved it? Or I don't deserve you?'

'This isn't about my mother. This is about me.'

'And what about the kids? What about me?'

'You'll be fine. You have it all under control.'

An image of the harp floats into view. How am I going to lug that around? How am I going to manage Scarlet's moods and fads? I *don't* have it all under control. And what about *my* mother?

In all this confusion I realize I am pacing the room. I need to get out and clear my head. I shrug on my dressing gown, ignoring Rob's pleas to stay and listen, and tiptoe downstairs. I walk barefoot through the kitchen and out of the back door into the garden.

It's cooler out here. Autumn is heading our way. I love autumn. Colours and crispness. Halloween and bonfires. New beginnings. New chances.

Moonlight spills over the paving stones and I sit on the bench and examine the sky as if it holds all the answers, which it possibly does. A plane blinks its way slowly across it.

Africa.

For a year.

And it hits me. He's been planning this for some time.

I hear a movement. A fox or a cat. But it's Rob, sitting down beside me and taking my hand in his. He twiddles my ring.

'Why?' I ask him. 'And don't say *because it's there*.'

'Well, it is there.'

'So it *is* a mid-life crisis?'

He thinks about this. 'Maybe.'

'Is it me?'

He thinks about this too. 'Maybe.'

The mid-life crisis I can deal with, sort of, but this? Twelve years ago, it was just me and Ruby, after Nathan left us, his home and his job, for a colleague in the City. They went travelling too. It was only supposed to be for a year but that was a big fat lie. They never came back. Then Rob and Scarlet burst into our lives and we've been a family for a long time. Now he wants to leave us too. To go travelling. For a year. So why should I believe anything that comes out of his mouth?

'Maybe?'

'Not definitely,' he adds. He takes my hand in his, that familiar hand, realizing that my lip is wobbling and tears are pooling in my eyes. 'To be honest, Chrissie, I just want to be on my own for a bit.'

'Don't we all? It's normal to feel like that with two fifteen-year-old girls in the house. It doesn't mean you can bugger off for a year, for God's sake!'

'No, Chrissie,' he says quietly. Firmly. 'You don't understand.'

'Try me.' I make a really big effort to look at him through my tears but he's all blurry like a ghost.

'I don't think it's normal to feel like this,' he goes on. 'I mean, you don't feel like this. You love being around people, helping them sort things out, problem-solving.' He squeezes my hand. 'That's why you want to go to Eve's. To swoop in and save her. And no, before you ask, that isn't a criticism. It's who you are.'

He knew that when he asked me and Ruby to move in with him and Scarlet. He knew that when we got married, our two girls bridesmaids, our mothers like sparring boxers. How can he be throwing this at me now?

'Do you still love me?'

'Yes, I still love you.' He grips my hand tighter. 'I definitely do.' A pause. Then: 'But I don't really like myself much right now.'

'I'm finding it hard to like you much right now too. I'm beginning to wish you *were* on Tinder. Then it might all be over and done with and I need never know.'

'But you *want* to know everything. And I'm not saying that's wrong. And I'm a rubbish liar. And I don't want anyone else. And—'

'Really? You don't want anyone else?'

'No. Really. No one else.'

'Just your bike.'

'Just my bike.'

And I rest my head on his shoulder and feel his body next to mine and wonder if I know him at all.

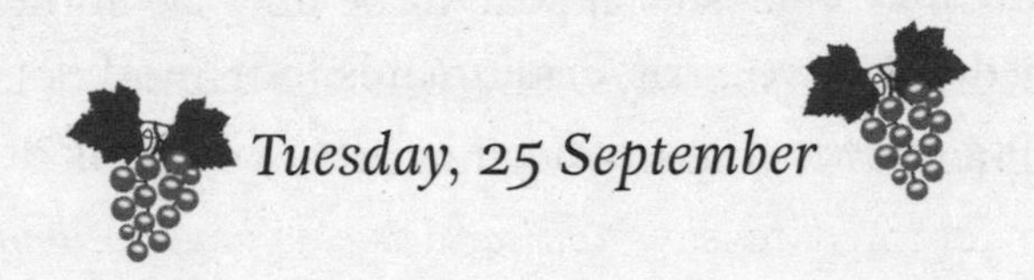

Tuesday, 25 September

TUESDAY IS MELINA'S day at our house. She cleans, she irons, she does odd jobs. We really couldn't live without her; she's a miracle. Though a tad brusque. Some might say rude.

I've taken the executive decision to work from home this morning, despite her imminent arrival. I can't face going into the office and seeing everyone, with this bombshell hanging over me. Melina will let me get on with it and do her own thing.

But when she turns up at her usual 9.30, dragging several bulging bin bags with her into the kitchen, unfazed, as if this is perfectly normal, I realize my assumption might have been mistaken.

'I am evicted,' she announces.

'Evicted?'

'Yes. Landlord tells me I must leave. So I leave.'

'That's terrible. He can't just do that. And – wait a minute, you live with Jason. Jason owns the flat.'

'Yes. He dump me.'

'Oh. Right. Sorry to hear that.'

She shrugs, doesn't appear to be all that bothered. 'He is plonker,' she says. She fills the kettle. 'I leave belongings with you. In your house. I hope is OK?'

I'm tempted to say, *You can leave as many belongings as you want, seeing as Rob's buggering off with his bike and gear – and I'll be chucking out the exercise bike and all the rest of his stuff, the way I'm feeling right now – so there'll be plenty of space.* I'm tempted. But of course I don't say this.

'No problem,' I tell her. 'Is that all you've got?'

Melina has lived in this country for five years. Surely she's accumulated more than a few bin bags?

'Is everything.'

'Right. And have you got somewhere to stay?'

'I stay with friend, Anna. She has nice sofa from IKEA but tiny apartment. I find somewhere else soon. Or I go back to Poland. To my grandmother's farm.'

Et tu, Brute? is what I'm thinking. 'We'd be very sorry to see you go, Melina,' is what I say. 'I'm sure you'll find somewhere else to live.'

She tuts one of her tuts that contain so much more than I could ever guess at. So I press on with my work and let Melina crack on with hers.

Half an hour later, she passes behind my seat at the kitchen table, where I have been battering away at my laptop and have just taken a five-minute break to do some googling. I feel her pause and read over my shoulder.

'Why you googling about bad wine?'

I tell her about Des and Eve. She's met them, whenever a visit of theirs has coincided with her day here. She's always shown an interest in their work. She's even been the recipient of some of their bottles.

'Is very bad wine,' she says.

'I know. I'm trying to work out why. They have the best position. Fantastic soil. They prune the vines properly. Treat for bugs. Why is it so horrid?'

This is a rhetorical question; I don't expect Melina to have the answers.

'If it's not vineyard, then must be winemaking process.'

But, as ever, I underestimate her. 'Of course, it must be. So—'

'Do they press own grapes?'

'Yes, they have a wonderful old press.'

'Wood rots. Metal rusts. Maybe has much copper? Some copper is OK, but too much is very bad. Also, old presses are too harsh. They squash grapes too much. This makes bitter wine. Do you have bottle?'

'Yes, I have bottle. I mean, *a* bottle.'

'We can taste now?'

'Now?' I check the clock on the wall above the door into the hallway. A wedding present from Rob's mother. I've never liked it. 'A bit early, isn't it?'

'I need to taste.'

'All right. Let me find one.'

I know exactly where the bottles are stored. In the cellar, along with the old stair-gate and various DIY bits acquired over the years whenever Rob has begun a project never to be finished. I keep the bottles down there for emergencies. In case I decide to make a boeuf bourguignon or we've run out of every other type of alcohol and the corner shop is shut. Or we need to start a fire.

I traipse down there and choose a white, as this is slightly less bad. But still bad enough. Within minutes of retrieving it for Melina, she has uncorked it, sampled it, and given her verdict.

'They need new press. Modern presses are more gentle. They make more better wine.'

'So what should my parents do?'

'They can send grapes to another winery? Are there more in Devon? Somewhere close to their vineyard so they can move grapes quickly?'

'Right. Wow. Thank you, Melina. That's really helpful. I'll look into it.'

She shrugs. Gets out the hoover and charges off with it, into battle.

I PHONE EVE. Tell her we'll be down on Friday.

'Oh, darling,' she gushes. 'Thank you so much. I knew you wouldn't let us down.'

I feel her whoosh of relief.

'This year looks all set to be vintage of the century.'

Well, it *could* be vintage of the century if they got the next bit right. Do I tell her this? Yes. I have to.

'Eve...?'

'Yes? What is it? I know you want to say something. Spit it out.'

'Spit it out? Nice pun from a winemaker.' My pathetic attempt at levity before I wade in with the steel-tipped boots.

'Yes,' she says. 'Quite. But... What is it?'

'You know how you're supposed to spit out wine when tasting it?'

'Always seems like a waste to me, but yes, of course I know.'

'Well, Eve...' Here goes. 'I want to spit out your wine quite a lot.'

Silence. Apart from crackles on the telephone line. Must be windy down there. They really need to call out an engineer. Still silence.

I carry on. I've come this far. 'Do you think now's the time, possibly, you know, maybe, to... check on your winemaking process?'

The line goes so quiet for a beat that I wonder if we've been cut off, but no. Eve can keep her mouth shut no longer.

'Whatever do you mean, Christabel?'

'This isn't a criticism, but—'

'This is definitely going to be a criticism.'

'Hear me out.'

A sigh. I can hear her tiredness quite clearly above the crackles. But I must persevere.

'Your wine, well, it isn't as... It isn't as good as it could be.'

She sighs again. I think she's about to protest but she takes me completely by surprise.

'I know,' she says. 'It's absolutely terrible. And now we have all these grapes to press and I'm so worried that this year we're just going to have twice the amount of frightful wine that we usually have.'

'Oh.'

'I'm not stupid, Christabel.'

'No. No, of course you aren't. But I do have an idea.'

'You do? Let's have it, then. No time for delay. Tell me.'

So I tell her.

I SPEND THE rest of the week, in between sidestepping Melina's bin bags and avoiding Rob, trying to sort out a contract to have the grapes pressed elsewhere. It turns out the press really is beyond salvaging and they should cut their losses and pay someone else to do it, as I learn from Melina a lot of small vineyards do. But this is proving tricky for two reasons. Everyone is hard-pushed this year with the surplus of grapes. And it costs money. Money which is in short supply for Eve and Des.

By the time we go to work and school on Friday, it looks like the first of these problems could be sorted. According to Eve, the new owner of the Chudston Estate, next door, has *some contacts* at the winery up the valley. Apparently they *owe him a favour* which he has *called in*, making me picture him as Al Pacino.

Which still leaves the lack of cash. Eve and Des will have to find the money to pay the bill so this means I need access to their books and accounts. Spreadsheets rather than juicy grapes are calling me back to Home Farm.

And while the vineyard's problems are being addressed, that still leaves the worry of explaining Rob's plans to the girls this weekend, while we are away from home, which he and I are both hoping will provide the perfect opportunity.

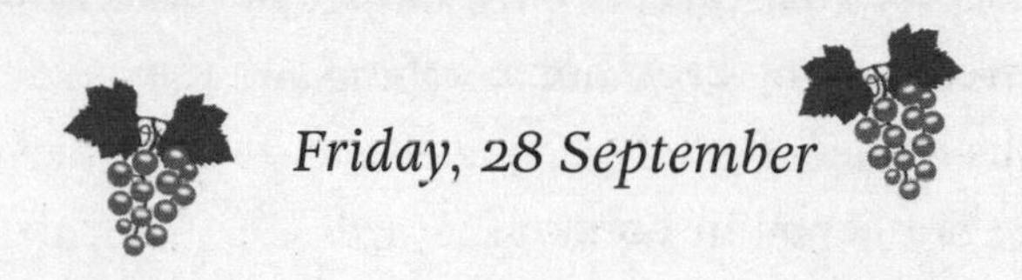

Friday, 28 September

This is how we end up in a queue on the South Circular, leaving London at the busiest time of the week, Friday rush hour. The girls on phones, Rob staring out of the window, me driving, biting my lip so hard I can taste a smattering of blood. That is how we end up in a tailback approaching Stonehenge as the sun sets over Salisbury Plain. For a moment I get a whiff of what Rob is going on about; adventures other than the A303. Far and beyond. Another land, another country. Another continent.

After making it through Somerset, into Devon, and onto smaller roads, then lanes, then a single track, we finally turn into the gateway of the shambling old house of my childhood. The moon is big and bright, the stars in schoolbook formation, even Mars putting on a show of fire, while a glow from within lights up my mother and Des in the kitchen window, heads bent together over the table. A cosy tableau of which I'm immensely jealous. I've never wished I could come back here. But now I do. And the truth of that prickles behind my eyes. Why has it taken me so long to recognize the insane beauty and peace of this place? Why have I never seriously considered moving back home before?

Is this home?

Am I not happy in London?

I thought I was. Until the other night. When Rob told me he didn't want to be with us any longer. At least not for a year. Which is a flaming long time.

He wants to go away. And it hurts. It really, really hurts. And then there's the worry. The fear that – like Nathan before him – Rob might never come back.

But no time to dwell because an enormous dog is poking its head through the window of the car.

'Hello, Luther.'

After shrieks of welcome, from the dog and from my mother, and after bear hugs all round from Des, we are hurried into the kitchen and wine is forced into our hands, even the girls'. Before I have the chance to object, Eve says: 'It's perfectly allowable for fifteen-year-olds to have a glass of wine. There's no law about it. Not in your own home.' Meanwhile the girls thank the gift horse and neck the booze before it's too late.

From being grumpy in the car, they have now perked up. Scarlet's soon lying in the dog basket with Luther, the elderly Irish wolfhound, stroking his ears like he's a (ten-stone) puppy. Ruby's showing Des a video of her school orchestra performing the *Pirates of the Caribbean* film score. Rob has wandered off to bring in our stuff from the car, which leaves Eve and me alone. She ushers me into the hall. There's a large cupboard under the stairs where she still keeps the old Bakelite telephone with its crackly line. You can shut the door and have quiet conversations, which was perfect for the days before mobile phones – and just as useful now, what with the signal being so dodgy in this valley.

She switches on the light, a bare bulb hanging bereft of a shade, and shuts the door so we are very confined. Just the two of us in a weird time capsule. Seventies flowery purple wallpaper, old tins of Quality Street and Crawford's biscuits, the smell of jasmine.

'Tell me what's going on?' she urges in a stage whisper.

'How's your arm?' I whisper back.

'Stop deflecting,' she says, normal tone resumed. 'And the wrist's not too bad. Nothing painkillers and wine can't handle.' She holds up her plaster-casted arm like it doesn't actually belong to her, this woman who is never ill or damaged or broken in any way. She winces slightly and lowers it again. Uses her good hand to grip my shoulder, all the better to gaze deep into my eyes with that glint I find hard to refuse, using all the dark arts of the mesmerist. 'Tell me.'

So the two of us sit cross-legged on the floor inside the cupboard, which might as well be the portal to Narnia with the other-worldliness I'm feeling. And now Eve is producing a bottle of wine and two glasses from a secret stash, like a magician pulling a rabbit from a hat, blowing off the dust and using the corkscrew on her Swiss army knife that is somehow always to hand.

The wine is sharp and bitter but I plough on regardless. It's amazing what you can drink when you're confined in such a small space with your mother and she's on a mission. But Eve isn't saying much. She's employing that knack of hers, that calm, intense poise that hunting cats use and which always has this effect on me: I spill the beans. I tell her bit by bit what's happened. Rob's revelation. Africa.

I suppose I'm hoping for backup, motherly support. After all, I know she's not exactly Rob's biggest fan. They're different souls. With different priorities. Different principles. Surely she'll be on my side? She is my mother, after all. And so it is quite a surprise when she asks: 'Do you love him?'

I only wait a second. 'Yes, I love him.'

'Well, in that case, though it might not be the best timing – in your book, that is – you have to let him go. If you love him.'

'I do. I do love him. I just don't like him very much right now.'

She makes a dismissive scoffing noise. 'There's plenty about Des I don't like. He eats too much, drinks too much, spends too much. He's loud, crude and over-the-top. But I love him and if he wanted to go away for a year I'd let him, though he wouldn't get any further than Totnes. And, if the tables were turned, he'd let me go.'

'But I wouldn't *want* to go.'

'Really? You've never had a hankering to travel? To watch the sun rise over the Indian Ocean? To ride a camel? To travel the Silk Road?'

'I wanted to go to Tenerife this summer. There was a great all-inclusive deal...' I trail off. I sound beyond boring. I do have a certain amount of self-awareness. 'But I love London, Eve. I love our life. And Rob clearly doesn't.'

'Rob is unhappy. He's an ad man, for goodness' sake.'

'I thought you didn't like Rob. Why are you sticking up for him?'

'Of course I like Rob. And I'm not sticking up for him. I'm simply looking at the bigger picture and so on. If you let him do this, he'll come back to you, and your relationship will be all the happier for it.' She tops up my glass. 'End of sermon. Let's find the others and get those beds sorted. Early start tomorrow.'

I am knackered so I'm not going to argue now. I don't have anything to actually argue about with Eve. I just feel narked. And worn out. But mostly narked. With Rob. Bloody Rob and his bloody bike.

I help Eve up and she gives me a hug, cramped and stooped as we are in the cupboard. I get a mouthful of her long grey wavy hair and inhale that heady scent of jasmine. For a moment I think she's going to say something else. But I sense a hesitation, and any words get lost in her brain somewhere, never making it out into the damp warmth of our confessional.

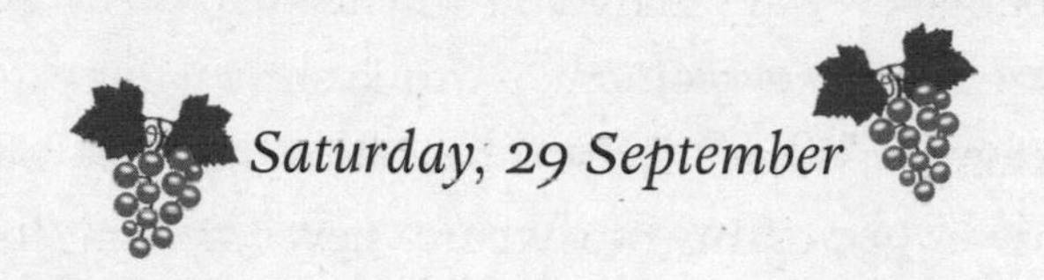

Saturday, 29 September

On Saturday morning I open my eyes to a soft dawn light, having forgotten to draw the curtains after flopping into bed, exhausted, gone midnight. A glimpse of distant hills. Frayed power lines. The thatched roof of the barn. And beside me, an empty space. Still warm. Hopefully Rob's on an errand to bring tea.

The countryside is very noisy. Birdsong. Tractors. Dogs. Gunshots. Must be from next door. The new owner. Old Joe never had shooting on the estate. And surely pheasants can't be mown down till 1 October? This guy's a bit keen.

Bang! Bang! Bang!

I think of those pretty, stupid birds and feel a wave of sympathy with the girls' newfound zeal for animal rights, though I suspect if Des were to offer Ruby a bacon sarnie she'd put that zeal aside for another day. And then, with a jolt, I remember the conference happening today. Panicked, I text Declan.

All OK?

Stop stressing!

How rude!

Good luck with the harvest.

I know he'll be fine running the event but I can't help the worry. Always the worry to get everything absolutely, perfectly right.

By the time it becomes clear that a cuppa is not going to materialize, I'm showered, dressed and parched. Too much wine with my mother. In the cupboard. Her wine. Bad decision.

As I enter the kitchen I'm greeted by Luther and a chorus of 'Hi!'; my girls are washing and drying up. Rob is nowhere to be seen. So much for our plan to talk to them.

'Hello, sleepyhead.' Des envelops me in his meaty arms and my mother puts a glass of orange juice and some headache pills on the kitchen table.

'Join us when you're ready,' she says. 'Rob's made a start with the first of the volunteers. He was up before any of us.'

'He was?'

'He wanted you to sleep in a bit,' Eve says. 'Which is nice.'

Her expression is hard to read. Some unsaid words still lurk but she's not going to release them just yet. Which is not like her. Not like her at all.

'Yes,' I agree. 'Very nice.'

Suddenly everyone's in a rush – Mum, Des, the girls – and I'm alone in the kitchen with only old Luther for company, sitting up close to me, hoping for toast crumbs.

'You need a bath, Luther.'

Luther sighs, drools a bit, continues his death stare.

THERE'S AN ARMY of volunteer pickers already at work by the time I reach the hill. It's a clear day. A blue sky, a few fluffy clouds, a cool breeze, lovely picking weather. Which is just as well; up close I realize that, apart from the London contingent, there's not one helper under pensionable age. However, they all seem to be made of stern stuff, issued with gloves and secateurs and much enthusiasm, baskets waiting at their feet to be filled with ripe, juicy bunches of grapes – a real hive of activity.

'These off to be pressed, then?' I call out to Rob as he heads past me downhill, lugging a crate of grapes.

He nods. 'Can't stop,' he shouts over his shoulder, all busy-busy.

I watch him stride towards the barn where the picked grapes await transportation to Chudston Winery, twelve or so miles away up the valley – a contract I've negotiated. I smile, satisfied to see my organizational skills paying off.

Ruby's helping Rob with the ferrying to and fro.

'Isn't that a bit much for her?' I ask him a few minutes later as he whizzes past again.

'It's all right, love. She's used to heavy loads with her harp. And she doesn't want to hurt her string-plucking hands on the grape vines.'

I wonder, briefly, if this is possibly the most middle-class thing I have ever heard but I swipe that thought away.

Scarlet, meanwhile, is snipping busily, working in tandem with... wait a minute... *Melina*?

'Melina? What are you doing here?'

'Hello, Chrissie. I decide I must come. I call your mother and I say I will help.'

'Right. OK. Well, that's very kind of you.' I don't have the mental capacity to pursue this matter any further right now. I can't get over the fact she is actually here. In Devon. On my mother's land, picking grapes.

'Barbara, lady with big hair, she has spare basket,' Melina says. 'You ask her and she will give it.'

I'm too stunned to speak so I approach Barbara, the lady with the big hair, and she directs me to a pile of baskets at the bottom of the row. Why do I feel like I'm in a dream?

My mother pairs me with Clara, a woman from her t'ai chi class. She has quick hands and light limbs. So I get stuck in, do my best to keep up with her, even though she must be three decades older than me. She chats constantly, a steady stream, in a West Country burr that stirs something long forgotten, that tells of ploughed red fields and wild hedgerows. It's hypnotic and reassuring.

TIME PASSES QUICKLY. My back tugs a little. My knees creak. And now, here's Eve, sidling up to me suspiciously rather than in her usual strident way.

She opens her mouth to speak, clamps it shut. Starts again. What is going on with her?

'It's coffee time,' she says eventually. 'Can you help me?'

WE GATHER IN the courtyard. Ruby and Rob have put out plastic chairs and there's a couple of picnic tables so that the olds can have a breather, which includes me. Luther waits patiently while I hand round the coffee and biscuits, for which Eve apologizes.

'Shop-bought, I'm afraid. Not much I can do about that with this hand.'

Nobody's bothered. There's much chat and camaraderie, the caffeine/sugar combo doing the trick. If Rob wasn't about to bugger off to Africa for a year, this unexpected scenario would actually be enjoyable.

But he is. And so it's not. And when are we going to tell the girls?

A sudden gust of wind swoops past, ruffling leaves and flapping hair. It's gone before we have a chance to complain and here's Des, giving us a pep talk.

'Keep it up, everyone. There's ham or cheese ploughman's for lunch soon. And nuts and dust for any vegans in our midst.' He winks at Scarlet, expecting her to laugh.

'That's not funny,' she says, stony-faced.

But the wind blows away her words and we watch something like tumbleweed bowl across the yard.

'Desmond,' Eve says.

'Yes, my love?'

'Back to work now.'

'Of course, my cherub.'

And off he ambles, back to the vines, oblivious to his crassness, and my heart aches a bit to see how old he looks from behind. Should he really be doing this manual work, what with his aches and pains? Wouldn't he rather be dabbling with his paintbrushes?

ANOTHER TWO HOURS of picking and it's harder than I imagined. I realize how unworked my hands actually are, soft-skinned from too much time in the office and not enough soaking in dirty dishwater. I'm cultivating a blister. Nobody else seems bothered, apart from the odd stretch here and there. Half an hour till lunchtime; I can make it.

Thankfully the sky's clouding over and it's cooling off but I've slowed down considerably. Melina's filled ten crates already. She catches me watching her while I'm surreptitiously shaking out my hand, giving it some air.

'I come from farm,' she says. 'I help grandmother with pigs. And now, in UK, for five years I clean every day. Hours of cleaning and bleaching and scrubbing. You think this is hard? This is easy.'

'I'm not complaining—'

'Your mother she is workhorse but she is old. She needs help. I help her. I ask if I can move here maybe.'

'But—'

'Scarlet and Ruby must help clean your house. They are lazy slugs.'

'But Rob...' This time I stop myself as Scarlet's close by.

'Dad's what?'

'Er... Look, Scarlet. We need to have a chat, the four of us.'

'What's he done?'

'He hasn't done anything yet. It's what he wants to do.'

'He's not going on about another new bike, is he?'

'It's a bit more than that.'

I'm sorely tempted to tell her but I don't get the chance to explain; Des is banging a gong for lunch, which is probably just as well because Rob and I agreed to talk to them together. Only Rob has been mysteriously busy. Obviously concerned about the fallout of his impending revelation. Obviously avoiding it.

As we troop into the barn, all of us looking forward to some hearty food, he won't even catch my eye. The coward. Luther holds up the rear, nose close to my midriff, believing me to be the weakest link. Maybe I am.

BACK ON THE hill for the afternoon shift. We're making steady progress, vine by vine, moving in pairs down the rows. Scarlet is doing her very best to keep up with Melina, though I notice Melina helping her so they can keep the pace going. Rob, with Ruby shadowing him, is treating the whole thing like a training exercise, back and forth to the barn, staggering under the yoke of grapes, the only thing missing his bike. Des is overseeing the crates being loaded onto a truck for the first journey to the press. A truck loaned by the new owner next door. This new owner appears to be some sort of super-neighbour because he's also lent a couple of his own labourers, Tomasz and Michal.

'Polish,' Melina tells Scarlet as they take a moment to watch the men while they get stuck in.

Despite my burgeoning blister, I find the repetitive work comforting; the snip and rhythm, the bending and stretching, helping me avoid contemplating the inevitable discussion, the return home tomorrow and what will happen after that. This big thing – Africa – is lurking offstage. Thankfully, my partner Clara is rabbiting non-stop. The village post office. The latest bus route closure. Her grandson's ADHD diagnosis. On and on and on. There's not a chance to think about anything else.

'Did you feel that?' she asks me, standing up straight and looking towards the darkening sky. 'Rain,' she adds, unnecessarily.

Yes, I did feel that. A few splats of the wet stuff. Across the vineyard waterproofs are ruffled out of backpacks and Eve has ordered Ruby to distribute a ragbag collection of capes and anoraks for those who've come unprepared. It seems we will have to carry on.

'Just a squall,' says Clara.

AND SHE'S RIGHT: ten minutes later the clouds have cleared, leaving behind a breeze and sunshine. Now, hopefully, the grapes will soon be dry and won't leave any water in the press – a known problem in winemaking.

Des can't understand it because the weather forecast did not predict this. Or his barometer. Or his gout. But he insists we take a break to give the elements a chance to do their magic.

'It's going to be a long night,' Clara murmurs.

WE'RE GATHERED BACK in the barn with the tea urn and cake.

'Shop-bought,' Eve apologizes again. She's damp, dirty and decidedly dejected.

'Can't we leave the picking till tomorrow?' Ruby asks Des.

'Definitely not,' Des says. 'Time is of the essence. The sugar content and acid levels are at their peak. It's just a short window of opportunity. Once they're dry again, it's back to the vines.'

'How much is left to pick?'

'We've got two acres. We've maybe done a quarter.'

'Is that it?'

''Fraid so. The Pinot Noir will be a few more days yet before they're ready but the Chardonnay needs to be picked this weekend. Normally we have about three tons, but this year it looks more like five.'

'How many bottles is that?'

'A lot,' he says.

Ruby waits for something more specific but it's not forthcoming.

Business acumen: zero.

Before I suggest creating a spreadsheet, we hear a nerve-jangling scream followed by a scuffling of boots outside in the yard.

Scarlet. I'm about to go and fetch her when she appears, breathless, in the entrance to the barn.

'Scarlet? Whatever's the matter?' Eve is straight over to her granddaughter, good arm around her, worry written all over her face and in her gestures. I can't remember her ever showing me such concern.

'There's a... pair of... dead birds... in the loo.'

'Oh, those,' Des says, unhelpfully. 'Those are the partridges I shot earlier in the week.'

'But *why*?' Scarlet looks bewildered. Shocked.

Why does she think? How naive our children can be; for all their apparent streetwise London ways, they know so little about life, death and the country.

'To make them taste more tender,' Des answers.

'You're going to *eat* them?'

'Of course we're going to eat them.'

'*I'm* not going to eat them!' Scarlet exclaims.

'Then don't. All the more for the rest of us.'

'I'm not going to eat them either,' Ruby says.

But Scarlet doesn't hear her sister's support because she has stormed off in that typical response of hers. She'll be trying to find a couple of bars of mobile-phone coverage to group-chat her mates and vent her spleen. Or possibly having a sneaky roll-up behind a hedge, sending smoke signals into the ether.

'Why are you shooting partridges?' Ruby asks, round-eyed with disbelief.

'Because it's too early for pheasants,' Des replies, as if that's perfectly logical to a fifteen-year-old from south London.

TWENTY MINUTES LATER and Des claps his big hands, chivvying us with his never-faltering cheeriness. 'Come on, troops.'

'I'll just pop next door and see if the neighbours have any spare hands,' Rob suggests. 'After all,' he adds, turning back to face me, 'your mum's always saying what a great community this is.'

'It *is* a great community.' Eve has acute hearing when she wants.

Despite the team talk, looking out upon the rows of vines it's clear there are a lot more grapes still to be picked and there's an audible sigh from the group.

'Well, let's see how much civic responsibility this dude has,' Rob says, heading off to find out. It's a bit of a trek to next door so he jumps in the car and disappears through the gate and up the lane, leaving me wondering how on earth he will cope cycling across that great continent, crossing the equator, from Cape Town to Cairo. Eleven countries. None of which he has ever visited.

An hour flashes by so quickly we barely notice how tired we are. Ruby continues to do the donkey work, shifting the crates to the barn single-handedly in Rob's absence – where is he? – while the rest of us carry on picking, a slower pace than before, apart from Melina, who is a machine.

I'm heading back across the yard after a visit to the partridge loo, when in pulls the truck driven by Tomasz, back from the winery up the valley. Only he offloads more than the empty crates. A battalion of labourers pile out – mainly men but also a couple of women.

'I bring help,' he announces to anyone who will listen, though there's only Eve – doing a few yoga stretches – and me near enough to hear, everyone else beavering away up the hill.

Then Rob returns with a stony-faced but slightly calmer Scarlet, arms crossed, in the passenger seat. He winds down the window. 'I've brought the cavalry,' he says, pleased with himself, as if it's anything to do with him, the messenger. He parks and heads straight up the hill to help Ruby, Scarlet reluctantly in tow, while the men get themselves organized, fussed around by Des and company.

And then a Range Rover pulls into the yard, parking up by the barn, dispersing a cloud of dust.

The driver gets out, slamming the door and surveying the scene, a caricature gentleman-farmer type kitted out in tweeds, boots, flat cap, the works. The new neighbour. The new neighbour who looks – ohmygod – somewhat familiar.

'What the hell is *he* doing here?' I ask my mother.

'Oh, didn't I mention that?' Eve asks, innocent as a fox with feathers in its mouth. 'No time for chatting now. Back to work. Chop chop.' And she tries to bundle me away before I make a public affray.

But I put my foot down and this is how I come to be standing in my socks on the kitchen flagstones in front of the Aga slugging from a bottle as I face my ex-husband.

'HOW'S THE WINE?' Nathan asks.

'Don't.' I eyeball him and take another sip. 'Just don't.'

He helps himself to a glass from the cupboard, knowing exactly where to look, and reaches across me to pour himself some of the wine, which he then downs. 'The best way,' he says.

I ignore this, shut my eyes wishing he'd disappear back to where he came from, wherever he was before he decided to move in next door. 'Since when have you been interested in farms?'

'I grew up on a farm, remember.'

'Of course I remember. You bloody hated it. Couldn't wait to leave.'

'Well, that's something we had in common.'

'That and only that. Only you made a habit out of leaving whereas I had to stay put. What with having a young child. *Our* young child.'

'You could have come back here.'

'Why should I have had to? I wanted to live in London but you made that very difficult for me.' The bastard. The utter bastard. 'Why did you have to buy next door? It's my home, for goodness' sake.'

'But it's not your home. You hate it here.'

'That's not the point.'

'Isn't it?'

'Of course it isn't.' Honestly, I can't believe the audacity. And I don't know which is worse. Nathan buying next door or Nathan standing in his ridiculous clothes in my mother's kitchen.

Actually, I do know what's worse. And that is the fact he hasn't seen his daughter in years. Where's he been all this time? Last I heard he was in New Zealand. A decade ago. With a woman called Charlotte.

And finally, the penny drops. All over the flagstones.

'Was that Ruby I saw? Carrying baskets?'

'Yes, that was Ruby.'

'She looks so grown-up.'

'She's fifteen so technically still a child.'

'I'm sorry,' he says. 'I've been a bastard.'

Oh.

Well.

I wasn't expecting that.

But it's true. So true.

'Yes, you have, Nathan. You've been a complete and utter bastard. All this time and no word, no money, nothing. You can't just say you're sorry and expect everything to be fine.'

He's about to speak and I remember how Eve has been on the verge of saying something since our arrival yesterday. She knew she should tell me about Nathan, but she deliberately didn't do so. When I find her I will ask her why exactly she omitted to mention that my bastard-of-an-ex-husband-shit-for-brains-absentee-father-of-my-daughter is back on the scene.

At this moment I'd like to beat him about the head with the brace of dead partridges but that would be a waste of their pitifully shortened lives. Besides, I can't look at him any more and the sooner the work's done, the sooner he'll be off this property and back to his own stinking farm.

I turn and leave him alone in the kitchen, shove on my boots and stomp back across the yard, hoping to head off Ruby before she catches me with her unknown father. Because I have no idea what to say to her when she finds out. Which she will do.

And then there's Rob. And Scarlet. I could throttle my mother for not warning me.

As dusk falls, there's a decided chill in the air. Des calls it a night, though I suspect the new workers will keep going. I slip inside the house before anyone else, grab the half-empty bottle of wine that's still on the kitchen table, and head for the bathroom.

And maybe I'd feel slightly more human if there was actually enough hot water for a bath, but there isn't, so I have to make do with a lukewarm shower.

Afterwards, wrapped up warmly in joggers and a sweatshirt, I creep back downstairs, feeling bad for abandoning the girls – but then reminding myself that they're in their grandparents' house and I've only been gone half an hour. I'm not exactly disappearing for a year. Or for many years, like some I could mention. Bastard Nathan.

I'm in the hall when I hear his voice. Unmistakable. Not convivially loud like Des, but boomingly annoying. I just can't face him now. Not yet. I hide myself in the telephone cupboard and help myself to another bottle of wine and take a swig.

It really is bad wine, but needs must.

And it's quite cosy in here, with a pouffe and a blanket. A seventies cocoon. I remember hiding here as a child, reading *The Famous Five* and *Malory Towers*. The girls used to make dens in here as well. They'd write secret messages to each other. Their own code. Sisters from different misters. And different mothers. But sisters always. I've never felt as homesick as I do right now. Not for our cosy London house, though – for here. Is it possible to be homesick when you're actually home?

What feels like seconds later but must be longer, I jolt upright. My neck is stiff and there's drool across my cheek. The bottle is empty. The house is quiet. Where is everyone?

Shaking myself awake, I stretch and emerge into the hallway, my eyes adjusting to the darkness. A strip of light is visible under the door to the living room so I head on in, to find Ruby and Scarlet wearing old dressing gowns and towels for turbans, spread out on the sofa under blankets and throws. Luther lies like a pampered prince between them. Rob is on his knees before the inglenook fireplace and Des's canvas that hangs above it, as if in worship of the Goddess Eve in all her splendid naked glory. He is not actually engaged in some kind of pagan ritual but leaning over the fire trying to resuscitate it, making a hash of the old newspaper trick, which really is not one for an urbanite to try. Not if he wants to keep his eyebrows.

'If Des catches you doing that, he'll have a fit,' I tell him. 'You know how paranoid he is about fires.' I'm about to offer to do it myself, but hang on... 'Where *are* Des and Eve, by the way?'

'Pub,' the girls say in unison, eyes focused on *Strictly*.

'Really? They could've asked us if we wanted to go.'

'They did,' Rob says, leaning back on his heels. He looks exhausted.

And again, that thought: how the hell will he manage the challenge ahead of him? All those wild animals: lions and elephants and hungry hippos. All those wide open deserts and death-trap mountains. Civil wars and insurgencies. Heat and exhaustion and mosquitoes. A marathon trek across a vast continent he's never visited. One he's only seen on David Attenborough and *The Lion King*.

And perhaps, if I'm totally honest, I'm rather more worried about myself. How will I cope without him?

'I thought you'd rather stay in,' he goes on, interrupting my spiralling-out-of-control thoughts. 'Besides, you were talking to his nibs from next door. What's his name again? Lord Lucan? Farmer Giles?'

Before I can reply, explain myself, say anything, in fact, the door bursts open and Nathan appears with kindling and newspaper. 'I was just heading back home when I noticed the chimney smoking,' he says. 'Thought you might like a hand. It's notoriously difficult, this one. It's jealous.'

'Jealous?' Rob's as confused as I am.

'It's something the French say. When you've got more than one fire going at a time. One of them takes all the draught.'

'Where's the other fire?' Scarlet squints at Nathan. If only she'd wear her glasses she'd see him for who he is.

'There's a log burner in Des's studio,' I tell her.

'Is he painting again?' Ruby asks.

And for once, Nathan is without words. He's actually stumped. Because there is his daughter, in all her tired, worn-out glory. He stares at her. Stares some more. Doesn't say anything. Not a word.

I have to break this silence open, smash it like a champagne bottle against the hull of the Good Ship *Family Dysfunction*.

'I can do the fire,' I tell Nathan. 'You get off. We mustn't keep you any longer from your Saturday evening.'

'Well, all right. If you're sure.'

'Quite sure. It's amazing what I can do when left to my own devices.' I can actually feel my eyes glitter menacingly at him.

'Right. Yes. Of course.' He backs out of the room, half reluctant, half relieved, one eye on Ruby. My precious jewel. My precious daughter.

And now seems as good a moment as any to talk to the girls about Rob's plans. Anything that'll distract me from having to face up to Nathan's reappearance and what the repercussions of this might mean for us as a family. Maybe if I tell Rob about Nathan, he'll decide to stay? But then he'd be miserable. And I'd be miserable. And I really don't want misery to be the legacy we give to our daughters.

It's just a shame that it takes me so long to get the fire going. And that I'm a tad squiffed. Best leave it till tomorrow. There's a lovely peace drifting through the room as it gently warms up, and I'm lulled onto the sofa, a girl on each side and Luther on top of me.

Blimey, this dog is heavy.

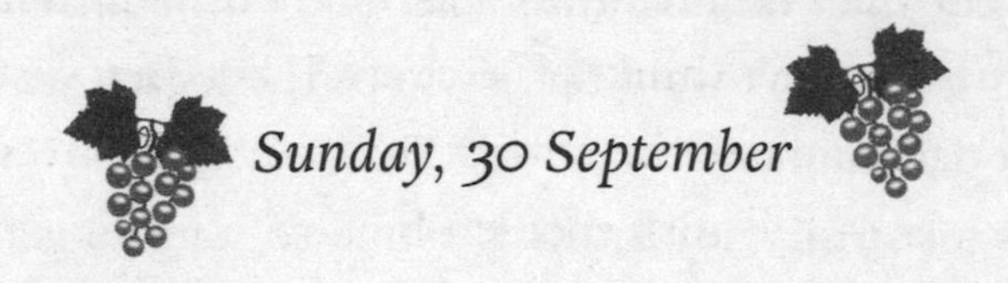

Sunday, 30 September

I WAKE MISERABLY with a banging head. Why do I never learn? I only did this the other night; now here I am again. That bloody wine.

I roll over into the empty space next to me. Pipes clank so presumably Rob's already in the shower across the landing, nabbing the hot water before it's snaffled by his daughters and wife.

I sigh. I really must speak to Eve about the central heating. A boiler instead of the ancient Aga. Workhorse it may be, but spontaneous? No. But of course there's no gas in the village... if you can even call it a village; more of a hamlet, really, a smattering of dwellings running alongside Billy Big Bollocks' estate. My mind is going into overdrive.

'Mum? You all right? I've got you some tea.'

'Oh, Ruby, thanks. That's kind of you. I was miles away. Well, right here to be more precise, thinking about the central heating system.' I take the tea from her and shuffle over a bit.

'I didn't know there was a central heating system.' She sounds surprised. It is surprising.

'Well, there isn't really. Not as we – normal, civilized people – would think of a central heating system. Anyway, get under the covers, Rube. You're shivering. There's still a warmish spot left by Rob.'

She's wearing her brushed-cotton tartan pyjamas and her feet are sporting the finest woolly socks, rainbow-coloured, hand-knitted by her grandmother. Eve's trademark. Ruby flexes her toes.

'Nana Eve made a pair for me and a pair for Scarlet. What do you think?'

'They're lovely. Cosy. Get under the covers though, love. You're freezing.'

'I might be getting a cold.'

'Really?'

'Nana Eve gave me something disgusting to drink.'

'Not some of her wine?'

'*Mum.* No. Some... "tincture" she called it. Herbs.'

Herbs. Eve's a big fan of herbs.

'Who was that man yesterday?' Ruby segues startlingly.

'Which one?' I try to buy myself time. 'There were quite a few.' Hopelessly. Because I know exactly which man she is referring to.

'The farmer.'

Bingo.

'That's exactly who he is. The farmer. He owns next door.'

'What happened to Old Joe?'

'He sold up once his wife passed away and moved to Florida with his new girlfriend.'

She's quiet for a moment, probably thinking about Old Joe and his girlfriend sunning themselves in Tampa. Possibly wondering why I'm being so cagey about the new owner.

'What's the new owner called?' she asks.

Damn.

'Nathan.'

She does a double take. 'Nathan?'

Damn, damn.

'Er... yes. Nathan.'

At this moment, this critical moment, the dangerous conversation is saved by Rob bowling back into the room. He's wrapped in a pink candlewick dressing gown that I think might have had mice nesting in it because it's all nibbled and shredded up the arm.

Ruby laughs at him, thoughts of strange men with the same name as her birth father completely gone.

'Great, you're up, Ruby,' he says. 'All ready to help with the picking?'

'She's not well.' I speak for her. 'She's getting a cold. She needs to rest.'

'Oh, sorry, no. You'd better stay put. Is Scarlet awake?'

'Awake? Scarlet?' Ruby laughs again and I catch Rob wincing slightly and wonder if what he told me about the difference between our girls is true.

'Noted. By the way, the Lord of Devonshire is sending round his labourers. That's neighbourly of him, isn't it?' He looks at me, must see the mixed emotions written across my face despite me trying my very best to pretend this is all quite normal and I'm not hiding the fact that the new next-door neighbour and Ruby's birth father are one and the same man. 'Isn't it?' Doubt is creeping in, but he doesn't pursue it. 'Right. I'll go and shake her.'

'I'd give her a coffee if I were you. Three sugars. Then you might have a fighting chance.' Ruby turns over then, pulls the covers up to her ears and it's clear she's had enough. Though I'm not entirely sure what she's had enough of. But one thing at a time.

'Rob, maybe we should have that family confab now?'

'Family confab?'

'Your trip?'

'Now?'

'We can't keep putting it off.'

'Right then. Now.' He disappears to wake Scarlet.

TEN MINUTES LATER the four of us are in the bed together, just like old times. Saturday mornings and Christmas Day, Rob and me up one end, Scarlet and Ruby down the other. Only it's not the same; not when they're fifteen, one with a cold, the other with sleep deprivation.

'Rob has something to tell you.' I shut my eyes, sip the coffee that Rob has made for us all, keep my head very, very still and my eyes tightly closed – so tightly they ache – so I can avoid his glare of annoyance or panic or whatever it is he might be feeling right now because I've handed the baton over. But hey, we wouldn't even be having this talk if it wasn't for him and his madcap ideas.

'What is it, Dad?' asks Scarlet.

Once he begins to speak, I open my eyes and watch the girls, waiting for their reaction. I have no idea how they will take it.

'You know when you wanted to learn to play the harp, Ruby?'

'Yeah...?' Ruby's wondering where this is going. As am I.

'Well,' Rob continues, 'you were really determined that was what you wanted to do. It was no use Mum and me persuading you to take up the flute or the violin. It had to be the harp. We never really understood why; it was just your dream. And now you're living that dream.'

Ruby sniffs and I hand her a tissue. Yes, she's really living the dream.

'And Scarlet. You know how you wanted to be a vegan and nothing would put you off, not even me having a go?'

She nods. 'Meat is murder,' she says, simply.

'You were determined,' he says. 'Animal rights is your passion.'

Among many other things.

'Well, I've never really had a passion,' he goes on. 'I've spent the last twenty years working in a job with the sole purpose of getting people to buy things they don't actually need. As if they don't already have enough things.'

'The world's richest 1 per cent get 82 per cent of the wealth,' Scarlet pipes up. 'Most people can't afford anything.'

'*British* people then,' he clarifies.

'What about food banks?'

'OK, point taken. What I'm trying to say is most people in the West don't need more stuff to make them happy. All they need is *enough* stuff. And, granted, some people don't have enough stuff and that's not fair. And my job just buys into all that.'

At this moment I can't help but chime in. 'Rob, your point is...?'

'I'm just coming to that,' he says, determinedly patient.

'What is it, Rob?' Ruby asks earnestly.

He looks from one girl to the other. 'I want to do something that will probably seem selfish.'

They wait. They're not going to help him here. And *I'm* certainly not either.

'I'm going to cycle across Africa.'

'Africa?' they both wail in unison, Scarlet's eyes wide in astonishment, Ruby's brimming with tears.

Then, 'How long will that take?'

Rob does at least have the decency to sound contrite when he says, 'A year.'

Scarlet swears and I don't have the heart to tell her off because she immediately covers her mouth with her hand and apologizes. It's a word I'd like to have said myself but I'm the grown-up.

Ruby is silent. A lone tear slips down her pale, rashy face. 'A year?' she manages to croak.

'I know it's a long time,' Rob says. 'I mean, it *is* a long way.' He starts to name the countries he intends to ride through. 'South Africa, Namibia, Botswana—'

'Why?' Ruby's voice is very quiet, husky, confused, but as clear as can be.

'Yeah, *why*, Dad?' Scarlet has also quietened, bewildered and shocked by her father's announcement.

Rob thinks about this for a moment. Puts his arms around both girls and pulls them close to him, gently. They resist at first, then let themselves sink into him, little girls again cuddling up for a bedtime story.

'I suppose people will think it's a mid-life crisis,' he says. 'Maybe it is. But one thing I know is that you three will be fine without me. And a year is nothing. It'll fly by.'

'A year takes forever,' Ruby says.

'We'll be in Year 11 by the time you get back,' Scarlet adds.

'What about Christmas?' Ruby pulls away from Rob so she can get a good look at him, as if looks alone could change his mind.

Scarlet does the same. Goes for the jugular. 'What about our birthdays?' she says.

Rob takes a deep breath, decides not to answer them directly but from a different angle entirely. 'I want you to be proud of me,' he says. 'I want to achieve something. I want to follow a dream I've had since I learnt to ride a bike.'

This is the first I've heard of his dream but I don't say anything because all I can focus on is those 'I want's clanging inside my head.

Ruby's mind is racing ahead now. 'Who are you going with?' she asks.

'Just me and the bike,' he says.

'But aren't you scared?' Ruby's scared of going to the Co-op by herself, so this is extremely hard for her to contemplate.

'Of what?'

'The lions and all that,' she says. 'Where are you going to sleep?'

'I'll be camping.'

'*Camping?*'

'If I can't find somewhere safe to pitch my tent, I'll find a hostel or a guest house.'

And this goes on for a good half-hour, back and forth, here and there, dodging between the three of them, while I let them get on with it until the questions and queries fizzle out and the girls listen quietly as he gets more and more animated and it's as if he's already there in his mind; Africa, thousands of miles away from here. He's ready to go. He has a real plan. He is altogether much more organized than I realized.

Finally, silence. The sort of silence only a teenager knows how to employ. Dark and moody and likely to be highly explosive at some time in the future.

But Scarlet breaks it with, 'Good for you, Dad.'

I am so flabbergasted that I don't say a thing. What's happened to wild, tempestuous Scarlet? Why isn't she shouting and screaming at her father for abandoning her? For abandoning us? His family.

And Ruby says nothing. She rolls over again and I don't know if those sniffs are due to the cold or because she is crying.

'I want to sleep now,' she says. 'Can you go?'

'Course, Rube,' Rob says. 'We've got a harvest to reap.'

'GUESS WHAT, NANA Eve,' Scarlet asks, the four of us reconvened in the kitchen where my mother is washing dishes, humming to herself in that distracted way of hers, while Des feeds some scraps to Luther. '*Nana Eve.*'

'Yes, my darling?' She carries on scrubbing.

'Dad's cycling across Africa! For a year! An actual whole year! Can you believe it?'

'Well, I never,' Eve says. 'That *is* very hard to believe.'

I feel myself bristle. I might be mightily fed up with Rob's plan, but Eve could sound more encouraging in front of Scarlet and Ruby, which I am quite aware is contrary of me.

Maybe Eve picks up on my vibes because she stops washing up for a moment and turns to address my husband. 'That's very ambitious, Rob.' She throws him a look, supposed to convey just how impressed she is with this revelation. Only, my mother isn't a very good actress and Scarlet and Ruby will cotton on any moment that their Nana Eve knows about this plan already. Fortunately something more pressing distracts them.

'What's that smell?' Scarlet narrows her eyes.

Ruby inhales. Pulls a face.

'Don't tell me,' Scarlet says. 'It's the partridges, isn't it?'

'It's not the partridges,' Des says.

She sighs dramatically with relief. Which is daft because it's clearly meat of some kind, which begs the question, why are dead partridges any worse than dead chickens or cows? It's the old country-versus-city thing again, I suppose. But I'm not going to say anything.

Unfortunately, just as I think we've got away without a lecture on the environmental and economic impact of meat production, Des pipes up.

'It's the rabbits I shot earlier in the week,' he says, while throwing Luther another scrap, which the old boy catches with surprising ease, showing a lifetime of practice.

'Rabbits?'

Rob rushes Scarlet out of the kitchen and into the boot room, forcing her into her wellies before war is declared.

'They were free-range,' Des calls after her. 'Lived a good life, eating up our vines.'

But Scarlet doesn't hear. Or if she does, she doesn't reply. Instead there's the cold, hard bang of the back door slamming behind her.

EVE STAYS INDOORS, while Rob, Scarlet, Melina and I get started in the vineyard, joining the dozen or so people already working away out here. I count four of the stalwart villagers, including Barbara with the big hair and T'ai Chi Clara, plus eight of next door's workers, who introduce themselves one by one: Tomasz, Michal, Julia, Aleksy, Zofia, Piotr, Gabriel and Borys.

And someone else. Further up the hill. The lone wolf picking and snipping with speed.

'Morning, Chrissie,' Nathan shouts, bright and breezy when I'd like to trample him in the dewy earth until his top-of-the-range farmer coat is ruined and, while I'm at it, shred his ridiculous cowboy hat with my secateurs.

'This is a watershed moment!' he calls out, bulldozing his way down the hill towards my spot.

I'm trapped. Workers below me. No exit route. He's standing before me now. In my space.

'A "watershed moment"? What do you mean by that?'

'For English wine. This bumper crop. I know how important it is to your family.'

'It's a shame the wine is so bloody awful,' I say before I can stop myself – and immediately feel like a traitor. I am a traitor.

'They've done remarkably well setting up this vineyard over the last few years,' he rattles on. 'And this is a brilliant harvest. But you were right to intervene.'

I'm about to tell him that my intervention was only down to Melina, who realized the bad wine was due to the dodgy old press, but I don't get the chance even to draw breath because he ploughs on regardless.

'They've got Pinot Noir and Chardonnay,' he says. 'But the holy trinity is missing one.'

'What are you talking about?'

'Pinot Meunier.'

'Why are you telling me this? All these years and you're talking about *grape* varieties? Our daughter's inside – with a cold, I might add – and apart from the briefest of apologies, you're yabbering on about Pinot Minot?'

'Pinot *Meunier*.'

'That's what I said.'

He sighs, like it's costing him a lot in patience. Him! The cheek of it. But before I have the chance to get too outraged, he's moved the conversation onto wobbly ground, which is partly my fault for bringing it up, but how could I not?

'Is Ruby all right?' he asks.

'Is Ruby all right?'

He's taken aback by the venom in my voice, the anger in my face. I was always the sensible one. The controlled one. But now... Now I think I might actually be – scaring him?

'Right,' he says. 'I can see we're not going to have a sensible chat now.' He backs off a couple of steps. 'We'll leave it for another day.'

'See you in another decade or so. When Ruby's pushing thirty with her own kids.'

He opens his mouth to reply and then clamps it shut – why is everyone acting like goldfish around me? – and stomps off, back to his position further up the hill. He carries on picking, bent over with his backside towards me so I have an almost overwhelming desire to charge up to him and kick it with my wellies, but I don't have the energy. I just want this job over and done with.

Des appears next to me – a brief break from work. His huge presence is comforting.

'You've got a face on you,' he says. 'I suppose that's something to do with Rob buggering off. Your mother told me all about it. I don't agree it's a good idea. He's shirking his responsibilities, as far as I'm concerned.'

'To be honest, Des, I'm miffed about Rob, of course I am, but it's the other one that's got me all worked up.'

'Ah. Nathan.'

'Yes. Nathan. Why did neither of you think to mention he'd come back? That he'd bought next door, for goodness' sake?'

'We did think about telling you. We thought about it rather a lot, actually, but sort of parked it to one side, if you'll forgive that awful expression.'

That 'awful expression' is one of Rob's favourites. Along with 'squaring the circle', 'touching base offline', and 'joined-up blue-sky thinking'. A need to make something more impressive than it actually is. Which I suppose is thanks to his profession. Marketing. Making people believe they want stuff they don't need.

'We *were* going to tell you, but then Eve broke her wrist and then there was all the worry of the harvest and... Well, now you know.'

There's a pause. I do nothing to fill it. I let Des scrabble around.

'Chrissie. My darling girl.' He holds my shoulders; gently, tenderly.

There's not another person in the whole wide world whom I would allow to call me 'girl'. But he's been the best father he could. And I thought that was what Rob was doing for Ruby. But it seems I never knew Rob at all; he's just like Nathan.

'Chrissie, listen to me.'

'Do I have a choice?'

'You always have a choice. That's something your mother and I have been adamant about.'

'I know, Des, sorry. I don't mean to moan but you can see how all this has thrown me.'

'Yes, I realize that. I also realize that Nathan has been a man of utter fecklessness. But—'

'Does there have to be a but?'

'Sadly, yes. There always has to be a but. And the but is that Nathan has lent us his workforce, even said he'll pay them. He's gone beyond and above being neighbourly.'

'That's guilt for you,' I retort. 'That's why he's being "neighbourly". To make up for being such a prick all these years.'

'Perhaps.'

'And there'll be some other ulterior motive. Don't be conned by him, Des.'

'Really, Chrissie, you are such a cynic.'

'I'm a realist. I'm talking from experience. Personal, bitter experience. How can you be so forgiving?'

The sun beats down. The wind blows. My lips are dry. My head hurts. I'm cross. Fed up. Tired. But mainly cross. I put my head down and snip, snip, snip the low-hanging fruit and only feel a little bit bad for sending Des off with a flea in his ear.

THE GONG CLANGS for coffee break. I flounce down the row of vines quickly, before I have to face the odious ex, though flouncing is quite tricky in wellies.

I find a lonely hay bale just inside the barn entrance and sit down away from the throng. The locals queue up for DIY coffee then move out into the sunshine and bask on the plastic chairs, while next door's workers light up fags in the yard, Des directing them away from the barn to the picnic benches.

'You can't let heritage like that go up in flames,' he's always saying about the thatched-roof outbuildings.

They do as they're told, chatting away in Polish, welcoming Melina enthusiastically into the fold, and it's strange but nice hearing her speak in her mother tongue and I let my thoughts drift away with the sound of their voices. Then I remember about Melina's grandmother's farm and wonder at that other life. How did she end up washing our kitchen floor and cleaning our loo?

'She's quite something, your Melanie,' Nathan announces as he bounds up to me, interrupting my thoughts and sitting himself down on my hay bale without an invitation, slopping coffee onto my fleece, which he doesn't even notice or apologize for.

'*Melina*. And she's not *mine*.'

'But she is your cleaner.'

'Yes, she is our cleaner.'

'Melina the cleaner.'

'Yes, ha ha. No one's ever said that.'

'Really?'

'No.'

He sniggers. Idiot.

'And anyway, she's more than our cleaner. She's our friend. Which is why she's here.'

Though I feel ashamed to call her 'friend' when really I know so little about her. When she looks happier than I've seen her in a long time.

'She's clever,' he says.

'Yes.'

'So you obviously know she has a degree in science?'

'Of course.'

'And a master's in pedology?'

I blush. I have no idea what pedology is. Something to do with feet?

He notes my embarrassment. Sniggers again. 'Pedology is the study of soil,' he informs me.

'Right,' I mumble when I really want to tell him that of course I knew all that, but I'm too ashamed to comment. I thought she was a pig farmer. But there's no way I'm admitting that to the man sitting next to me. I shuffle over as far as I can go without falling onto the concrete barn floor.

'Like I said, we're friends.'

'So you know how worried she is about Brexit?'

'Something your lot voted for.'

'My lot?'

'You posh farmers. You'll lose all your subsidies.'

'I'm actually a Remainer.'

'Of course you are.'

'I am.'

'You are?'

'Anyway, what I was trying to say was, if she returns to Poland, will you manage without her? Your cleaner? Your *friend*?'

'What are you getting at?'

'Your mother told me about Rob's little adventure.'

'You make it sound like a day trip to Paignton Zoo. And Eve had no right telling you about my personal life.'

'Are you ashamed or something?'

And there it is, that word. Shame. Am I? Am I worried what people will think? Or am I generally devastated that my husband wants to abandon us? To go to Africa. For a year. With his bike.

'If Melanie – sorry, *Melina* – goes back to Poland then you'll be stuck, won't you? Working full-time... two teenage girls... no husband—'

'How dare you.'

'I'm showing concern.' He shrugs, like he can't understand my attitude.

'*Concern?*'

'All right, granted, it's kind of late in the day,' he admits. 'But what I'm trying to say is I'm here for you.'

'You're *here* for me?'

'And Ruby.'

Ruby. And there we have it.

I grip the hay bale with both hands, trying to steady myself, trying to get my thoughts into some kind of order. Yes. Clutching at straws. It takes all my control not to shout at him but I can't. I don't want anyone to hear this conversation. It's my business only. Mine and Nathan's. But I *will* let him know exactly what I think.

'You finally want to play a part in Ruby's life then, do you? Is that it? After all this time? You'd like a go at playing Daddy? Well, you can bugger right off. Again.'

'I want to make up for... you know. Losing touch.'

'You mean buggering off.'

'Yes, all right, I mean buggering off.'

'Why, Nathan? Why did you bugger off? The job in New Zealand was supposed to be for a year. What happened?'

Silence. He doesn't know how to answer. But he needs to. God knows how much energy I've wasted on wondering.

'I went off the rails with Charlotte,' he mumbles.

'Pardon? I can't hear you.'

He turns to face me, looks at me. Which is such a weird feeling. It's been so long since I looked back into those eyes I fell in love with at school. The ones I thought I could trust.

'She wasn't interested in Ruby,' he goes on. His face is flushed with embarrassment. 'I tried to make it work, you know, when I first moved out. I tried to get Charlotte involved with Ruby but it was just so difficult. She's not an easy woman. And I couldn't swallow my pride and say I'd made a mistake. It was like I had to push on, to prove that I didn't break our marriage on a whim. Then we got this chance to go to New Zealand and I thought we'd be back after a year and... well...'

He stops for a moment, foundering. I'm not going to help him out. I leave the silence well alone and wait for him to carry on.

He clears his throat, a sort of strangulated useless cough to hide his shame. Oh God, I hope it's shame.

'I was weak,' he says.

I find myself nodding, in agreement for once. 'And?'

'And by the time we were in New Zealand, Ruby was so far away I could somehow put her to one side. When the year was up, it was easier to carry on and do another year. And then we did some travelling and I heard you'd got together with Rob and I suppose I thought you'd moved on and it was too late for me to try to start being a dad again.'

'You should have tried harder.'

'Yes, I should've tried harder but then Charlotte was ill and I was torn between a rock and a hard place.' He's staring at his shoes now. Still on the hay bale beside me. I feel sick with anger. The urge to shout and scream is almost overwhelming; the barn is spinning, my head hurting. I want to tell everyone what a useless bastard he's been. But I take a breath, two breaths, three breaths, place my feet firmly on the floor, try to keep steady.

'Ruby's ill in bed right now so can't speak for herself. Nor should she have to. But I can speak for her. She doesn't need you. She needs me. Her mother. Who has never ever let her down. She doesn't need you. She doesn't need Rob. She doesn't need Melanie. *Melina*. I'm enough. My family's enough. I'll say it again in case you didn't hear me the first time: we don't need you.'

'You don't need me, yeah, I get it.' He sighs. The lone wolf who huffs and puffs but who will not blow my house down. 'But have you asked Ruby what she thinks about getting to know me?'

'Why would I do that?'

'Because I want to get to know her.'

I don't know what to say. I literally don't know what to say.

'Just let me have a chat with her.' He takes my silence for hesitation, tries to wear me down. 'Let me hear it from her.'

'No,' I say firmly, my voice found. 'I told you she's in bed. She has a cold. It's not appropriate. It's not going to happen.'

'She's not in bed. She's over there with Eve, handing out what looks like very nice home-made cake.' He points at Ruby, on the other side of the barn with my mother. Young and vulnerable. There's no way I will let this man hurt her by disappearing again.

'Don't you dare even think about it,' I hiss.

'Oh,' he says, smacking his forehead like a pantomime villain, realization hitting him. 'You haven't told Ruby about me, have you?'

So THE OFFICIAL meeting between birth father and daughter does not happen until of course my mother decides to invite everyone, including Nathan, for lunch. And Nathan, of course, accepts.

Wellies and jumpers are left in the steamy boot room, hands are washed and hungry pickers troop in socked feet into the kitchen where we are greeted by a gamey smell. Rabbit stew, baked potatoes, roast parsnips, carrots, swede and peas. Plus some kind of vegetable loaf.

Eve catches me scanning the room. 'Ruby went for a lie-down,' she informs me. 'No need to check on her. I've only just been up and administered some tincture.'

'She didn't mind?'

'Why would she mind when she knows it'll make her feel better?'

'No reason,' I reply, thanking my lucky stars I don't have to deal with the whole Ruby/Nathan scenario right now in front of a full house.

'Please be seated,' Des commands. 'Anywhere you like. We don't stand on ceremony here.'

They certainly don't.

It's rather cramped but most of us manage to squeeze around the huge farmhouse table, some happy to eat from plates on their laps, sitting at the window seat that overlooks the yard.

Des ladles out stew into Eve's hefty hand-thrown bowls. Another fad of hers.

'Tibetan roast,' she announces somewhat grandiosely, holding up the veggie loaf I'd seen on the side: a green-brown brick-like slab on a platter. 'For the vegetarians and vegans amongst us.'

'How many Tibetans went into that dish?' Nathan laughs over-heartily at his pathetic attempt at a joke and Des joins in, stopping abruptly when he catches my thunderous expression and shoving a forkful of the bunny stew into his mouth, concentrating on scooping the potato innards out of the skin.

I bite my lip, take an overambitious slug of the wine, not caring about the shocking flavour as it hits my taste buds. Surely this year's will be an improvement?

There's some chat about the recipe for the roast: bulgur wheat, mushrooms, spinach, sage, red wine – the latter at least being good for something. When the platter is passed around the table, Nathan pulls a face as if he's being offered the testicles of a Tibetan monk.

Eve takes the conversation off at a tangent, tells us all why we must support Free Tibet. Then we have a toast, a little bit of Shakespeare delivered by Des – 'Give me a bowl of wine. In this I bury all unkindness' – using lavishly splashed-out red and white, distinguishable by colour if not by taste, though it's all going down quite quickly. Only Rob abstains, with the handy excuse of being designated driver back to London. We plan to leave early this evening to stand any chance of being home before eleven.

Des, mental wheels now nicely oiled, makes a speech worthy of a best man. Eventually, after several viticulturist jokes that nobody except Melina finds genuinely funny, another Shakespearean toast – 'Good company, good wine, good welcome, can make good people' – and a few firm pokes from Eve, he finishes talking. There is a lull in conversation as food is consumed and I look at Melina and realize that I've never witnessed her laugh quite like that, from the belly. I don't know her at all.

Before I can berate myself for this, I see Ruby, shuffling across the flagstones in a fluffy dressing gown and rainbow woolly socks: white-faced, dark-eyed, ravenous. She wedges herself between Eve and Melina while Des passes down another of the rough-hewn bowls heaped with food for her.

'Feed a cold,' Des says, but this is a difficult gap to fill. Because once Ruby has tucked in and chewed for a bit, she finally notices the big man sitting diagonally across the table, staring intently at her: an older, uglier, more brutish version of herself. I see Rob looking from one to the other, before turning to me, holding my gaze tightly with his own, raising a questioning eyebrow.

I nod. A small, definitive gesture that no one but my husband can see. My husband whose face has visibly paled, whose hand shakes ever so slightly as he lifts his glass of water to his pressed-together lips.

Early evening: journey home, fading light. As we say goodbye in the driveway, the barn in darkening shadow behind us, the vineyard stretching up the hill, somewhat bereft of grapes, a deep, booming voice calls out, bouncing around the yard.

'You off?'

When I look up, there he is, Nathan, on the roof above my room, with Tomasz, fixing a loose roof tile.

'Give me a sec,' he orders, 'and I'll come down and say goodbye.'

Ruby, wrapped in a duvet, lumbers into the car, only the briefest of backward glances before slamming the door. Scarlet reluctantly takes her eyes away from Tomasz's taut backside, sliding in from the other side next to her sister. She winds down her window, which is the perfect height for Luther to poke his head through. Des restrains him from clambering in after her, while Eve imparts words of wisdom and insanity to their granddaughters.

Nathan and Tomasz are now back on terra firma and, while Tomasz puts away the ladder in the barn, Eve thanks Nathan profusely, keeping one eye on Rob who is fussing around repacking the boot. She doesn't comment on this. She doesn't have to. She knows that I know Rob will never be the sort of man to scramble up a ladder to fix a dislodged roof tile. But she has the decency to go and talk to him, to thank him for helping, to wish him well.

Meanwhile, Nathan touches my shoulder gently and unobtrusively – not his usual brash style at all. 'I do want to make it up to you, Chrissie,' he says quietly. 'I did you and Ruby a bad wrong and I want to put it right. Or at least try to make it up to you both.'

'If only it were that simple,' I tell him. 'But I can't do this now. I won't.'

I leave him standing there so I can say goodbye to Eve and Des. I am always happy to be hugged by Des. But I am more reluctant with Eve. I hugged her in the telephone cupboard two days ago. That's usually enough to be going on with. Not because I don't want to be hugged by her. I do, despite her inability to warn me about Nathan, a man she has always loved, far more than Rob. I don't want to be hugged because I don't want to leave her. She has tears in her eyes. She looks older, frailer, a shock when she's always been such a warrior goddess.

'This too shall pass,' she whispers into my ear. 'This too shall pass.'

I cling on to those words. Eve's mantra. And yes, it's true, this will pass but sometimes you really don't want to have to wait. And sometimes you want things to carry on just the way they are.

THE TRAFFIC IS not so bad tonight. No queues across Salisbury Plain. No road closures. No accidents. Rob drives. Non-stop. A frown of concentration. Hostile body language. No words. Only sniffing from the back, courtesy of Ruby, and an unusual silence from Scarlet.

We pull into our street, trapping a scrawny fox in the car headlights before it slinks by and disappears behind the wheelie bins, on its way to the cemetery. I bat away thoughts of the foxes in Devon, foxes who might be plumper, but who are more likely to be gunned down or torn apart by hounds. Town and country, two parts of my life. A clash of cultures. Different ways of living. And what about Melina with her degree in science and her years in London scrubbing floors? Not that there's anything wrong with scrubbing floors. It's just that I don't want to do it.

Am I a horrible person?

We fall into the house, dump the bags in the hall. Scarlet and Ruby trudge up the stairs, already pyjamaed-up, like the two little girls they used to be, travelling to and from Devon. Some things never change. Some things always change.

I shove on a wash, a hot wash to stand a chance against that red mud. Normally Melina would sort it out on a Tuesday morning. But... She's decided to stay in Devon. To help with the harvest.

'Your mother and father need me,' she said yesterday.

And I'm put out. Put out because Des and Eve are so happy to have her with them. And because yet another person is deserting us.

Am I a horrible person?

'You go on up to bed,' Rob says. He's standing in the kitchen doorway, right where I stood at the beginning of this week on the verge of his life-changing revelation.

I want to say thank you, yes, I will go on up to bed. I want to manage a smile at least. I definitely want to pour out my grief and anger and frustration all over him, but I can't. What Rob and I have now, whatever it is, is not the same as before. It's a different shape. Saggy and slack.

So I say nothing, fetch a glass from the cupboard, move to the sink, watch the glass fill with water from the tap. London water that they say has gone through seven people before it even gets to your lips. Maybe it's already been through me.

And there it is again. That hankering. Fresh spring water that you have to filter to remove any floating bits of sheep poo. Fresh water that tastes of Devon. That tastes of thatched roofs and steep hills. Red cliffs and rolling waves. Not concrete and traffic and deep-fried-chicken shops.

As I pass by Rob at the kitchen table where he's already unfolding his maps, I sense for the first time some reticence in him. Some reluctance about this proposed trip. A sigh. Or a flicker of worry. Some indescribable feeling. Maybe it's the sight of that vast continent, that huge land mass spread out before him? Maybe he's doubting himself? I mean, there's all sorts going on in Sudan. How's he going to avoid that? Or maybe he's doubting me? Leaving me on my own with the girls. Can he trust me, knowing that Nathan is standing, legs astride, just offstage? And if it wasn't for the fact that Nathan is an utter shit, maybe he would have cause for concern. But no. Never. Not with Nathan. Never ever. I mean, I might be tempted to live back in the country again – it *would* be emotional support for the girls. And for me. I could help my mother and Des. Get this wine business running properly.

I might.

If there weren't so many things against it.

Mainly Nathan.

But.

No.

I have resisted and resisted all these years, ever since leaving on the train with my backpack and fifty quid in my pocket saved from the summer's work next door. On the farm. The bloody farm next door.

If only it weren't for that shadow in the wings.

Lying in bed, I can feel Rob's muscles taut and tense. He should be tired. I'm tired, and I didn't have to drive. We're all tired and Ruby is stuffed with cold. No doubt it'll be Scarlet's turn next, then Rob's, but not me, as I never get the chance. Maybe this year I will let myself succumb.

We're beyond tired, the two of us lying here, side by side, in the dark. Beyond the reach of sleep. Beyond each other.

I turn away from him and feel my tears soak into my pillow and hope it'll all go away. That by morning the tears will have dried up, like residual rain running off the red earth of home.

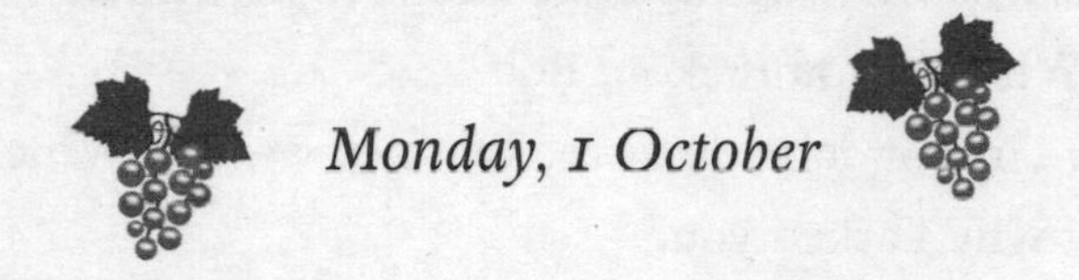

Monday, 1 October

MONDAY MORNING IS a rush of gobbling down toast, scrabbling for lost shoes and snapping at each other. Not even the chance to get a sausage casserole, vegan or otherwise, into the oven. I hate this disorder. Mondays should be a good start on which the rest of the week hangs. But it'll go tits-up at this rate.

'Rob!' I grab him before he leaves with the girls.

Ruby's already in the car while Scarlet is preening herself in front of the hall mirror, furtively applying mascara as if I didn't know what she was doing. As if I was never fifteen with lads to impress. One in particular who I really don't want to remember right now, though I haven't forgotten his tanned face, blond highlights and toned arms – all that work on his parents' farm, the one he couldn't wait to escape.

'Chrissie?' Rob asks.

'Sorry. Miles away.'

'Are you OK?'

Is this a genuine question requiring a genuine answer, or is it one of those throwaway ones people use for small talk? Is this what we have become? People who do small talk. 'What do you reckon, Rob?'

'Er, I'm not actually sure,' he says, warily. 'Which is sort of why I asked you.'

'Don't be facetious. It's not your best quality.'

And this is really not going well. Not that I particularly wanted or expected it to go well. I don't know how I wanted or expected it to go. I don't know anything.

I take a deep breath, steady myself, grip the edge of the table. It needs to be sanded, polished, taken care of. So many stains and fissures, dings and dents.

The front door bangs right after Scarlet's shouted, 'Bye, Chrissie, see you later!'

Not waiting to hear my 'Bye, love.'

The house is quiet. Very quiet.

'We need to talk,' I tell Rob. 'You and me.' I point to him and then myself as if I need to clarify this. 'I'll meet you after work at the Greyhound. Tell the girls to make their own way home and that they can have a takeaway while we're out. Give them some cash.'

He looks like he might protest but pulls himself up short, thinking better of it. Which is wise. A good decision.

I leave him looking slightly flummoxed by the kitchen table (maybe I could shabby-chic it? Distress it?

Paint it like a rainbow?), but he's soon distracted by the beep of his phone so I leave him to it and let myself out into the crisp freshness of the back garden. Once I hear the door bang again and the sound of the engine firing up, I make a phone call of my own.

'Declan?'

'Aha!' Declan exclaims, Alan Partridge style. 'The wanderer returns. Well, not exactly returned. I've got your favourite: a flat white. Only it's going cold because you're not in your usual 8.30 spot at the desk opposite me.'

'I'll be there. I just need you to hold the fort in the meantime.'

'No problemo.'

'And thanks for handling the conference. Your text updates kept me from fretting.'

'I know you too well, and when you eventually show your face in here, I'll be wanting some straight talking, which is saying something for a gay man such as myself.'

'Yes, Declan. Don't worry. We'll do lunch.'

'You never "do" lunch.'

'Well, today I am. We are. My treat.'

'I'll forgive you anything, in that case.' He laughs. The Declan cackle that never fails to cheer me up, however annoying and in-your-face he can be. 'All your sins will be absolved.'

'Sins aren't the problem here, my friend. Unless they include abandonment, bad wine and a rogue cleaner.'

'Sounds like the title of an extremely pretentious art-house film. The type my latest beau is so fond of. Last night he took me—'

'I don't need to know where he took you, right at this moment in time, thank you very much, Declan. Save it for lunch, if you must.'

'Yes, ma'am. I must. Though it could be a long lunch.'

'Goodbye, Declan.'

IT'S ELEVEN O'CLOCK by the time I reach the office, a little flushed and breathless from the last couple of hours.

Declan nabs me before I've even had the chance to take off my coat and sit down. 'Thought you'd been gobbled up by the hound of the Baskervilles.'

'I came across someone far more hideous.'

'Bite worse than his bark?'

'How do you know it was a he?'

'Isn't it always?'

'Hmm. Not sure that's entirely fair, but you have a point.'

'Well?' He looks expectantly at me. If he were a hound, he'd be a Luther type; oversized and gentle and always drooling for more.

'Wait till lunch. We need to focus on work. I've got some stuff to tie up.'

I ignore his 'I bet you have' expression and dig in. Two hours till lunchtime.

'I WASN'T EXPECTING anything this fancy,' Declan says as we're shown to our table.

A trendy bistro with an eclectic style and menu. The sort of place usually inhabited by Rob and his ilk. Declan's more of a McDonald's/Subway kind of man. I usually have a packed lunch. So this is nice. Though gobbledegook. All quenelles, foam and deconstructed rhubarb cheesecake.

'Do they do fish and chips?' Declan turns the menu over to scan it.

We really should be better at this menu malarkey. All those events and conferences we put on. But to be honest, the undertakers, the accountants, the Rotary clubs; they're usually happy with ham-and-mustard sandwiches as long as they're cut into triangles and sprinkled with mustard cress.

'I fancy sausage and mash.'

We eventually find a responsibly sourced salt-crusted John Dory draped over heritage baby turnips tossed with a whisper of samphire. And a macerated artisan chorizo on a bed of foraged chervil, chard and chicory with a cloud of crushed potato.

'Wine?' He's always hopeful.

'Oh, I think so.'

'Fizz?'

'Why not?'

He calls over the waiter, points randomly at a bottle on the menu.

'Good choice, sir,' the waiter says and swans off.

'So how was the harvest?' Declan asks, not entirely focused on me.

'Bumper.'

'That's good. Isn't it?'

'Yes. It is good. But it would be much better if they knew how to make a decent wine.'

'Apparently it's a watershed moment in English winemaking.' He's back in the room, attention restored.

'Not you as well.'

'What do you mean?'

'I've heard that statement once this week already.'

'Must be true then. Especially as I heard it on Radio 4.'

'Radio 4? What happened to Radio 1?'

'I decided to grow up.'

'You mean you wanted to impress your "beau"?'

'Maybe. Yes. Obvs. But they did really say it was a watershed moment for English and Welsh wine.'

'So I hear. That cold winter we had killed off all the diseases and bugs. Then there was all the rain. Followed by a long, hot growing season. Turns out these were perfect conditions.'

Then I tell him about Melina's revelation regarding the grape press. I tell him about the Polish pickers and the local volunteers. About the contracting-out of the winemaking. I repeat the gist of Nathan's lecture yesterday, the holy trinity of grape varieties, two of which we have at home, and that even if Devon is cooler than other wine-growing countries, this means naturally high acidity and low sugar levels. Making for tart table wines – but ideal for sparkling wine.

'You're beginning to sound like an expert, Chrissie,' Declan teases.

'Hardly. But I would like to be able to help out where I can. To learn more about the business – you know, the path from grape to bottle.'

'Vine to wine?' He looks coy for a moment. An unusual expression for Declan. 'I actually know a bit about that,' he admits.

'You mean you like to drink it?'

'I mean I spent a couple of months on my gap year working in a vineyard and winery in Tuscany.'

'Tuscany?'

'I was Interrailing, stopped off at a vineyard. Fell in love. With a farmhand. And the grapes.'

'You're kidding?'

'It was the best time ever,' he says, going into a trance of reminiscence, only interrupted by the waiter who appears with a bottle, popping the mushroom cork with a flourish, pouring a splash for me to taste on Declan's insistence. *You're paying for it*, his eyes tell me.

So I try it. I sniff it and get a hint of English countryside, orchards and hedgerows, fresh-cut grass and honey. Then I take a sip.

'Oh!' The bubbles hit my nose as my taste buds explode with the crisp, fresh flavour of the wine that fizzes under my tongue. 'This. Is. Nice.'

The waiter pours us a glass each and leaves the bottle on ice. We chink flutes. Say our usual *chin-chin-bottoms-up-cheers-m'dear.*

But the wine.

The wine is a revelation.

'*Here is wine, / Alive with sparkles*,' he says, using a lofty, poetic voice. 'Keats,' he confirms when he sees confusion on my face. 'You think I'm a philistine, don't you, Chrissie?'

'No, of course I don't.' Maybe I do. A bit. If I'm honest. But, like everyone else I know, he's full of surprises. 'What exactly is this we're drinking, Declan?'

The wine menu has been whisked away and so he reaches for the bottle and holds it like a sommelier for me to inspect.

'I chose this particular wine on purpose,' he says. His eyes are as sparkling as the bubbles in our glasses.

'You did?' I take out my reading specs and feel my mouth break into an almighty smile. It almost hurts because it's been so long since I did that. It's been nothing but frowns, tears and mopes and right now I am relishing this fizz of expectation.

'Yes, I did,' Declan says, returning my smile with his delighted beam. 'Because it's English.'

We begin our eating journey or narrative or whatever nonsense it is. The food is actually very nice. Why couldn't they just list the ingredients and tell us if they are poached, mashed, grilled or fried? Anyway, we dawdle over lunch while I tell him about Rob. And about Nathan.

Unusually, he's surprisingly contained, listening intently. No expletives or exclamations fly out of his mouth. He just holds back.

'What shall I do, Declan?' I'm not really expecting an answer but he sort of gives me one nonetheless. He can't stay quiet after all.

'If there's one thing I know about you, Chrissie,' he says, 'it's that you always try your hardest to seek out the answer to a problem. You don't rush in. You take your time. You play the long game.'

'Do I?'

'Yes, Christabel. You do.'

'Do *not* call me that. My name is Chrissie, as you well know, and I'd chuck the last of this wine in your face if it wasn't so good.' I'm only half joking.

'Soz,' he says, puppy-dog eyes. 'Couldn't help myself. I mean you're not in the least like your namesake.' He gives me that cheeky grin that I've come to love from all these years working with him. He's always been so much more than a colleague.

'You mean I'm a conformist, not a radical?'

'I do.'

'Oh.'

'You sound disappointed.' He reaches across the table to squeeze my hand.

'Disappointed, yes. Surprised, no.' I squeeze his hand back. 'I know Ruby and I are two of life's plodders. We get things done, but through routine and good old keeping calm and carrying on. Scarlet – and Rob, I suppose – they're more... maverick.'

'Rob? Maverick? Hardly. Feckless, maybe.'

'Feckless? You're not the first to say that.'

'Anyway,' he carries on, 'we can't all be the same, Chrissie.'

'I know that. Horses for courses and all that. But...'

'But what?

'Well, without wanting to sound too dramatic, right now, I actually sort of don't want to really be... me.'

He grabs my other hand now, grips me in a deadlock stare. 'Who do you want to be, Chrissie?'

'I want to be someone more like my namesake.'

'More radical?'

'Yes, you could say that.'

Deeds not words.

He rubs my hands with his own manicured ones. 'Then you know what you have to do.'

Yes, I suppose I do know what I have to do. I manage a nod.

'Don't look so glum, my lovely. What else is keeping you here?'

'In this restaurant? The wine?'

'No, you numpty! In London. In this life.'

A rare moment of hush while I listen to the hum of the other diners, the chink of cutlery on crockery. Bubbles of laughter. But I don't answer Declan. I don't know what to say.

But he does. 'Chrissie, I would really, *really* miss your daily presence in my life but you could have a fantastic new challenge in Devon. Don't let Rob be the only one to have a mid-life crisis. You could actually do something worthwhile, like help your parents. Show your daughters that if a thing needs doing, you do it. Even if it means throwing your life up in the air and seeing which way the wind blows.'

I imagine my life – my house, my job, my family – chucked into the air, like some kind of *Wizard of Oz* twister. Would it crash down in a land of Munchkins and flying monkeys?

This is what I'm thinking.

But this is what I say: 'Shall we get another bottle?'

I don't wait for an answer. Instead, I catch the waiter's

eye. Mime the international sign language for *Another bottle please* and he's back in a blink and Declan and I are on our way to putting the wine world – the whole of the big fat world – to rights.

'Here's to Brit Pop,' Declan says as the bubbles go up his nose and fill his mouth with fizzy delight.

'To Brit Pop.'

Throw your life up in the air and see which way the wind blows.

By the time I reach the Greyhound, I have to admit to being half-cut, which isn't the best way to enter peace talks with Rob. He's there before me, leaning on the bar, bottle of cold lager in hand. He's come on his bike so he's sweaty, in Lycra, and asks if it's all right if we sit outside till he cools off. I'm feeling quite flushed myself so I say yes, that's fine, and ask for a black coffee.

So it's just the two of us outside on a bench with that familiar view across the gentrified road up to the common, where we've lived for the past ten years. We've seen the area evolve from slightly edgy to rather chi-chi. It used to be working-class Londoners, school teachers and nurses. Now it's all media types, yummy mummies and marketing men. Exhibit one. My husband. Designer lager and a thousand-pound bike chained up beside us.

'Are you a tad drunk?' he asks.

It's hard to say no because I've just managed to trip over my own shoes and slop some very expensive Fairtrade organic Columbian coffee over my dishevelled dress. I take a cardie out of my bag in an act of distraction.

'It's getting chilly,' I add by way of explanation.

'Shall we go back indoors?' he suggests.

'No. I like it.'

'Right. You actually OK? I mean I realize I've dropped a bombshell on you.' He waits for me to agree, as disagreement on this point is highly unlikely. 'I also realize I'm being a completely selfish arse.' He smiles that smile that won me over back in the day when he asked me out on a date to a preschool parents' meeting.

'Sort of and yes and yes.'

'So what do you want to talk about? You know – specifically.'

'Right. Well.' I pull myself together, slurp a big mouthful of bitter, strong coffee. I'll never sleep again, but I need to sober up because this is important. As important as it gets. You plod along for so long and then something changes. This is my moment of change, the point where my life stumbles upon a fork in the road, and I have to make a decision. A decision for me. And for the girls. Ruby and Scarlet. I'm mother to both of them. How can this man, who I thought was the best father in the world, think it's OK to go off for a year? A whole year on his own. With his bike. Across Africa.

And, OK, it's not forever. Hopefully. Nothing's certain. And it's also really not OK. The girls are fifteen. On the cusp of womanhood, and I am being left alone to deal with any fallout. And the question hangs there: what if I say no?

Do I ask this? Do I throw it up in the air and see which way the wind blows?

'What is it, Chrissie?'

His tone is soft, gentle – like that of the old Rob who has been absent for, well, quite some time, only I hadn't realized. I've let things slip. Taken my eye off the ball.

'Tell me,' he urges. 'Anything. You know you can tell me anything.'

'I thought I could, but now I'm not so sure.'

'Tell me.' He holds my hand.

'I was wondering what you would say if I said no? You can't go?'

'Then I'd say fine.' He squeezes my hand, differently from the squeeze Declan gave it earlier but a squeeze all the same, and I don't know if this is voluntary or a spasm of despair.

'But it wouldn't be fine. Would it.' This is a fact, not a question.

'No.' That squeeze again. 'I don't think it would be.'

A breeze billows up the road and I pull my cardie tighter around me. 'And what if *I* said I wanted to have a gap year?'

'I'd say, can it wait till I've had mine and then you can have yours?' He bites his lip, trying not to snigger – one of his bad habits, laughing when he's nervous. 'That's not a euphemism, by the way,' he adds. 'Just to be clear.'

I ignore this. Now is not the time to be aggravated by my husband's silly habits. Don't sweat the small stuff, as Declan would say.

We both take a moment. He finishes his beer. I finish my coffee.

'Shall I get us another drink?' he suggests.

'Do I need another drink?'

'Dutch courage?'

'For you or for me?'

'For both of us.'

'Right,' I say. 'This is daft. Just tell me. I know there's something you want to say.'

'OK.' He takes a very big breath of chilling air, dramatic and noisy, his sniggers all at bay. 'I've booked my plane ticket for three weeks' time.'

'Three weeks? You never said you were booking them.'

'I decided to go for it. Before I changed my mind.'

Deeds not words.

'Right.' I have to try and let this sink in. Three weeks. Twenty-one days. Africa for a year. But I have to ask: 'Why didn't you tell me how you were feeling before? We should've been able to talk about it. I didn't realize that you were 100 per cent definitely going. That you were so unhappy with your life. Our life.' An uncomfortable pause that he waits for me to fill. 'I suppose I thought there was a chance you might change your mind.'

'I'm sorry, Chrissie,' he says. 'I haven't changed my mind.'

'Right. So what do I do? How does Ruby get home with her harp? How many people do I have to inconvenience so I can leave early and pick her up? How do I manage without Melina? How do I hold down a full-time job and look after two teenage girls one of whom—?'

I stop myself just in time.

'One of whom... Isn't your own? Is a troublemaker? Isn't Ruby?'

'That's not fair, Rob.' I shudder. Was I going to say that? He shouldn't put words in my mouth.

'I don't mean to be blunt but this isn't about you. It's about me.'

'That is quite blunt, to be honest. And, actually, it's also a load of old rot. Of course it's about me. Everything you do, every decision you take, every mid-life crisis you decide to have, has an effect on me and the girls.'

He looks like a chastised little boy. The one staring out from the photograph frame on his mother's piano. Ingrid spends much of her life chastising people. Disapproving. Judging. I don't ever want to end up like her.

'I'm sorry,' he says.

And somehow, whether intentionally or not, Rob turns this around so that I am suddenly comforting *him*, holding his sweaty head against my shivering breast.

How did this happen?

Throw your life up in the air and see which way the wind blows.

As I hold him I imagine throwing up our lives: Ruby's, Scarlet's and mine. And I imagine them blowing south-west and coming to rest in my Devon home.

'I've got an idea,' I tell Rob.

I PHONE EVE later that evening, enthusiasm for my blossoming idea fuelled by that heady cocktail of booze, caffeine and adrenalin. But before I have a chance to pitch her my plan, she screeches out her news. 'Hallelujah! The rest of the grapes have almost been picked!' A pause for breath, then, 'It's nearly dark but they're determined to stay out until it's all done and then Nathan's driving the last crates to the press.'

I can imagine my mother holed up in the cupboard in her woolly socks, long wild hair and a glass of vino in her good hand. Which reminds me of what Declan and I discussed earlier as a possibility for the future.

'Have you thought about sparkling wine?'

'Sparkling wine? You want us to get on the Prosecco bandwagon too?'

'No. Well, yes, sort of. But I was thinking more along the lines of champagne.'

'But you can only have champagne in, well, Champagne.'

'Yes, but you can make something bloody similar. You've already got two of the grape varieties needed.'

'I know. The holy trinity is only missing Pinot Minot.'

'Pinot *Meunier.* Have you been talking to Nathan?'

'Only briefly, dear. He's been working alongside the others all day. He's suggested the very same thing to Des and me and we're actually thinking it's a jolly good idea. Turn half of this year's crop into bubbly and plant some Pinot *Meunier* for the future.'

'That's quite ambitious.'

'But you were suggesting it!'

'It was only an idea.' Bloody Nathan bloody interfering when *I* am Eve and Des's daughter and it is down to *me* to help them, not him.

'Well, ideas have to be acted on, don't they?'

'Deeds not words?'

'Exactly, Christabel,' she says.

'That's what I was phoning to tell you. There's something else I want to ask.'

'Oh?' I detect a prickly note in her voice. Wariness or suspicion?

'I'm thinking about moving in – to Home Farm – with the girls.'

Silence.

'Just for the year.'

More silence.

'You know, until Rob gets back.'

'Moving in here?'

'Of course.'

'Oh, right, I see.'

'And?'

'What about your house?'

'We can rent it out.'

'What about the girls? Have you asked them? I remember what you thought about rural life aged fifteen, and that was before the Internet and mobile phones.'

'It'll be tough, I know, with their GCSEs coming up. They'll probably hate the idea, but in practice they love being with you and Des. They could go to the secondary easily enough. There's a school bus still goes through the village, right?'

'Yes, it does.' She sighs. I can almost feel it down the line hitting me in the face. 'Speak to them.'

'The school?'

'The girls. Don't tell them it's a *fait accompli*. Get them on board. Show them the positives.'

'I think I know how to do that, Eve. I spend my whole life looking after other people, making sure their sandwiches are cut into triangles and their carrots into batons.'

This stumps her for a second. 'Right,' she says, hesitant, then inhales what sounds like a deep breath of optimism. 'If anyone can do it, it's you, Christabel.'

I don't *think* she's being facetious but before I can confirm she says she must go and check on the pickers. So we hang up, and I'm not sure why but Eve didn't seem as thrilled as I thought she'd be. It's the conversation I need to have tomorrow that I'm more concerned about now, though. How's that going to pan out?

THE NEXT DAY after school, Rob and I sit down with Ruby and Scarlet at the kitchen table, scene of much squabbling and laughter and celebrations and moods. And the thing is with fifteen-year-old girls, you never quite know how they are going to react.

There are two surprises. One from each of them.

Scarlet says: 'Really? We can really move in with Eve and Des and live in their house and help run a vineyard?'

And Ruby says: 'Over my dead body.'

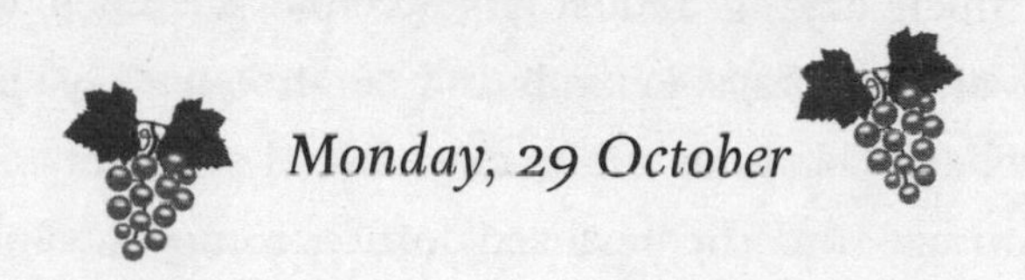

Monday, 29 October

FORTUNATELY, RUBY'S DRAMATIC mood swings are relatively short-lived, downgrading to a general stroppiness that we more usually associate with Scarlet. I suspect Rob is secretly chuffed about this. Though maybe I'm being unfair.

Ruby has spent the last four weeks in tears – for her school friends, for her harp teacher, for her swing band, for her house, for Rob, for her life which is not worth living any more. Scarlet, on the other hand, has kept up the enthusiasm she first showed when a move was discussed. I say discussed; Eve, I'm sure, would say we presented it as a *fait accompli* – though I made Rob do most of the work and let it be known quite categorically that this 'trip' was nothing to do with me. That I was in fact very happy with our London life but that if he was buggering off to Africa (I didn't actually use this phrase out loud, though I definitely did in my head) then we should have our own adventure, especially one with a purpose – to help Eve and Des turn around the business.

There's no going back now. School has been left with much crying and shirts Sharpie-scribbled with names and hashtags. Friends and neighbours have been farewelled. The house is packed up, the contents put into storage and the rest sent off in removal vans to Devon. From next week our home will be rented out to a lovely family from Syria, whose story puts ours into perspective. My resignation at work has been handed in and my notice worked out. So apart from saying a teary goodbye to Declan, I don't feel too sad to be going. If anything, there's a sort of relief. A freedom.

I do sort of wish they'd done a proper farewell party at work, though – something a bit more meaningful than the box of doughnuts and the Buck's Fizz that Declan bought for the office at lunchtime. And yes, I know I'd made him swear not to spring any surprises, but I suppose I was secretly disappointed there wasn't champagne and three cheers and much hearty singing of 'For She's A Jolly Good Fellow', and that I had to spend the rest of the afternoon stocktaking.

And then there's my husband.

Finally, a few days ago, we waved off Rob and his bike at Heathrow. It was a difficult day. The girls were very down, I was doing my best to hold it together – as, to be fair, was Rob – but the problem was his mother. Ingrid insisted on meeting us there and so we never had our own private family goodbye. It was sort of like the end of *Brief Encounter*, when that chatty woman ruins the special moment between Laura and her lover.

And then he was gone.

Now we – Ruby, Scarlet and I – are on our way to Devon early on a sunny autumn Monday morning, the week ahead of us free as it's half-term.

'Climate change is a bad thing for the world,' Scarlet says as we head back down the A303. She's sitting up front with me. Ruby is in the back. 'But it could be a good thing for English winemaking.'

'Obviously you'd never mention that to Nana Eve.'

'Obviously. I'm not a dumb-ass.'

Ruby snorts at this. We ignore her.

Scarlet continues. 'More sun means more sugar which means more alcohol which means you don't have to add sugar before fermentation.'

Since finding a book on winemaking in Oxfam last month, she has been googling away, preferring to stay indoors and help at home rather than going out with her friends – who are all 'saddos'. Her friends have always been important to her so I'm not sure if this is her building up walls for self-protection or if she is genuinely pleased to be leaving. She hasn't so much as put a brush of mascara on her eyelashes. And her hair is permanently shoved up in a bun-type thing, which is quite different from her usual just-woke-up-but-spent-three-hours-doing-my-hair-this-morning look.

'Oh, will you just give it a rest,' Ruby says.

'Are you premenstrual or something?' her sister asks, some of her former combativeness still bubbling away below the newly calm surface.

'None of your business,' Ruby snaps.

And this is what I've been most worried about. That one of them will have such a hard time that I won't be able to manage without Rob. That Eve will think I'm capitulating to teenage whims when I only want to be supportive. But I never thought the one having a hard time would be Ruby.

Meanwhile, Scarlet will not be put off. 'We have a cooler climate but this is balanced by a long ripening period which allows time for the flavour of the grapes to develop more. So the taste is bright and fresh, crunchier and crisper.'

'Shut up, Gordon Ramsay.'

'Gordon Ramsay's a chef,' Scarlet says, quick as a whippet. Haughty. Deadly once more. 'He makes food. Not wine.'

'Well, I don't know any wine people.'

'Jancis Robinson,' I shout out, like I'm at a quiz. 'She's a wine critic.'

'Never heard of her,' Ruby says.

'Because she's a woman,' Scarlet says.

'Actually I think it's because English wine's had a bad press,' I offer.

'I'm not surprised, if it's anything like Nana Eve and Des's.' The voice of doom from the back.

'Well, that's changing,' Scarlet says. 'It's the new thing now and we need to ride this wave.' She is passion personified.

'But their wine is still crap.'

'Ruby. Come on, love.'

'What? You told me it was crap, Mum. And I've seen your expression when you drink it, remember?'

'Only the first few sips. Till my face goes numb.'

She sputters out a laugh then. Scarlet and I join in. The car fills with bubbles of joy. But bubbles go flat. Bubbles get popped. And before we reach the Somerset border the girls are back to arguing over who is sleeping where.

'Isn't it enough that for the first time in your lives you can each have your own room?'

'Not when it's in Devon,' Ruby says. 'And if Nana Eve insists on keeping that embarrassing naked painting of her in the living room, I'm going to sneak down one night and burn it on the fire.'

What was I thinking the other week? That Ruby should have more passion? I really should be more careful what I wish for.

By the time we reach Devon, they are both asleep

and I have the headspace to ponder the enigma that is my husband.

He whispered into my ear as we left him at Departures, *Sorry, Chrissie. I'll never forget you letting me do this.* And he held me tight, looked me dead in the eye. *Will you be OK?*

How I'd have loved to have said, *And* now *you're asking. Don't be laying guilt at my feet.* But the girls were both there, not to mention his mother, and it was going to be a long time before we would see him again. Did I really want the last words of mine that echoed in his ears to be full of nags?

We'll be fine, I told him. And while saying those words I felt a surge of power, like electricity or some deep force from within the earth – though it could have been the rumbling of aircraft taking off. But right in that moment I knew those words were true. We *would* be fine. I'd done it before when Ruby was little and I could do it again now with the two of them; both capable, strong young women. Most of the time. When they want to be.

By the time we approach the village, I am slightly less sure on this point because Ruby and Scarlet are awake again, arguing back and forth over the bedrooms. And just as we hit the brow of the hill, a ping tells me I have a Facebook message, so I pull over before we lose reception and there it is: a photo of Rob in one of the Cape vineyards, a view of Table Mountain behind him.

He's in his Lycra, sunglasses on, windswept, smiling, a glass of bubbly in his hand. With a message.

> Wine tourism is big biz here. Been growing grapes since 1600s. Lots of new winemakers making great stuff, including what locals call a really 'quaffable' fizz.

I'm not sure how to react to this. We've been growing grapes in Britain since Roman times? We also have a new generation of winemakers? We have some brilliantly 'quaffable' wine? (I use the term 'we' in the broadest sense.) Is this a competition? It's certainly needling me. I was expecting him to be roughing it but there he is, with a glass of wine. Relaxed, tanned, but most of all, happy.

After the usual shrieks and woofs, we arrive at our new home at lunchtime.

Eve is at the Aga, stirring a cauldron of broth with her good hand while the other is still strapped up in a sling. The kitchen smells of cabbages and farmyards but I'm assured the soup is vegan.

'Made from actual vegans?' Des asks. He is laying the table whilst glugging a glass of red.

Ruby cracks a smile and Scarlet rolls her eyes, but with more irony than usual.

Eve studiously ignores him and carries on stirring the pot.

Stirring the pot is something she is making a habit of lately.

Take Melina: her feet well and truly under the kitchen table and the rest of her well and truly in my bed.

'She replastered the ceiling, so I thought it was the least I could do.'

'Offer her my room?'

'She said it had a nice view.'

'It does have a nice view. My view.'

'I thought you'd be better down the other end so you can be more self-contained, what with it being by the girls' rooms and the other bathroom.'

'Right.'

'By the way,' she says, casually offhand, 'Nathan's coming round tomorrow morning. He says he has a proposal.'

And Nathan makes two.

LUNCH DONE, AND Melina is washing up as if she has stood at this sink for all time.

'I like very much living here,' she tells me when I grab a tea towel from the Aga rail. 'My room has beautiful view of fields and sheep and I imagine being at home with my *babcia* who is now very old.'

The girls, with Melina's calm and patient help, have finally decided on their bedrooms. Scarlet actually is the one to say Ruby can choose. And Ruby strangely goes for the smaller one.

'What about your harp?' I ask her when she and I are standing in there, surrounded by her half-unpacked belongings.

'Des says I can have the study to practise in. He says he likes the sound of it. And he's spending more time back in the studio anyway.'

'Really? Have you seen his paintings?'

'Yeah, they're really good. He's stopped with the naked women and he's doing landscapes.'

This is the best conversation I've had with Ruby in a while. I'm helping her make the bed and once she's got her duvet cover on, she smiles for the first time in ages. But she notices me notice her smile and turns it quickly into a scowl.

'You'd better help Scarlet with her bed,' she says, dismissing me. 'She gets all stressed out doing her cover.'

I don't know if this is an olive branch of any sort but I only push my luck a little by lunging in for a half-hug and then doing as I'm told. Though when I get to Scarlet's room I find Melina already helping her.

LATER, WHEN THE girls have gone to bed, exhausted, I put on my pyjamas and dressing gown and head downstairs for a ginger tea. I'm so wired I don't know if I'll ever sleep, though my bones are telling me I ought to give it a try.

Eve is there at the kitchen table. Her arm is now out of its sling but she's wearing one of those foam straps to support it.

'Is it sore still?' I ask her.

'Not too bad. Just stiff, really. From lack of use.' She wiggles her fingers to demonstrate then goes back to sorting out her pills into one of those weekly containers.

'I didn't know you took tablets?'

'They're supplements, mainly. And I still take the herbs, of course.'

'Right.'

'Don't have ginger, my darling. Camomile is much better this time of night.'

'Camomile tastes of grass.'

'It's very relaxing.'

'It makes me retch.'

'Oh, Christabel,' she says. 'Always so stubborn. That's where Ruby gets it from.'

I'm about to protest. I'm about to say Ruby's not stubborn when I have to admit to myself that maybe there's an element of truth here. And as for me, I want to ask her why I'd let Rob go away for a year if I was stubborn. But Eve cuts me short.

'It turns out I do have osteoporosis,' she says as if she can't quite understand it, like it's some kind of conspiracy between the NHS and 'big pharma'.

I'm sitting back at the table now with my ginger tea. I've made her a camomile. It stinks.

'Oh, Eve,' I say. 'I'm sorry. Is that serious? I don't really know much about it, to be honest.'

'The doctor says I'm at risk of more fractures so she wants me to take this medication.'

'Well, then you should.'

I try googling osteoporosis but, surprise, surprise, no signal.

'Look, Eve, now we're living here too, can we find out about getting broadband? The business would really benefit. It's so useful. Essential, actually. And then there's Rob. He's going to be blogging about his journey and we'll be able to read what he's doing. And the girls can FaceTime him. You know, speak face to face with him on their phones.'

'Really, Christabel, what's the point of bringing them to live in the countryside if they're going to spend the whole time glued to their phones?'

'I want them to stay in touch with their father. And their London friends. And I want them to make new ones here.'

She sighs.

'It's how it is now, Eve,' I say as calmly as I can. 'Whether we like it or not.' And whether we like it or not, the reality is that we are living in Devon while Rob crosses Africa. While we are dealing with dogs and pheasants, Rob could well be facing wild animals that would think nothing of eating him for lunch.

We sip our tea, both lost in thought for a moment.

'I've got a leaflet somewhere,' she says, breaking the impasse.

'About broadband?'

'What? No. About osteoporosis.'

She rummages amongst a pile of papers on the dresser top and brings over an NHS leaflet for me. I take it from her and scan it.

'It says to avoid further fractures you need to take regular exercise.'

'I certainly do that. Luther and I go for a walk around the field and into the village every day, come rain or shine. And I'm doing t'ai chi and my daily yoga.'

'Good. Right. And you have to eat healthily.'

She snorts derisively. 'I've always eaten healthily. I was a pioneer of wholefoods back in the sixties, for goodness' sake.'

'Lots of food rich in calcium and vitamin D?'

'I eat tons of green veg, but I suppose I don't really do cheese or much dairy...'

'In that case it suggests a daily calcium supplement.'

'But you know me and pills. I really don't want to be putting something into my body I don't need.'

'You're always taking supplements.' I point at her container. 'This is just a vitamin. The clue's in the name.'

'I suppose so,' she admits, reluctantly. 'Remind me what else it says?'

'It says you must give up smoking and reduce alcohol consumption. You haven't smoked in years, have you?'

She looks guilty. 'No. Not really. I mean the occasional one.'

'Eve, really? You just said you don't want to be putting something into your body you don't need. You don't need tobacco. Or booze, for that matter.'

'Yes, all right. I know fags and booze aren't needed but when you live with someone like Des, it's hard not to indulge.'

'It's probably not great to be living on a vineyard either.'

'No.'

We sigh in stereo. Like mother, like daughter.

'I don't have to drink it, though, do I?' she says.

'You don't. Though it might be trickier to abstain if the wine actually tastes good in the future.'

We share a wry smile.

'My early menopause is to blame,' she says.

Oh yes. The early menopause. I haven't forgotten that.

'Not to mention the family history,' Eve continues,

tapping her long fingers against her tea cup so I get another waft of grass.

'Family history?'

'My mother,' she says, as if I should know Granny had osteoporosis when no one ever told me that. 'So, Christabel, you need to look after yourself. And Ruby too, of course. Before you know it you'll be hitting the menopause and she'll be pushing out a baby.'

Great. Something to look forward to. 'Eve, really.'

'I'm being practical. You like me being practical.'

'True.' She has me there. 'And while we're confessing, I have something to tell you.'

'Oh?'

'I've booked an engineer to come on Friday.'

'An engineer? Whatever for?'

'Broadband.'

'Oh, Christabel.'

Tuesday, 30 October

TUESDAY MORNING, AND Eve is bustling round the kitchen, sliding a baking tray out of the Aga and resting it on a cooling rack. It smells like Christmas. Cinnamon and nutmeg. We haven't even got out of October yet.

'Flapjacks,' she says. 'Make some coffee, would you, darling?'

'Did someone say coffee?' Des is here, covered in streaks of vibrant colour. He goes to kiss me but I dodge out the way and indicate his filthy hands.

'Just a bit of paint, Chrissie.'

'I'd rather you kept it to yourself, Des, thanks all the same.'

He pretends to envelop me and I manage to sidestep him. 'Someone's got out of bed the wrong side this morning.'

'You mean someone's got out of the *wrong bed* this morning.' I clank about making coffee.

'Ah,' he says, knowingly. 'Still annoyed at your mother for giving your room to Melina?'

'Yes. No. Whatever.'

'Really, Christabel, you sound like Ruby and Scarlet,' Eve chides. 'What on earth are you sulking about? Melina's transformed that bedroom into a work of art.'

'Work of art?'

'She does have an eye for colour,' Des says. 'None of that magnolia for her.'

'I don't use magnolia. I use off-white.'

He smiles at me. Then his smile mutates into a frown of concern as he recognizes the hurt in my expression. 'Whatever is the matter, my love?' he asks.

Before I get the chance to answer, the door bangs open and there he is, like Lord Flashheart – Flash by name, flash by nature – legs astride, ruddy-cheeked, taking up all the space and oxygen in the room.

'I've brought the post,' Nathan says. 'Something smells good.'

THE FOUR OF us sit around the table, hot coffee and warm flapjacks, but a chill in my heart. Eve and Des are so relaxed with Nathan. He is so relaxed with them. I can't really process what's happening or what is to come. Or why Eve has forgiven him so readily for walking out on her child and grandchild. Was it because she knew him when he was a young lad? He was always round here, part of the family. They hit it off. Had a rapport.

He'd do odd jobs around the place. And she knew how much he loved me. And he did love me. And then he didn't. He fell in love with someone else and buggered off to the other side of the world. But I reckon Eve still believes it was my fault he left. That something was lacking in me. Or that I did something. Or didn't do something. It's so unfair.

I focus on Luther's warmth at my feet where he's resting his chin, his breath like a mini fan heater.

'So what's this proposal?' Des asks, pulling me back from the precipice of despair with a jolt.

Proposal? No proposal of Nathan's ever led to anything good.

'It's about a party, actually,' Nathan says. 'I've been speaking to Melina and she told me to organize a send-off for the pickers, before they head back home, and I thought we could use your barn.'

'*Our* barn?' I am taken aback. The cheek of it. He's got so many outbuildings he could shelter a small town in an emergency. 'Haven't you enough barns of your own?'

'None as pretty as yours.'

Eve and Des both smile, proud owners of a pretty barn rather than narked owners of a failing business.

'I never thought of our barn as pretty but I suppose it is,' Eve says.

And yes, all right, you can't deny its charm. An eighteenth-century granary built in cob with a thatched roof. Rough round the edges. What Rob would call 'rustic', using his marketing shine to buff it up, to promise more than he can actually give.

But no.

Just no.

'What a wonderful idea.' Eve studiously ignores me kicking her under the table. 'We'll ask the locals along too.'

This is absurd. 'Sorry to put a damper on the proceedings, but who's going to cover the cost of this?' I pipe up in desperation.

'It's the least we can do,' Des says. 'We haven't had to pay their wages, Chrissie.'

'Des, there's no money to put on a spread. I've been through the books.' I indicate the pile of papers on the table in front of me but then feel treacherous again, mentioning their – *our* – financial woes in front of Nathan, who really should know better than to ask us for help when he must have an inkling that Eve and Des are struggling. And now I'll probably get another reprimand from Eve for mentioning money.

'I'm not expecting you to foot the bill for this,' Nathan says, looking at me. 'I just thought your barn would be a nice setting. Actually it was Melina who suggested it. My barns are all full of stuff. "Junk", she called it.'

'Ignore my daughter, Nathan. She's being ridiculous.' Eve, as expected, is most put out. 'Of course you can have the barn. And we can run to a crate of wine and a keg of cider.'

'We really can't spare any more than that, Eve.' I'm being a cow, I know I am – those workers put everything into gathering our harvest and we should be thankful, but really, this is exasperating. Why is this man so welcome at our kitchen table?

'And I can provide a pig for a hog roast.' Nathan is leaning back in his chair now, legs akimbo, as if this is his own kitchen table.

I get a flashback to our relationship. How much space he used to take up. In the kitchen. In bed. In the car. And then, after he left, in my head. I might be a cow but he's a big fat bull.

'A hog roast would be splendid as long as it's away from the barn,' Des says. 'We don't want any stray sparks on the roof.'

'Of course,' Nathan says.

'Hang on,' I interrupt. 'How do you reckon Ruby and Scarlet will feel about a dead pig being rotisseried in front of them?' I think of the girls, imagining their horror – and then wondering when they're going to show their faces this morning, hoping it won't be just yet.

But these thoughts are shoved sideways when Nathan sticks the boot in. 'You shouldn't mollycoddle them, Chrissie,' he says.

I can almost hear the sharp intakes of breath from my parents. They know this won't go down well.

No, it won't.

'*Mollycoddle* them? Did I hear you correctly?' I ask this very quietly, through gritted teeth.

'Sometimes you just have to tough it out.'

'Tough it out? Like you did with our marriage? With our daughter?' I'm having to ball up my hands now, to stop them from shaking. To stop them from throttling his big fat neck. 'How dare you comment on my parenting.'

'I'm just giving you my opinion,' he says, arms up in the air like I might be about to whip out a shotgun and aim between his eyes. Oh, how I wish.

'Your *opinion*? What do you know about parenting?'

His body language changes. He has suddenly shrunk in stature. His legs are crossed. His arms by his side gripping the chair. He at least has the decency to blush.

'I don't know a lot about parenting, Chrissie. If you remember, I didn't have very good role models at home. It was only here, in this house, that I found acceptance and guidance.' His eyes narrow. He strokes the stubble on his chin. 'I let you down. I let Eve and Des down. I let myself down. But most of all I let Ruby down.'

There's a gaping hole of silence now, no one sure how to fill it. I almost feel sorry for Nathan. *Almost*. But I won't let myself. 'You left us,' I tell him, keeping my voice as steady as I possibly can.

'You were the one who told me to leave,' he says.

A shift in the room. A slip sideways.

I feel my face flare up with heat and nausea pool in my stomach. 'I told you to leave *home* when I found out about you and Charlotte. I never told you to leave Ruby. She hasn't seen you for ten years. Ten years! She doesn't even know who you are. You're just a name. Not even a memory. How dare you twist this!'

Nathan shakes his head as if I'm being ridiculous. The girl he used to know so different to the one now, and yet exactly the same. 'Let's not do this here,' he says.

'I'm not doing it anywhere,' I retort, shoving back my chair with such force it tips over.

Then I leave them to their pathetic party-planning and grab Luther's lead from the chair. He wags his tail, a steady gaze of adoration in his dark-brown eyes, and I can't remember the last time a human looked at me that way. We head out into the cold day and the poor old dog has to work those long legs to keep up. As we reach the gate, I stop to open it and Luther licks my hand.

'What is wrong with people?' I ask him, half hoping for an answer because I don't know anything. Tears sting my eyes and my heart feels crushed. Why of all places did Nathan have to move in next door?

'Woof,' Luther barks, enigmatic as ever.

Nathan has gone by the time we've returned from our walk, some of the cobwebs blown away. The kitchen is deserted apart from Melina, who is scrubbing the flagstones.

'Hello, Chrissie,' she says. 'The floor is wet.'

'You don't have to do this, Melina.'

'Who else will do it?'

'Me?'

'You have other fish to cook.'

'I do?'

'Ruby is unhappy.'

'She's awake, then?'

'Yes, I woke her and Scarlet.'

'Oh.' I want to tell Melina that waking the girls is not her job but then I realize the time. It's nearly midday.

'Do you know what's the matter with her? Has anything specific happened?'

'She has face like thunder.'

'Nothing else?'

'She doesn't tell me.'

Poor Ruby. My poor unhappy Ruby, abandoned first by one father, then by another. I did not tell Nathan to do that. I did not. I told him to leave *me*. Not *her*. And yes, OK, maybe I made things difficult for him, but I had to be strong. I had to focus on Ruby. My career. Then he went off travelling with Charlotte and that's pretty much the last I heard from him, and when Rob and Scarlet appeared, it was just so much easier to put all my eggs in one basket.

Does Ruby have an inkling who Nathan is? And why am I avoiding the inevitable conversation? But I can't do this today. She needs to settle in, get used to her space, the new school. And anyway, she's shown no interest in meeting her birth father. No desire even to talk about him. 'Rob's my dad,' she always says when anyone asks. End of. And it hurts me all over again that he's gone away.

'Where is she, Melina?'

'She has went with Des to see harp man about musical lessons.'

'Oh. Right. Yes of course.'

'You OK, Chrissie?'

'No. I'm actually not, Melina.'

'Sit down and I make coffee.' She tuts at the Aga. 'I do not understand why Eve has so much love for this old stove. Why not get nice clean electric cooker?'

She clanks away and makes coffee, strong and sweet, and I can't help it. All my bitterness and resentment froths up and spills out of my mouth.

'I'm so angry with Rob for leaving us. He's so bloody selfish.'

'He is going to Africa. Not to the moon.'

'I know that, Melina. But really? Right when the girls are about to embark on their GCSEs?'

She's sitting opposite me at the table with her own mug of coffee, staring into its depths like it's a crystal ball. I wish she'd find the answers in there. 'Tell me about Nathan,' she says. 'Why do you hate him?'

'I'm talking about Rob,' I correct her.

'But this is about Nathan.'

And so it is.

I tell her about Nathan. The gist of what happened in the past.

'Nathan is Ruby's father?' Melina actually looks surprised. She never looks surprised. She always takes everything in her stride.

'Her birth father, yes.'

'And now he lives next door.'

'Yes. He lives next door. And I hate the way Eve and Des, Eve especially, have welcomed him back like the prodigal son.'

'And did you tell him to leave? Many years ago?'

'I did tell him to leave. But that doesn't mean he should've shirked all his responsibilities. It certainly doesn't give him the right to tell me how I should bring up my daughters.'

And now, to my shame, I am crying. Quiet shudders rather than snot-filled blubs, but crying nonetheless. 'I'm sorry, Melina,' I manage to say. 'I feel so stupid.'

'You feel stupid? Why?'

'Because I'm going to pieces over this. And it's pathetic. I mean it's not like I've had to leave my country and everything. To clean other people's floors.'

'True.' She shrugs. 'I do not argue with that.' She gives a wry smile.

And I feel my lips reciprocate. My problems a little lighter for a shared moment.

'You must appreciate what you have,' Melina says. 'Two good daughters. Lazy, but good.'

I nod. She's right. I do.

'You must not worry about what you do not have. Rob has not forgotten you. You will hear from him soon.'

I nod again, though this time with a little less certainty. 'I hope you're right, Melina. I'll go up the hill again and check for a signal. See if he's emailed. Or messaged. Or blogged. Or texted.'

I'm about to get my coat when she stops me.

'There are letters here.'

For a silly moment, I think she means from Rob but of course they're not from Rob; they wouldn't have got here yet even if he had written a letter, which I don't think he's done since he was a child.

'Bills, maybe.' Melina opens the property section of the *Western Morning News* and there, hidden amongst its pages, lurk three telltale envelopes.

I PUT OFF searching for a signal and hunt down Eve instead. I find her and Scarlet in the study. They are behind the desk, in cahoots, Scarlet showing Eve a sketch in her notebook.

'Ah, Christabel. There you are. Scarlet's helping me plan the party.'

'We're going to hang bunting from the rafters in the barn,' Scarlet says, excited. 'And those paper hangy things. And fairy lights.'

She shows me the sketch; I can see the barn will look great and, much as it pains me to admit it, that having this party is a good thing to do.

'And EU flags!' Scarlet goes on. 'And Polish ones too. And we'll have straw bales and trestle tables and we've agreed not to have a hog roast but a vegan feast.'

Eve squints at me. 'I know that's an oxymoron but Scarlet has some wonderful ideas.'

'What's an oxymoron?' Scarlet asks. 'I can't even google it, Nana Eve, because there's no signal or anything.'

'Your mother is on to that, fear not.'

'Really?'

'Hopefully by the end of the week.'

'Brill!' she says, like a small child at Christmas. I've never seen such a happy face.

'Scarlet, you're amazing,' I gush. 'Helping Nana

Eve like this and just, well, being so positive about everything. I really thought you'd struggle.'

'You thought *I'd* be the nightmare but actually it's Ruby?'

'Something like that.' My eyes start welling again.

'There's no need to cry, Chrissie.' Scarlet gets up from the desk and comes round to hug me.

'I don't know what to do about Ruby. How's she going to manage at school on Monday?'

'I'll be there. I've always been there for her.' Scarlet's matter-of-fact, not in the slightest put out or after a special award; it just is what it is to her.

And she's right; she *has* always been there for her sister.

'I never give you credit for that, do I, love?'

'That's OK. You're an only child, it's different for you. But she's my sister. And you don't have to hold me quite so hard, Chrissie. I can't breathe.'

'Sorry, love.' I pull myself together and turn to my mother. 'But Eve. I need to talk to you about these bills.' I wave the three letters at her. 'Are there any more lying around unopened?'

'It'll have to wait till later, darling. We need to sort this party stuff out right now, what with it being on Thursday.'

'Thursday? As in *this* Thursday? That's two days' time.'

'That's right, Christabel. The day after Wednesday. Which comes after Tuesday. Which is today.'

'Thank you, Eve.' I'm about to leave in a huff when I stop myself. 'Why Thursday? Why not leave it till Friday or Saturday? Why the short notice?'

'They're leaving on Saturday. And besides, it's All Saints' Day on Thursday.'

'All Saints' Day?'

'The first of November. The day after Halloween.'

'And that's worth celebrating because...?'

'Because it's the Day of the Dead and, like, a massive Polish festival,' Scarlet chips in, excited at the prospect of a party, even if it is with adults. 'It's called... wait a minute...' She looks at the notes in her book... '*Wsz-yst-kich Swie-tych*. Melina told me how to write it but I can't say it very well.'

'Well, that's... nice. I think.'

'It's not scary or anything, Chrissie. It's about remembering the dead. They put candles on gravestones in cemeteries to help the departed find their way through the darkness.'

'Where to?'

'The other side, I suppose,' she says, oblivious to my facetiousness. 'Like heaven and that.'

I must stop this. I must embrace her enthusiasm.

'And there's bread, eggs and honey as part of the feast but I don't mind about the eggs as long as they're free-range and I don't care about the honey as long as it's local.'

That's very good of you, I want to say, but I am the grown-up here. And who knows? Maybe a party isn't such a hideous idea. It will at least give the girls something to look forward to. 'It sounds marvellous, Scarlet. But one thing?'

'What?'

'We don't have to dress up, do we?'

'It's not Halloween.'

'Oh. Gosh. I forgot about Halloween.'

'Don't look so worried, Chrissie. Me and Rube are too old for Halloween. This sounds so much better.'

'You reckon?'

'Course. Be open to new possibilities. Who knows what might happen?'

And I don't miss the slight smugness on my mother's face.

A COUPLE OF hours later, and Des and Ruby are still not back from seeing his harpist friend. She was very close to her teacher in London, so fingers crossed she'll like him. God knows she needs some distraction from her current angst; she can think about finding a youth orchestra to join and meet friends that way, as well as through school.

New school Monday.

Not the school I went to, where Nathan and I were inseparable, but it's a good community college, with a sixth form which should encourage the girls to have aspirations. Lots of hippy young people go there, the offspring of tree-huggers and soap-dodgers, Steiner graduates and home-schoolers venturing into the real world. They specialize in the arts. Melina says the arts are important but the girls should also put their efforts into maths and science. Melina has a lot to say these days. And I'm listening to her more since we arrived here. Is that because I've finally realized, as well as being able to coax a stain out of a delicate woollen jumper, just how much else she knows?

When I get a moment, I'll talk to Ruby. Find out how she's getting on. Straight to the point. No dodging. No swerving. But right now I need to work through the parental unit's business accounts. Not much of a business if my first scan of the numbers is anything to go by.

I do hope Ruby likes this teacher.

A FURIOUS BANG and much stomping used to mean it was Scarlet's hormones on the loose. But today it is Ruby. *Crash!* goes the door of her new bedroom. I can hear it from the kitchen.

I rush off to hunt for Des, find him dazed and confused, standing stock-still in the hall.

'What's happened?'

'Ruby didn't think much of Malcolm,' he says, bewildered. 'I can't think why.'

Oh, for Pete's sake. There could be a multitude of reasons, knowing Des's circle of friends and acquaintances – a motley assortment picked up over many years hanging about in pubs and restaurants, in the art world and Eve's hippydom.

'Tell me about Malcolm, Des?' I ask him, tentatively, unsure if I want to know the truth.

'Malcolm? What can I say about Malcolm?' This is a rhetorical question. He's pensive for a moment while he tries desperately to gather his thoughts into some coherent response that will satisfy me and save his friend's dignity. 'Malc's a top gent. Always polite and considerate.' He does an embarrassed cough. 'Apart from the odd fruity word.'

'Fruity? How fruity?'

A pause. More pondering. 'Oh well, you know, fairly fruity, but he wasn't as fruity today as he is in adult company,' he declares. 'He does have standards.'

'Right.'

Another pause. 'And the occasional emission.'

'Emission?'

'He's prone to a bit of wind. Both ends. It didn't endear him to Ruby, which is such a shame because once you get past the foul language – and the occasional whiff – he really has impeccable manners and he's a very good harpist.'

I shut my eyes for a second. Centre myself. Think of poor Ruby who's used to an elegant concert harpist with an impeccable, friendly yet robust teaching style.

'That doesn't necessarily mean he will make a very good teacher.'

'No,' Des agrees. 'I might've misjudged that. Do you think I should have a word with her?'

I shake my head. Rather vigorously. So vigorously, in fact that I feel a bit dizzy. 'Maybe not right now, Des. I'll go and see her.'

A TENTATIVE KNOCK on her bedroom door.

'Ruby? Can I come in?'

'If you must,' she says, in a woe-is-me warbly voice.

I open the door gingerly, mindful of the booby traps that lie in wait on the other side – discarded undergarments and empty mugs and lonely socks; what has happened to my tidy, organized daughter? – and sit down on the bed where she is lying, prostrate as a Pre-Raphaelite Ophelia, staring blankly at the ceiling.

'Do you think Melina would plaster this?' Ruby says, pointing upwards, weakly, pathetically, deathbed-ily, as if it's taking up all the energy she has ever had. 'I *hate* looking at those cracks. I keep imagining they're worms and it makes me feel weird.'

'I'm sure she would, Rube. If you ask nicely.'

'Of course I'll ask nicely,' she says, un-nicely.

I can't help it: my eyebrows shoot up and I can't reposition them without her noticing. I brace myself for the explosion. But it doesn't go off.

'Sorry,' she says. 'I know I'm being a cow, Mum, but I don't know how to stop.'

This takes me by surprise. I hadn't realized just how much I've been tiptoeing over eggshells these past few weeks. And although I'm not quite sure how to respond, gut instinct tells me to go along this path with her. Tread carefully, take her lead.

'Oh, Rube.' I kiss her forehead and remember her newborn smell. Her girlhood. She's the same as she always has been – it's just that she's been possessed by teen spirits. And we're all dealing with a new life, Rob's absence, the appearance out of the blue of Nathan. Even if Ruby still doesn't know his real identity. Bloody Nathan.

I've been an idiot. Handled it all badly. I need to fix this. I *will* fix this.

But maybe not just yet.

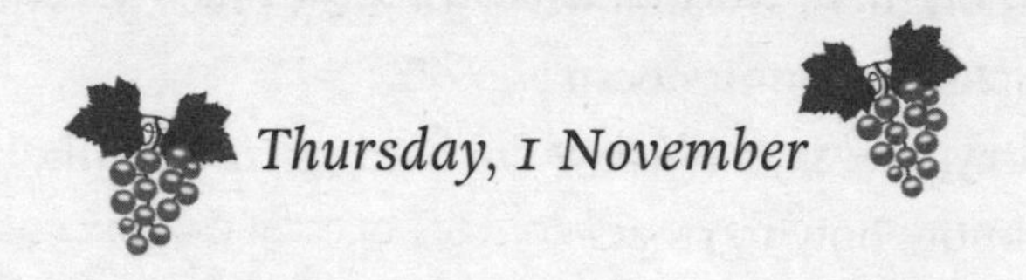

Thursday, 1 November

EARLY THURSDAY MORNING, All Saints' Day, I'm in the Co-op in Chudston on a mission to buy olives, falafel, crisps, anything vegan I can lay my hands on. Eve has given me £200 in cash. She said it arrived in an envelope on the doormat earlier, no idea who it was from or who delivered it but she told me never to look a gift horse in the mouth. So I'm doing as directed and, to be honest, I haven't the bandwidth to question who might be giving us money right now. And there's something rather soothing about filling a trolley with food. I even throw in some bottles of cava because I seem to have found a taste for fizz.

Des and Ruby are picking up cider from a nearby farm while Julia, Zofia, Borys and Scarlet decorate the barn, which includes some thatching repairs on the roof; it turns out there are places where there is nothing between the overhead beams and the sky above.

Eve is inside, beavering away in the kitchen, baking bread, while Melina is making a vat of borscht.

'It's called *barszcz*,' she tells me as I return with bags of shopping. 'I need more of time to make it properly vegetarian. I hope my friends do not hate me for making bad *barszcz*.'

'They'll love you, Melina.'

'We are judged by our *barszcz*. I cannot disappoint my grandmother.'

'It smells amazing, Melina. It looks divine. They'll be delighted.'

'Not when they taste your parents' wine. I hope they bring much beer.'

Eve chuckles at this comment. Why does Melina get away with this when I would be held to account for such negativity?

Hours later, and it turns out that our Polish friends do bring beer. Much beer. And *kompot*. And vodka. And more food. And lots of energy and fun, and for the first time in ages I let my hair down and enjoy the spirit of the evening, all the better for Nathan's mysterious absence. Even Ruby cracks a smile and joins in the dancing. And with the folk music playing, and the fairy lights twinkling, and the warm food and the wine, it's hard not to be entranced by the beauty of the barn. Who *wouldn't* want to have a celebration here? If I shut my eyes I can imagine newlyweds spinning around on the floor in each other's arms, their first dance. A barn dance. A ceilidh. A gavotte. A Para Para. A polonaise.

Weddings. Could we do weddings? We could do weddings.

'You want to dance with me?' Tomasz holds out his hands.

I instinctively check around me; I don't know why – maybe because I can't remember the last time a man asked me this question. Probably the school disco, I realize; Nathan dressed like Liam Gallagher in ridiculous shades, swaying to 'You're Gorgeous' or another of those nineties ballads, with me held tight in his arms. He was a lanky sixteen-year-old. Tomasz is much older, he's lived a life, is rough round the edges and strong, and off he whisks me before I've gathered breath. I'm feeling quite giddy by the time we've spun around the room a few times, me doing my best not to tread on his big feet, trying to let the music take hold of me the way he is holding me firmly in his hunky, confident arms. Round and round we go, until I have to beg to stop so I can steady myself and get a drink. From the sidelines I watch as he takes Melina in his grip, or maybe it's the other way round; whatever it is, they fit together perfectly, spinning and laughing, full of energy and fizz.

The air is heady inside the barn, folksy and earthy and otherworldly. And if the dead were to wake up and take part I shouldn't be surprised. You can almost smell the old grain that used to be stored here – though that could be the freshly baked bread. All this mingles with the hay bales and the *barszcz*. The spices of the apple *kompot*. The jars of local honey. The potato and cabbage dumplings. The chrysanthemums. The heat of dancing bodies. The bursts of laughter. The buzz of life sparking up to the rafters. Up and beyond into the clear night sky, smoke curling up amongst the trees. The hoot of an owl. The honk of a surviving pheasant. The smell of wood fire and countryside and the crispness of autumn. It is magical. All we need is some fizz of our own making to toast the dead, but that is a while and a dream away.

In the meantime: 'More *wódka*?' Melina asks, pink-faced, eyes glittering.

It's late now. The locals have gone, exchanging tearful goodbyes with their continental friends, all too aware of their less-than-certain return next year. There's a deep sadness to this occasion for us all.

'Churchill himself promised support to the Polish troops who were unable to return home after the war,' Des says, huskily. 'Poles have been living in the area for generations now.' He blows his nose flamboyantly into a vast handkerchief.

'Why couldn't they go home?' Scarlet asks.

'Poland was under Soviet control by that point and they were afraid of being taken as political prisoners.'

'Thanks for the history lesson, Granddad,' Ruby says. She's half joking, half sarcastic, which is an improvement.

'How can we learn about our present or indeed our future if we don't know about the past?' he asks, a question of his I've heard many times before.

Melina is here now, listening. 'The past is where our dead live,' she says. 'Now we go to graveyard to light the candles. You come with?'

'But you don't know anyone buried there. And it's Church of England.' I can hear the primness in my voice, creeping in despite the joy of the evening, the music, the feast, the dancing.

'Our beloved dead are in Poland. We are here. So we do this as symbol, no?'

'How wonderful.' This is right up Eve's street. 'I'll fetch some torches.'

'No need,' says Melina. 'We have lanterns.'

'Lanterns?'

'Piotr and Aleksy make them today. Come on. We must go now.'

So we gather together, solemn and silent, while Piotr and Aleksy hand each of us a stick with a hook screwed into the end. And from each hook hangs a jam jar with wire round its neck. Inside each jam jar is a tea light. One by one, the candles are lit – Des on fire watch – and off we process; out of the barn, across the yard, through the gate, down the lane, past the few houses in this small village which has no shop, no post office, no pub, but which is the proud home of a beautiful red-stone Norman church, St Mary Magdalene. It's surrounded by an old graveyard, a lychgate and a path lined with yews. The gravestones are arranged higgledy-piggledy, huge slabs of granite leaning at all angles, the names, dates and epitaphs eroded by exposure, blurred by the passing centuries.

I check on Scarlet and Ruby, who might be concerned at the prospect of ghosts and ghouls, but both are transfixed by the beauty of the gathering. The bright clear moon. The glow of the lanterns. And as the jam jars are unhooked and placed on the graves one by one, we're surrounded by dots of light, flashing like fireflies.

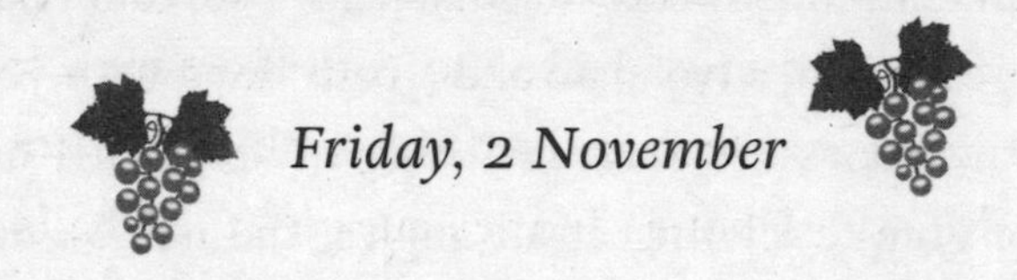

Friday, 2 November

FOR ONCE I didn't drink too much last night; the atmosphere was enough to keep up my spirits. Today I wake feeling more optimistic. I don't look at the space beside me straight away. I don't reach out for the cold sheet.

And Des has brought me a cup of tea and his big cheery smile, as bright as it has ever been. 'Another day, another chance to spread a little joy in the world.'

'How do you do it, Des?'

'What's that, my honeybun?'

'Be so... happy?'

He releases a Brian Blessed '*Ha!*', followed by, 'Now that's a question!'

But I'm waiting for an answer.

'I was given the gift of joy by my dear darling mother, and then I found Eve and little you. And now I have my granddaughters here. Why would I not be happy?'

He beams me his super-smile, the one that has eased a lifetime of negotiations with Eve. 'Also,' he says, 'I'm painting again. Come and see.'

DES HAS NEVER been an artist precious about his space; his studio isn't sacred. I used to come in here a lot as a child, even as a teen. I liked to watch him paint his commissions. For hotels and restaurants. Civic halls and community centres. Big splashes of corporate colour. But these...

'Des, these are spectacular!'

'Do you really think so? They're a departure from my usual work, I know. Not that there's been much at all for the last thirty years. Commercial stuff, yes. But not my own art.'

The canvases before us now are nothing like his own art either. Nothing like the huge paintings of the sixties. There are no doe-eyed young women. No bulbous breasts. No curvy bottoms. These are less brazen, finer, a little more impressionistic. The colours are remarkable – subtle yet somehow bold. How does he do that?

'They're completely different,' I tell him. 'But still so... you. I love them.'

He practically does a jump for joy.

'I've never seen you paint landscapes. It was always portraits.'

'That's what sold,' he says. 'Portraits paid the bills. For a time. But this is what I studied at the Slade. I did a grand tour in my youth. Painting *en plein air*. The *duomos* of Italy. The poppy fields of Belgium. The avenues of France.' He sighs, distant memories fresh once more. 'I wanted to be a Pissarro or a Monet but I became more of a Vladimir Tretchikoff or a J. H. Lynch. I was one step away from doing Pierrot clowns.'

'They *were* popular. You can't knock it.'

'I know. Except fashions change.'

'They're changing again. We need to get your paintings back out there. Your mid-century work should be very collectable now. We just need to give people a nudge.'

'You mean like a retrospective? Should I be hustling back into the art world?'

'I was thinking more of the everyday punter. Some middle-incomers after an original piece of retro kitsch on their kitchen wall.'

'Retro kitsch? Is that what I am?'

'Not you, Des. Your old paintings. People love all that nostalgia. Generation X-ers can't get enough of the stuff. It reminds them of happier times when Valerie Singleton and John Noakes were on *Blue Peter* and the Osmonds were on *Top of the Pops*. I've organized loads of events for them.'

'The Osmonds?'

'No, Des. The Gen X-ers. Fondue soirées, ABBA nights, *Abigail's Party*. They want pineapple and cheese chunks on cocktail sticks. Twiglets. Babycham. Biba dresses and flares.'

I think about the telephone cupboard under the stairs. The seventies vibe. I only remember the latter years of that decade but I find comfort there too.

'They forget about the inflation and the three-day week,' Des says.

'That's because they – we! I'm one of them! – were kids then. It was our parents – you Baby Boomers – who had to deal with all that stuff. But look at those parents now. Houses paid off, full pensions, while my generation are taking care of them as well as our own offspring, who will never be able to afford to leave the family home. Forget Gen X, we're the Sandwich Generation.'

Des stands before me; an old, vulnerable man.

'Is that how you see your mother and me?'

'Oh, Des. Sorry, no. I don't mean to suggest you're a burden.'

'A burden?'

'What I mean is, people my age are generally pushed for cash. But our kids will be even worse off as they'll never be able to afford their own home. The future is so uncertain for them.'

'And Eve and I?'

'Eve and you loved the Boomer lifestyle but... Well, you didn't invest wisely, really, did you? You were too Bohemian. And I wouldn't have you any other way.'

'That's not entirely true now, Chrissie, is it?'

'No, it's not,' I admit. 'I do wish you both took a little

more notice of your incomings and outgoings, but I also realize you're not about to start now, when you never have. Which is partly why we've moved in with you. To help turn around the business.'

'To keep an eye on us?'

'It works both ways. You can keep an eye on us too.'

He hugs me then and I breathe in the turps and oil and the woodsmoke smell of this man who has been my father since Jimmy wanted to be a long-haired lover from Liverpool.

'You give people joy, Des. And you could be the answer to the winery's money problems. We need to raise capital not only to pay bills but to buy equipment. And to upkeep the vines, maybe plant some Pinot Meunier.'

'Do you really think the old paintings are worth anything? Should I be getting in touch with Christie's?'

'I thought we could start with eBay.'

'Right. EBay.'

'To test the water.'

'And what about these?' He indicates his landscapes. 'I think they're a bit Paul Nash.'

'I have no idea who he is.'

'He was predominantly a war painter.'

I gaze at the greys and browns and reds for a while longer. 'There's something unsettling about them.'

'Unsettling? Hmm. That's all right. It's good to be unsettled every now and then.'

I try to immerse myself in the strokes. The textures and tones. The more I look, the more I see. 'They're rather surreal, aren't they?'

'Indeed they are. Nash was making sense of the senseless. But I don't want to look backwards in time. That's what troubles me about the old paintings. The –whatchamacallit? "Retro kitsch"?'

I nod. A tad embarrassed, but money is what is needed here now.

'I want to look forwards,' he says.

'To what?' I'm thinking dystopia. Climate change. The end of times. 'The Apocalypse?'

'Not actually the Apocalypse, no. I'm just predicting what the future might be if we don't get our act together.'

'And is this what you want to paint? What about all that joy of yours? I can't see much of that here. Is this Eve's influence? You know, all this... political stuff?'

'Not at all.' He feigns shock and horror. 'I am my own man, you know.'

I don't say anything. I let him go on.

'I suppose even the most joyous of us have some darkness within. I can express mine through painting. One must be able to vent somewhere. One must have a passion.'

'So Eve says.'

'Well, quite. Your mother's right about that. "Express your passion, do whatever you love, take action, no matter what".'

'Did she say that?'

'No. Tretchikoff. But it could've been your mother.' He laughs. 'And while we're on the subject, you shouldn't give her such a hard time. She really is trying her best for the girls, to make sure they settle. All these years she's hoped you'd move back and now it's finally happened, I think it's thrown her somewhat. She's rather desperate for it to work. And that goes for me too.'

'I feel like I'm intruding on her life though.'

'Nonsense. She's just shifting and shuffling to make room for you. I know for a fact that she is thrilled to her very core to have her family with her. You both need time to adjust.'

He kisses me on the forehead and I wish I were little again, no more worries other than finding another Enid Blyton from the library to read. Now there are no libraries and my problems are a whole lot bigger.

'Right, well, I hope that's all it is. I'll give her some slack.' I look back at the half-finished painting. 'It's brilliant, Des. This late flourishing in your career. You're an inspiration.'

And it's giving me an idea but no time to use him as a sounding board because Scarlet bursts in.

'The engineer's here!' she screeches.

Anyone would think it was the Messiah.

And now she's yanking me by the arm out of the studio, shouting, ''Scuse us, Granddad!', allowing me just a glimpse of Des, paintbrush in hand, intense focus all over his lovely old face.

Later, once the engineer's done his magic, and connected us to the universe – *Ta-dah!* – and once I've caught up on my emails, it occurs to me I haven't seen Ruby for a while. Where is she?

I can hear footsteps thundering down the stairs. Maybe that's her. Though it sounds more like her sister.

Ah. It is.

'I'm taking Luther for a walk,' Scarlet says, shoving on a jumper and hat.

Luther scrambles out of his basket and stretches, wagging his tail half enthusiastically, half reluctantly.

'That's nice. It's cold out, so wrap up.'

She disappears into the boot room and I follow her in, watch her put on her wellies and parka.

She makes a grab for Luther's lead and he stands submissively letting her clip it onto his old leather collar. Then she turns to say goodbye and catches something in my expression. 'You OK, Chrissie?'

'Me? Yes, I'm OK. I was just wondering where your sister is.'

'Floating upside down in the river if there's any luck,' she says with a sigh, then changes tack when she sees the horror on my face. 'But probably mouldering away in her bedroom on her phone now she's got Internet.'

'Scarlet.' I shake my head.

'Sorry, Chrissie,' she says, not looking particularly sorry. 'She's dragging us down.'

She's about to leave with Luther when I stop her. 'I know she's being difficult,' I say calmly. 'But—'

'But, what? She's doing my head in. She's being such a pain in the arse.'

Scarlet is getting worked up now. I know the signs all too well. The reddening of the cheeks. The biting of the bottom lip. And so I just come out with it because maybe that way she'll cut her sister some slack.

'I need to talk to you about Nathan.'

She's surprised for a moment, but rolls with it. 'Put your coat and boots on then,' she says. 'You can come with us and tell me.'

I almost say, no, I've got too much to do. But there's nothing more important than sorting this out. And walking is a good opportunity to speak, without having to make eye contact. Steady breathing. Fresh air. And I must stop procrastinating.

'Two minutes,' I tell her. 'While I check Ruby's alive, then I'll be with you.'

AT THE TOP of the hill, on a clear day, you can see the sea to the south-east, and to the north-west, Haytor. Today is not a clear day, so all we can make out is the public footpath, which disappears along the wall of the estate. I hope the owner doesn't loom out of the murk.

'Stop being so jumpy, Chrissie. You're making me nervous. Even Luther's spooked and not a lot spooks him.'

'Sorry.' I shake my head. 'I'm all over the place right now.'

'Did you find Rube?'

'Yes. She was mouldering away in her bedroom on her phone.'

Scarlet smiles, but doesn't say I told you so. She's never been one for rubbing things in, even during her more deadly moments, which really are dissipating in this new Devon air.

'Are you going to tell me then?' she asks.

'Tell you what?'

'Whatever it was you wanted to talk about.'

'Ah. That.'

'Is it to do with Dad buggering off?'

'Well, sort of.'

We swap a look, neither of us keen to examine what that means for the long term; it's bad enough right now, making do without him, resenting him.

'I need to explain who Nathan is.'

She gasps. 'You know him, don't you? Is he an old boyfriend?'

'You could say that.'

I tell her that Nathan was my first love from school, and that we met up again in London after he'd graduated and made a go of things for a few years, up until toddler groups and school waiting lists. And then he left.

'He's Ruby's *dad*?'

'Birth father. Rob's her dad.'

'Wow.'

Luther whines, unsure what's going on or why his walk has come to an abrupt stop. Or why Scarlet's mouth is still open but no more words are coming out.

'It was a surprise to me too. Seeing him here. Next door. And in our home.'

I give her a hug because that's easier than speech.

She leans into me and I wonder at this inner strength of hers that I never knew existed and I think of Laura, her mum.

'Let me say something and don't cringe or moan.'

'What?'

'Your mum would be so proud of you. And it's a privilege being your stepmum.'

'Chrissie, stop.'

She blushes but I can see the words move her and I should tell her more often. And really that's what I need to be doing with Ruby, too.

'But why has Nathan never stayed in contact with Rube?'

'That's for another day,' I tell her. Because it's something even I'm not sure about.

'You need to speak to Ruby now,' she says. 'Like *now*.' And she waits for me to turn around towards home before she treks on up the valley.

I FIND RUBY in the living room, sitting on the sofa, staring into space, holding a letter.

'Hey, Rube? You OK? What's that you're holding?'

She hands it over in reply so I sit down next to her and read it.

Dear Ruby,

I must apologize for the use of expletives. I think I might have Tourette's or it could be because my mother was a fishwife and passed on her bad habits. However, I can assure you that I will work on this dreadful part of my character and endeavour to use only the Queen's English, God save her, in future.

I must also apologize for my gastric problems. I have consulted your grandmother and she has dispensed some of her herbs which she insists will aid me a good deal. She has also advised me to stay clear of the Devil's food, otherwise known as wheat. So henceforth I shall be giving the Hovis a miss and will even cut out beer.

Ruby, you must know that there is no greater

sacrifice than this, to give up bitter, but I will do it for you as I can see you have talent. And talent is worth nurturing and supporting, and please, dear Ruby, give me a chance to be your teacher.
Your humble servant
Malcolm Everett-Smythe

PS. I will make myself drink wine from this day forward, forever and ever amen.
PPS. Even your grandparents' wine. What more can I say?

'That's quite a letter.' I hand it back to her. I'm not sure what else to add, but follow her gaze instead and see that it is fixed on the wall above the inglenook. The wall where my mother's embarrassing portrait is supposed to hang. Only it's not there. Just a huge rectangle of faded pink wallpaper.

'Ruby?'

'Don't ask me,' she says. 'I'd be the first to admit if I'd actually burned it.'

'Odd. Maybe Des is restoring it?'

'Maybe you should ask Scarlet.'

'What would Scarlet do with Eve's painting?'

'I dunno.' She shrugs. Rolls her eyes. 'She's sticking her nose into everything right now. Including moaning at me for being moany.'

'She's concerned for you, love. As am I. And I feel like it's all my fault. And Rob's.'

She starts to cry. So of course I start to cry too.

'I know you didn't want Rob to go,' she sobs. 'And I know it's not your fault.' More sobs. 'I don't even hate living here.'

'So what is it, Rube?'

'I just... I dunno how to say it...'

'That's OK. Take your time.' I stroke her hair. It has that greasy teen sheen to it. Must buy some better shampoo.

'I feel like a part of me is... sort of... wonky? Is that normal? Or am I mental?'

'You're not *mental*, Rube. And, by the way, you shouldn't use that word like that. It's derogatory, as you well know. You're just struggling right now because your life's been turned upside down.'

'But Scarlet's loving it.'

'I know. We all react differently though.'

She thinks about this for a while. I let the silence wrap around us. Watch the flames in the log burner. Breathe in the home smell: damp, woody. Possibly dust and old newspapers.

'I suppose,' she says. 'I do love Nana Eve and Granddad Des and Luther but... there's something wrong.'

'Right, love.' This is it. I can't put it off any longer. 'I'm going to tell you something I should've told you when we came down for the harvest. About Nathan.'

She looks me full in the face and I see the cogs turning, the pistons steaming, the synapses firing.

'Nathan's my father,' she says with a certainty that shakes the ground beneath me like an earthquake.

'How did you know?' I ask her, with palpitations and a churn of the stomach.

'I didn't know,' she says. 'At least not until now. Something just slotted together. It's not as if I look like Nathan. He's big, for a start. And I'm not. But there's something about him I recognize. His eyes maybe. The way he walks.' She takes in my shock. Pats my hand. 'I know you don't like him. So I don't like him either because I trust your opinion.'

Wow. So many thoughts whizzing round my head.

But one thought is uppermost for Ruby. 'Why did he leave us, Mum? It wasn't *really* just to "find himself", was it?'

'Oh, Rube.'

'Tell me,' she urges. 'I'd rather know.'

'He had an affair with a woman at work.'

'Oh.' She sounds disappointed. Her birth father reduced to a cliché. Just another bloke having an affair.

'Who?'

'Charlotte.' It still hurts even saying her name.

'So what happened?' Ruby presses me, needing to know.

'I told him to leave.'

She bites her lip, thinking this through, those amber eyes murky with confusion.

'He took it to the extreme,' I go on, wanting to hold her hand, make some gesture, but knowing what she needs right now is the truth, unclouded by any emotion from me. 'He went away with Charlotte to New Zealand for a year. But that year turned into forever.'

'Oh.' She takes a moment to think about this, decides it's too much for now and asks something more pertinent: 'Why did he come back?'

'They're not together any more. He wants to return to his roots. He wants to get to know you.'

'So he bought next door hoping to get in touch through Nana Eve and Granddad Des?'

'I think so.'

'Oh.' She starts to weep now. I let her cry, saying nothing, holding her close. Then when she stops shuddering, I nip to the kitchen to make us hot chocolate. And we melt marshmallows together over the flames of the log burner, sitting next to each other cross-legged on cushions.

'Did you really not move your naked grandmother?' I point at the faded rectangle on the wall.

'No, Mum,' she says. 'I have no idea where it's gone. But good riddance.'

'Yep. Good riddance,' I agree.

We grin at each other, friends again, and I know how stupid I've been to put this off. I'm lucky she's taken it so well, and from here on in, there are no secrets.

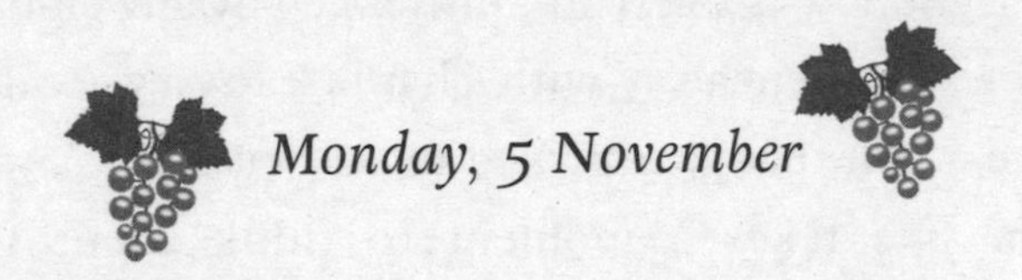

Monday, 5 November

MONDAY MORNING. I wake up with that feeling of trepidation you get when there's a big day ahead of you. Like it's *my* first day of school. I sigh. It's true what they say: you're only as happy as the least happy of your children. I feel nervous for Ruby, but also worried for Scarlet – that something or someone will pop that new-found bubble of zest.

Melina offers to drive them in for their first day, but after that it'll be the school bus. I feel guilty for accepting with such gratitude but I know they'll be calmer with her. So I manage to grab a quick hug from each of them before they trundle out of the door in their new uniforms, polished shoes and winter coats, lugging the usual bags of stuff.

'Don't be so worried,' Eve says, once the sound of my car has faded. 'They'll surprise you if you let them.'

'What do you mean, "if I let them"?'

'I'm simply saying, trust in them. They will find their path.'

‘I suppose.’ I hope. I pray. Anyway, right now we need to go down a financial path. ‘Let’s talk about your paperwork. Are you and Des free for a chat?’

‘He’s painting. He was up at six, feverish with creativity. It’s like the old days, when I first knew him.’ She looks wistful.

‘He’s a bit older now.’

‘He’s a lot older now, but one must make hay while the sun shines.’

The rain beats down outside. The windows rattle in the wind.

‘Gosh, I miss those Poles.’ Eve sighs. ‘It’s so quiet without them.’

There has been a strange stillness and sense of loss since the party. Because of a politician’s whim, they might never return to work the harvest here. It makes my heart ache, and I can do nothing else but focus on the girls. And these wretched books.

‘I’d better check on Des,’ she says, dragging herself from her daydream. ‘It’s time he had a break.’ And before I have the chance to ask, she says, ‘Don’t fret. We’ll have your chat in a bit, after coffee.’

She makes it sound like she’s doing me a favour. Really, this woman can be impossible.

Melina is back and tells me that the girls were fine. Which is a relief. A huge relief.

'They stick together like glue and many boys stare at them. Many girls too, though not so good.'

So maybe not such a big fat relief after all because now I'm paranoid that they'll be beaten up by the locals for encroaching on their patch. Or hit on by inappropriate lads.

Fortunately, I'm distracted by the meeting around the kitchen table, to which Eve invites Melina. The four of us make an unlikely team but there's no reason why this can't work. Well, there are probably hundreds of reasons why, but I am going to be positive.

I crank up my laptop and start taking notes. I am determined to make this professional if it kills me.

Over the next hour, despite protestations of backache, the bathrooms needing a clean and an impending t'ai chi lesson, we highlight the bills that need immediate payment, the bills that can be put off for another couple of weeks, and the loans that can be consolidated into something more manageable. I call Chudston Winery, who have our wine in their vats – a sort of ransom, and do my utmost to negotiate a discount if we can give them something in return. And before we know it Des has taken the phone from me, and offered to do a painting of their vineyard to hang in their cafe.

The owner is delighted and Des organizes a time to visit, to take some photos and do some sketches. It would also be an opportunity for Des to see another family wine business that actually works. Why Eve and Des have never bothered to do this before now is a mystery.

Back to the agenda, and the last item is the website and social media. 'Scarlet has willingly agreed to take it on,' I tell them. 'She's really good at this sort of thing.'

'It doesn't have to be wonderful,' Eve says. As if Scarlet isn't capable of doing anything wonderful, which is completely contradictory when Eve's always been Scarlet's greatest champion.

'It will be,' says I, Ms Hoity-Toity. 'It has to be. First impressions count, Eve. I know that's not your philosophy but you have to see it that way when it comes to the wine business.'

She's about to speak when Luther interrupts with his trademark low bark and his claws patter across the flags as he ambles arthritically to the door.

'Morning, Luther.' Nathan turns his attention to us. 'I hope I'm not interrupting.'

The barking stops and the tail wags. Traitor.

I want to tell Nathan that he *is* actually interrupting, but I'm aware of Melina, Eve and Des looking from him to me, all of them no doubt wondering how I will react, so I don't make an issue out of it. Instead I let him sit down. Watch him help himself to coffee from the cafetière, getting his feet under the table.

'We were expecting you at the party,' Des says. 'What happened?'

'I didn't want to interfere in their fun,' Nathan says.

'Party pooper,' Eve teases.

'Something like that.' He smiles what some people would call an enigmatic smile but I would call something far less mysterious. Smug, for instance. Or annoying. Or face-slappable.

'I don't suppose you know anything about that anonymous £200 in notes that found its way onto our doormat?' Eve asks, a little more flirtatiously than is necessary.

He smiles the smug, annoying, face-slappable smile again and throws in a continental shrug. 'Not a clue.'

'Nathan, you are naughty,' Eve says. And offers him a biscuit.

'These look delicious. Thank you, Eve. I'm glad you're back to baking.'

Oh, good grief. Stop now. Meeting closed.

LATER, WITH NATHAN gone, lunch consumed, and after much admin, I return to Des's studio. He's having a nap on his filthy chaise longue.

'Just forty winks,' he says.

'Sorry, didn't mean to disturb you.'

'It's time I got up and moving again. I forgot how exhausting painting can be.'

'You've been at it for hours.'

'I'm worried if I stop I'll lose that urge. I'm not stupid enough to believe you have to wait for inspiration; I know you have to work at your art or craft even when you don't want to, even if what you do isn't your best, because it's only by doing it, by creating something, that you have the basics to work with. But some days, like today, there's magic afoot and you can feel the blood pulsing through your brain, down your arm and onto the canvas. Well, not literally blood. I'm not one of those modern painters who use bodily fluids.'

'Des, please. I feel sick.'

'Sorry, honeybun.' He stretches and heaves his bulk to a standing position. 'Did you want something?'

'A couple of things, actually.'

'Let's have them, then.'

'First, the painting of Eve. Where is it? Are you restoring it or something? Only I'm worried Ruby might have pilfered it. You know how embarrassing she finds it.'

'Could never understand that.' He shakes his head, his shock of white hair falling over his forehead. 'But no. It's in the study. Scarlet's put it on eBay.'

'She has?'

'I relayed your thoughts and she offered to help. And Eve and I told her it was a quite brilliant idea. Testing the water to see if there's anyone out there who wants a piece of kitsch art for their kitchen wall.' He winks at me, the old devil. 'And what was the other thing you wanted to talk about?'

'Ruby.'

'Ah. Lovely Ruby Tuesday. She's not a happy young woman right now. Feels as if life has put rather too much on her plate.'

'Has she told you that?'

'She feeds me dribs and drabs, while she's practising her scales. In fact I suggested moving that harp from the study into here so she could play while I paint but she says it's too cold. She doesn't want a warped instrument.'

'She wasn't impressed with Malcolm either.'

'Ah.'

'But the letter might have swung it. She almost looked like she was prepared to give him another chance but couldn't bring herself to admit it.'

'Really? Right. Leave her to me. She can accompany me to the winery after school tomorrow to discuss that commission. A car's a good place for a chat.'

'I've talked to her about Nathan.'

'Ah. And?'

'She seems rather laid-back about it. Maybe you could find out more?'

'Of course, honeybun.' He winks. 'I'll do my very best.'

He gives me an absent hug, then picks up his palette and starts mixing colours. Our conversation is over for now. I tiptoe out of the room and leave him to it.

A LITTLE LATER, on the computer in the study, I check to see if there's any news from Rob, hoping for a message of some kind. He has posted his first blog. He's calling it 'From Table Mountain to the Pyramids of Giza', which isn't that snappy considering this is what he usually does for a living. But he's taken some stunning photos – Table Mountain, the Atlantic Ocean, the wine valleys, the rugged coast – though I suspect it's possible to point your camera anywhere there and the result would look like it came from the pages of a travel brochure.

He says how he loved the silence of the Western Cape but is struggling now with the unrelenting heat of the Northern Cape. Sweat is a problem. The burning sun. Aching muscles. Flies. He's wild camping. Feels safe from other humans, who are few and far between anyway, but it's the prospect of animals that would keep him awake if he wasn't so exhausted. Within the next few days he'll cross the Orange River into Namibia.

He signs off with the words: *Everything is different in Africa.*

But no messages. No emails. I suppose Internet opportunities are difficult to come by, though he's managed to post this blog. To distract myself, I check the eBay account set up by Scarlet. My mother's portrait has had thirty-four views, twelve watchers and as yet no bids. But there are still thirteen days for her to make our fortune.

It's almost five o'clock by the time the girls tramp across the yard and fall in at the front door, ties off, hair a mess, starving. I feel huge amounts of relief, knowing they are not only alive but actually quite communicative. Even Ruby. But I also know enough not to ask about school. I will wait for the drip feed of information.

There's some nice people. The canteen's decent. The bus is gross. Their timetables are OK. There's a swing band. A hiking club. And what's for tea?

'Melina's made spag bol,' I tell them. 'Meat and vegan.'

They grab some bread and jam and disappear to their rooms. And that's as much as I'm getting for now, but I'm happy.

'I told you girls will be fine,' Melina says.

But I'm not naive enough to believe this will be plain sailing. Oh no. There will be storms ahead.

After tea – eaten outside around a non-existent bonfire, washed down with the last of the reds while listening to distant fireworks, Des on edge with every bang – I chivvy everyone into the warmth of the study, where I show them Rob's blog. They crowd around the computer screen, exclaiming in awe and wonder – all except for Ruby, who creeps unnoticed out of the room. Not unnoticed by everyone. I follow her and find her under the stairs.

'My favourite place,' I tell her after letting myself into the cupboard to join her.

'Did all the walls use to be covered in this type of paper in the old days?'

'If by the old days you mean the 1970s, then yes, pretty much. Sometimes it would even be flocked.'

I go on to explain what flocked means, how it felt, the dust that would accumulate, while she looks suitably horrified. 'It wasn't all Arctic Roll and *Swap Shop*.'

This of course goes straight over her head, so she chooses to ignore it and ploughs on with her own thoughts.

'I didn't actually hate school,' she admits. 'The other students were all right. They showed Scarlet where to smoke. She went with them but she told me she didn't smoke anything because she doesn't really like it.'

For a moment, I have my Ruby back, grassing up her sister in that truthfully innocent way of hers. *Scarlet didn't flush the loo. Scarlet put her peas in the waste paper basket. Scarlet knows how to undo the parental controls on the computer.* And I see Ruby through Rob's eyes. Did he feel threatened by her? And what would it do to Ruby if she ever guessed that? But there's nothing I can do right now except be grateful she's talking to me, that she doesn't hate school, that she's not smoking weed or taking pills.

Oh, for the days when all I had to worry about was what to give them for tea. Dealing with the emotional stuff is so much harder but I must persevere. 'Have you thought any more about Nathan? I mean, how you feel about it all?'

'It's a bit confusing really. I feel sort of numb. Also quite sad sometimes. But also kind of excited. Is that normal?'

'I don't know how you're supposed to feel, Ruby. Your feelings are your feelings. But believe me when I say there's no such thing as *normal*.'

As if to highlight my point, we hear Des walk down the hallway singing 'Firestarter'.

She rolls her eyes at me and grins, then leaves me in our cubbyhole to do her homework upstairs in her room, at an old desk we found in the studio, spattered with years of paint, now upcycled by Melina.

I remain for a while, in the quiet of the cupboard with a bottle of red. It's amazing what you get used to when you keep at something. But I never want to get used to this bloody awful wine.

Later, in the kitchen, Luther sits patiently by the door in a pool of moonlight, waiting to be let out for his night-time pee.

'Come on, matey. Let's go.'

Outside, the air has a threat of winter to it. As Luther sniffs around, cocking his leg, I stand there in the middle of the yard, breathing deep. Farmyards. Mould. Sulphur. The moon and stars are enough to see by. Ahead of me, stretching up the hill, are the vines. Like ordered rows of mini Roman soldiers. It'll be time to prune before long and then who knows what next year's harvest will bring.

And I think of Rob, far away, on his journey across Africa, on his adventure. And here I am, back where I started. Before there's time to get maudlin, I realize I can't see Luther. But I can see a light bobbing along. A torch. Someone is coming up the lane. Why is Luther such a rubbish guard dog? He trots back up to me with a large man and two springer spaniels in tow.

'Evening,' Nathan says.

The bouncy dogs run circles round Luther.

I'm about to ask what Nathan wants but he doesn't wait.

'There's a hole in your fence,' he says.

'Right.'

'I thought you should know. You don't want deer getting in.'

I don't say anything.

'Don't worry,' he says. 'I'll sort it.'

I don't thank him, interfering bastard. But then again I don't refuse either. But I do have a question. 'Why are you lurking here in the dark?'

'You're welcome,' he says, put out by my line of attack. 'I was just walking the dogs. Thought it might be Des out in the yard.'

By now, Luther is waiting by the door to be let back in, ignoring the sniffing spaniels. I want to go back in too because this is awkward. I don't know why it should be awkward. But there's something about his expression. It's not slappable.

'Did you want to come in or something?'

He's stumped for a second, suspecting a trick. Then, 'You offering me a nightcap?'

'I was thinking more along the lines of a cup of tea.'

'Right then,' he says. 'That'll do.' And he claps his hands together, sending an echo around the valley.

We sit in the kitchen. We talk about his plans for the estate. Corporate awaydays. Arable farming. Renovating the outbuildings for holiday lets. Then I have to delve deeper into the past.

'So what have you actually *done* over these past ten years?'

He has a swig of tea, buying himself a little time, weighing up my mood, before going for it. 'Well, we worked in Auckland for a year. Then another, like I said. Then we did some travelling and somehow ended up on a sheep farm for a couple of years.'

'A sheep farm? What did Charlotte think about that? She couldn't exactly wear her heels and business suits there.'

'She grew up on the streets of Stepney. She's actually no stranger to hard work. Problem is, she likes to play hard too. That's partly why we stayed so far away, for such a long time. So she could, how shall I put it, detox.'

'I see. The illness. She had a... problem?'

'She did. To be perfectly honest, she still does. It's always a battle. She has these demons gnawing away at her.'

'Don't we all?'

'No, Chrissie. I know you had a bad deal with me but you're OK. You're sound. She's really not.'

I don't know how to take this. Should I be pleased? Angry? Or what? 'Are you still together?' Suddenly this is of paramount importance.

'Actually, no,' he says. 'She wants to be but I can't do it any more.'

'Right.'

A moment of stillness.

Then: 'Was it worth it? Leaving Ruby?'

He slowly shakes his head, brow furrowed, but he looks me in the eye. 'The honest answer is no, Chrissie. It wasn't.'

'So what was it all for?'

He thinks about this. He's searching deep but I don't expect him to come up with an answer. Certainly not one that I will be able to stomach. Because there isn't such a thing.

'I should've worked harder,' he says finally.

'You always worked hard, I'll give you that,' I tell him. Though of course it doesn't escape me that some of those late nights at work would have been spent with Charlotte.

'I meant I should've worked harder at being your husband,' he says, a slight catch in his voice. 'I should've worked harder at being Ruby's dad.'

He won't get any disagreement there but I don't say anything. I let him carry on. I need to hear this.

'I didn't feel very good at either of those jobs,' he says. 'And, to be perfectly honest, I suppose Charlotte offered me a way out.' He rubs his hand over his scalp, smoothing his wayward curls, an old habit. And I remember that time he washed my hair for me, after I'd given birth to Ruby. Tender and loving. Then he adds: 'I don't know if this regret of mine makes you feel any better?'

'No,' I tell him. 'Definitely not. It makes me sad. And angry.'

'Right. Well. I don't blame you, Chrissie. You have every right to feel those things.' He has a final gulp of his tea, drains the mug. Then, in a total change of direction: 'How's Forrest Gump getting on?'

'I presume you mean Rob.'

'Yes, I mean Rob. Where is he now?'

'Heading towards Namibia.'

'Good for him.'

'If you say so.'

'You're not happy with this arrangement?'

'No, I'm not happy but I'm resigned to it.' I sigh to emphasize my point. 'I'm thinking of our year in Devon as our own adventure. Not sure it's going that well. I mean, we've already handed over the winemaking.'

'But you still have a vineyard. And a business that can grow. And you'll soon be making your own wine again. Think of this not as a setback but as an opportunity.'

'You reckon?'

'I do. From what Melina and the others tell me, the barn party was a sensation. Fabulous setting. Maybe you could think about getting a licence to sell alcohol? Use it for events? That's your thing, after all.'

'I know. I was actually wondering about the possibility of weddings.'

Oh. That word. *Wedding.*

His right hand automatically moves to that finger on his left hand where once he wore a gold band. There's not even an indent now. It's as if it were never there. Like it never happened.

'Good plan,' he says.

Conversation fizzles out but his leg is fidgety and he's rubbing his finger again. I can tell he's itching to ask a question. And then he does.

'How are the girls settling in?' he asks. 'Scarlet seems all right?'

I swallow. I gulp. I breathe, breathe, breathe. I could let him have what for. Or I could try to be civilized. If I want this next year to work out I really must try my hardest to be civilized. Try hard, Chrissie. Dig deep.

'Scarlet's been a real surprise,' I manage to say.

'She does seem to be throwing herself into country life.'

'I know. Apart from the dead-animal thing she's really embracing rural living.'

'And...' He hesitates. 'Ruby?'

I can do this. So can Ruby. 'She'll be fine,' I tell him with ill-founded certainty.

And if he'd left it there, it might've just about been OK. But he doesn't. He has to go ahead and ask: 'Have you told her about me yet?'

'Yes, I've told her about you.'

'That I'm her father?'

'Her *birth* father, yes.'

'And does she want to see me?'

'What exactly do you mean by that?'

'Does she want any kind of relationship with me? Other than next-door neighbour.'

'You are an insensitive pillock, Nathan, you really are!' I yell, my calmness falling away. 'You need to give me some space, all right?'

'I'm just trying to make up for lost time, but you're making it impossible for me at every turn! Why can't we just be civil?'

Furious, I manage a 'Just go!'

So he goes.

Good riddance.

But the thought won't go. It buzzes around my head. At some point, Ruby will want some kind of relationship with Nathan. And what do I do when that happens?

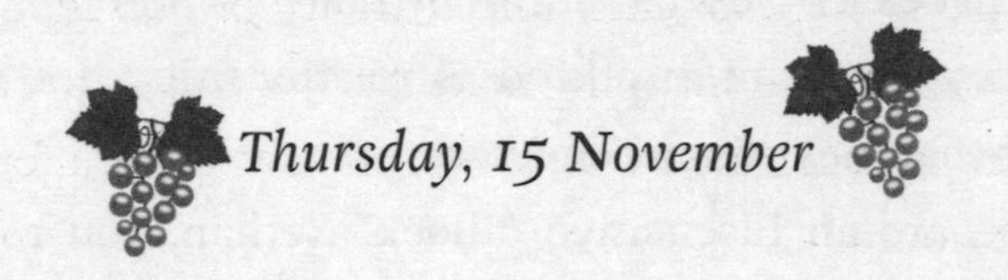

Thursday, 15 November

TEN DAYS LATER and I've barely seen Nathan, let alone talked to him. Life is sort of chugging along. The girls continue to get used to school. They catch the bus. They've made some friends. Scarlet has been embraced by a like-minded group and welcomed into their inner circle of activism. Ruby has found a young lad called Barney who plays the trombone in the swing band, unlikely to lead to romance but who knows. They're good chums already so that's fine by me.

Melina does the school run on a Wednesday with the harp in the back of my car – no mean feat. On Thursdays Malcolm comes to the house to give Ruby a lesson – persuading her to accept his teaching also no mean feat. Having him come here was the best compromise; at least that way she doesn't have to endure the probable stink of his house. And although he is a complete gent, I prefer having her within earshot.

'He's actually all right,' she tells me, after he leaves

this evening. 'I'm kinda getting used to him. He's different to Shona but then again everything's different these days.' She dips into a brief trance of nostalgia for her old life before snapping herself out of it and spurting upstairs to FaceTime Barney, who she hasn't seen for all of two hours.

So although everyone is carrying on, the big fat elephant in the room that we sort of addressed, Ruby and I, is still loitering.

Now Melina is about to serve our supper. Something Polish and cabbagey, *patatas bravas*, and chicken thighs plus some sort of vegan haggis – she is truly a European.

Des is cleaning up after another stint in the studio. Last week, he and Ruby visited the winery up the valley. Turns out he knows the owner's mother, Ruth, from way back. She could vouch for his pedigree as a painter and he's been given the go-ahead for the commission to paint the vineyard there for their cafe. This will help pay for the winemaking but there's still quite a shortfall, so we're banking on Eve. Three days to go and she's had 298 views, thirty-five watchers and twenty-two bids, the highest currently at £1,550. There is much excitement, the girls giving us regular updates on their grandmother's worth.

Eve, herself, is doing well with her injury, regaining mobility in her wrist and, with Melina's encouragement and her own herbal knowledge, being scrupulous about what she eats in order to strengthen her bones.

We sit down around the table and Des pours us each a glass of white. There are still a couple of cases left but soon the bad stuff will all be gone. And in January the first bottles of this year's vintage will be ready to drink. And then we'll have some idea if this could possibly be a viable business.

'You're quiet, Christabel,' Des says. 'Everything all right? Have you heard from Rob?'

'Not since last week when he'd made it across the Senqu River from South Africa into Namibia. He's paired up with a bloke from Doncaster who's raising money for a donkey sanctuary or something.'

'Is Rob doing any of this for charity?' Eve asks.

I feel a flush over my face – Why *isn't* he doing it for charity? – and before I get the chance to answer, Ruby dives in.

'He's thinking about it,' she announces. 'Scarlet's going to set up a giving page. But he doesn't know yet who to raise money for.'

'Isn't it a bit late in the day?' I ask. Why did none of us think of this beforehand? It might have made the whole saga slightly more palatable.

'It's never too late, honeybun,' Des says. 'Rob has thousands of miles ahead of him to cycle.'

We're all quiet for a short while, contemplating the vastness of Rob's journey and why he is there and we are here.

Food finished, Melina clears the plates – while Eve serves us all apple crumble and custard with its dairy-free alternative – then sits down and tucks in. She tells us that Poland used to export most of its apples to Russia but now Russia doesn't want them so the Poles are making lots of cider.

'Is very good cider,' she states.

'I thought you only drank vodka and beer in Poland?'

'No, Ruby. That is not so. We also make wine. Is very good wine.' She looks with disdain at the contents of her glass before downing them. She might as well be holding her nose while doing it. 'Some farms in the south near my home, they have started vineyards. Maybe is better for Babcia than pigs.'

'How old's your grandma?' I ask her.

'Babcia is seventy-five.'

'Does she have help?' I feel bad that Melina lives so far away.

'She has my Uncle Iwan and Aunt Agata.'

'Won't she retire?' Scarlet wonders.

'Maybe she can't afford to retire,' I jump in quickly. I'm aware as I'm saying those words that they sound completely ignorant.

Melina, as ever, is calm as you like, monotone and phlegmatic. 'Last time I go home, I see Poland has changed. The cities and the countryside look more prosperous than UK. Babcia tells me I must return. To work on farm maybe. Or to grow my own vineyard.'

We listen to her in stunned silence, none of us wanting to contemplate a life without this woman. We watch her as she gets up and walks to the window seat, picks up her bag and brings it back to the table. She rummages inside and produces a booklet of some kind. A prospectus.

'Plumpton College,' she says. 'Only college in UK where you may study wine. I want to study wine.'

'How to drink wine?' asks Des. 'I can show you that, Melina.'

'No, Des, I wish to study vine-growing and winemaking.' She hands him the prospectus.

'It's in Sussex,' he says.

'Yes. Four hours to drive maybe. I do one day a week for eight weeks. First week in December then start again in January.'

'Right. Wow.' I am particularly eloquent today. I am also reeling somewhat. Which is utterly stupid. Melina has every right to study more. She has every right to do something positive with her life. To go back to Poland. To forge a career.

'Good for you, Melina,' I make myself tell her. 'Good for you.'

And I really hope she doesn't think I'm being facetious, because I'm not. I'm really not. I'm just sad at the prospect of losing another important person in our lives.

But, I must remind myself, I have not lost Rob. He *will* come back. Only another ten months to go.

And then what?

I can't pursue this line of thought now because there's a double ping – one from Scarlet's phone, the other from Ruby's. They both screech, Ruby with more excitement than I have heard in a very long time.

'Nana Eve!' she shouts. 'You're now worth £2,025!'

LATER, WITH THE girls in bed and Des retired, I sit at the kitchen table drinking herbal tea with Eve, who is knitting a jumper.

'Should you be doing that?'

'It's good for my hand,' she says, not altogether convincingly.

'Where's Melina?' I ask her. 'Has she gone to bed?'

'She's taken Luther out,' Eve says.

I check the dog basket as if I have to see for myself and yes, it's empty. 'For a walk? A bit late, isn't it?'

'Is it?'

Eve is vague. Which is not unusual. She's often vague, her head off elsewhere, in dreamland, lost among the loops and purls of her knitting. Though sometimes I'm sure she pretends to be vague and lost so that she can avoid a conversation. Which is ridiculous because if she's of a mind to do so, she will say whatever she wants and not give two hoots about the repercussions. I think, possibly, this avoidance strategy is something she only employs when dealing with me.

'Eve,' I say, determined now to get to the bottom of this big nag in my head.

'Yes.' She carries on knitting, purple-framed glasses balanced on the end of her nose. 'What is it, Christabel?' The needles stop clacking. She peers at me over her specs.

'Why have you forgiven Nathan so readily? He's not been in contact with Ruby since she was tiny. It's not like he missed a school play or a dental appointment. He's missed practically her whole life.'

'Right. I understand that you're upset, I really do. But as I see it, Nathan is back and we need to build bridges between him and us.'

An impasse. Thankfully Melina returns with a puffed-out Luther. After a brief sniffy bark, he heads to his basket and curls up like a cat. A very large cat.

'Nice walk, Melina?' Eve asks, putting her knitting aside and wiggling her fingers.

'Very nice. Is cold but I have company. I see Nathan and he is walking his dogs. They are two of springer spaniels and very busy. Luther does not like them, I think.'

'Yes, they are indeed lively,' Eve agrees.

Why is Nathan prowling on the edge of his mahoosive

estate, wandering the lanes again, so close to Home Farm? He can't keep away. Is he after Melina? She does look pink-cheeked... The weather is crisp out there so it could be the cold rosying up her complexion. Or is it something else? Something I don't really want to consider now.

I say my goodnights and drag myself to an empty bed, taking a hot-water bottle that is wearing one of Eve's brightly coloured knitted covers. I'm hoping for a deep sleep, so I can switch off from worrying about Scarlet becoming an extreme eco-warrior, Ruby becoming a sad loner, Rob getting eaten by hungry lions. Everything is easier when I'm inhabiting the Land of Nod. I can dream of rows of vines bursting with plump grapes. A sparkling wine to die for. A successful business.

But the last thought that flits through my brain before it closes down for the night is whether there is something going on between Nathan and Melina. And if there is something going on between Nathan and Melina, what on earth will that mean for Ruby?

It all comes back to Ruby.

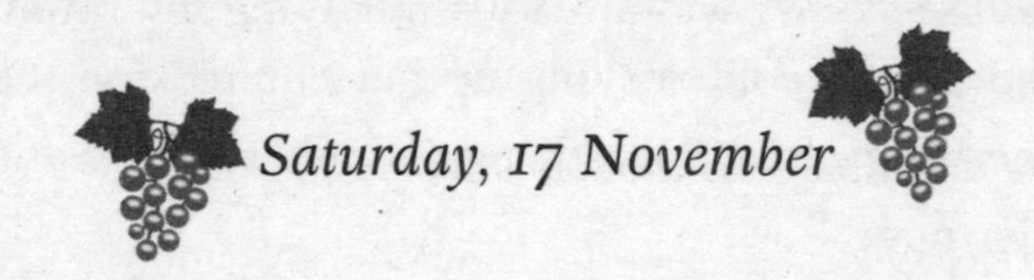

Saturday, 17 November

A DRIZZLY SATURDAY morning: woken by gunfire. Pheasants. Partridges. French hens, turtle doves, ten geese a-laying.

I'm hoping the girls will sleep through the one-sided onslaught. But apparently not. A knock at the door and in comes Ruby.

'Morning,' she says, somewhat bright-eyed.

Is she feverish? Coming down with another cold? Or is she just happier? She has definitely perked up of late. Appears to be more settled. I've tried a couple of times to encourage her to open up about the whole Nathan thing but she always manages to head me off. Meeting Nathan, knowing he's living next door, I thought she'd be keen to speak about him. To speak *to* him. To have some kind of meeting or other. But no. Nothing. Not yet. But I'm in no doubt that day will come.

'They're at it again,' she says.

'Sorry?'

'Next door. Killing stuff.'

'Oh, that. Yes, I know. Did they wake you?'

'No,' she says. 'I was already up, tidying my room.'

'You were?'

'You don't have to look so surprised, Mum.'

'Sorry.'

But it's all right; she's smiling. Then she asks: 'Do you think Nathan shoots up the pheasants too or does he just take the blood money?'

Now there's a question. After a moment's consideration I play it safe. 'I don't know. He never used to have a gun but now he's (I was going to say lord of the manor but I hold back)... the estate owner, maybe it's expected.'

'That doesn't mean it's right.'

'Country people have a different way of living.' I'm trying to be diplomatic. Which is tricky.

No comment on this from Ruby. Instead she retrieves a tray from the landing and carries it over to my bed. 'Your breakfast, m'lady,' she says.

On the tray is a mug of strong-looking tea and two doorstep slices of granary toast and jam. And a postcard.

'What's this?'

'Guess,' she says, trying to suppress a big grin.

Of course I know straight away who it's from. There's a picture of a vineyard and, when I turn it over, a South African stamp, dated more than two weeks ago.

Dear Chrissie, Ruby and Scarlet,
I hope you are getting used to Devon. I'm thinking of you every day as I cycle along the trail and roads through this incredible country. You feel very far away but I love you all.
Love Rob/Dad. Xxx
PS. I hope you're enjoying the blogs.

Short but sweet.

I give the postcard to Ruby. 'He sent this ages ago so God knows where he is now.'

She passes me her phone. 'This is his latest blog post.'

It turns out he's still in Namibia.

The cycling has been awesome through thinly populated lands, heading north-east on dirt and sand tracks, across the central plateau and up into the Namib desert. And the most incredible moment. A dawn visit to the world's highest sand dunes. Unbelievable. Why aren't they on everyone's bucket list?

It's hard not to think of Lawrence of Arabia riding a camel rather than Rob pedalling his bike. I struggle to imagine my husband, the townie, in the middle of a desert.

'When did he post this, Rube?'

She whips her phone off me to check. 'A couple of hours ago.'

'Where is he exactly? He must have Wi-Fi.'

'He says he's treated himself to a night in a hotel which included a wildlife buffet.' She looks at me – 'Scarlet won't like that!' – then hands back the phone so I can read for myself.

Tomorrow I'll be on the road to Windhoek, the capital. When there, I plan to experience the great beer and restaurants the city has to offer. And then the relief of long, flat stretches towards the border of Botswana.

Hotels. Wildlife buffets. Wi-Fi. Beer. Restaurants. Why is it that these are the words that stand out, shouting and singing at me?

But I will not show Ruby my disappointment. The sense of being let down. Made a fool of. He's having the holiday of a lifetime under the guise of a mid-life crisis, leaving me to keep everything together – kids, parents, life.

And it turns out that Ruby is still Ruby at heart because she gives me a hug and says, '"All shall be well, and all shall be well and all manner of thing shall be well".'

'Eve?'

'No,' she says. 'Julian of Norwich.'

'Who's he?'

'*He* was a *she*,' Ruby informs me, and it rings a bell. 'One of those nuns from hundreds of years ago. She was put in a cave or cell or something and wasn't allowed out. They passed her food and drink but I don't know how she went to the loo or anything.'

'Right.' I'm not sure where this is going.

'Weird,' she comments. 'And gross. But what she meant, this nun, is that she could put up with anything if she believed in God.'

'What happened?'

'She died.'

'Oh.'

'But she left all these writings. She was probably the first woman to write stuff in English. And people still read it now.'

'How do you know this?' I ask her.

'Barney told me,' she says.

'I must meet Barney. Ask him for tea one day next week.'

'He's coming over this afternoon. You can ask him then.'

'Oh, good. I will. Meanwhile, can you let Scarlet know about Rob's blog?'

She's about to do this when my own phone rings.

'It's Rob,' I tell her.

Ruby races to the bedroom door and yells out, 'Scarlet, it's Rob on the phone!'

So the three of us FaceTime Rob and it's really strange seeing his face – familiar and yet distant, living a life so different to ours. And it reminds me how odd it must be for him, seeing us in Devon, hearing about our latest news.

The girls speak loud and fast and Rob has to sit back and listen. I can't work out his expression – possibly a mix of loss and relief? After ten minutes of this barrage, he finally says, 'Can I have a word with your mum?'

So after they have said their goodbyes and left the room, I am alone with my husband. Who's in Africa.

'How are you?' he asks.

This isn't a throwaway question. I know he's genuinely concerned that I'm all right, managing OK, the girls still alive. And actually I *am* all right. I *am* managing OK and the girls are well and truly still alive.

I give him a résumé of the last few weeks: school, home, vineyard. I describe the autumn here, the changing colours, the leaves turning red, gold and yellow, before dropping to the soggy ground, the vines moving into their dormant phase for winter.

'How's the wine coming on?' he asks.

'Well, Des has been up the valley to visit and it's

fermenting nicely in the steel vats there.'

'That's great,' he says, 'knowing all that hard work's paid off.'

'There's a way to go yet,' I remind him. 'Some of the wine has to be bottled and the rest laid on the lees.' I feel a flush of pride about all I've learned these last few weeks at Home Farm.

'You're giving the sparkling wine a go, then?'

'We are.'

'Good for you,' he says. 'You're on the road.'

'I hope so.'

Then of course talk turns to the long road *he's* travelling. The punctures. The sore feet. How the dirt tracks are shorter than the roads but so bumpy that his teeth hurt. That some days there's so little shelter from the sun that he longs to be in rainy Britain. How he met this bloke, Jumbo, from Doncaster. How they help each other out, singing and chatting and telling stupid jokes and playing I spy. And he seems so far away that he might as well be on the moon, and how can I reconcile this person to the man I married over a decade ago?

'Have you heard from my mother?' he asks.

'No, I've not heard from your mother. Why would I hear from your mother?'

'No reason,' he says. 'It's just that I haven't been able to get hold of her the last couple of times I've called.'

'The last couple of times you've called?'

There's a sudden silence but I'm fairly certain I can make out the faint sound of his brain cogs whirring while he calculates how to get out himself out of this hole he's just dug for himself. He's had the time and the opportunity to phone his mother, but not his wife and daughters?

I'm not helping him out of this grave.

'I'm worried about her,' he says. 'You've got each other. You've got Eve and Des too. And Melina. Mum's got no one.'

I want to remind him that if she wasn't such an old battleaxe she might have some friends to keep an eye out for her but he knows this so there's no point reiterating it.

He steers the conversation back to his itinerary. The next leg to Windhoek. Then I hear a northern voice in the background and Rob says he has to go. They still have another sixty kilometres to get through today.

Then suddenly he's gone and it's as if he was never there at all.

AFTER LUNCH, A teenage boy, small in stature, lagged in winter clothes, appears from nowhere at the kitchen door. This must be Ruby's Barney. Before I can ask him, Ruby's stampeded down the stairs and hurled herself into the kitchen. She must've been watching out for him from her bedroom window, which overlooks the yard.

'Come in,' she says, out of breath. 'Mum, this is Barney.'

We do the intros and I try to do some small talk but Barney's hard work. Ruby rescues me and they disappear upstairs.

Melina, hands in the sink, looks at me, an unspoken question hanging between us – *Why are you allowing a boy in your daughter's bedroom?* – but I ignore it. Something tells me I don't have to worry about Barney. My Ruby will be safe with him.

She moves on to Scarlet. 'Your other daughter is walking dog,' she says. 'She is always walking dog.'

'She loves walking the dog and I'm very happy to encourage this.'

'Hmm,' Melina says.

I ignore this too and go in search of Eve.

IT TURNS OUT Barney only lives on the other side of the village. A big house on its own set back from the road to Chudston. He walked to Home Farm, which is why I didn't hear his arrival.

'His mother's on the PCC and organizing the carol service this year,' Eve says. 'They're a musical family.' She's in the study, searching for paperwork.

'You really ought to try filing, Eve. It would save you so much time and aggro.'

'I shall get round to it eventually.'

Subject dismissed.

'What are you looking for?'

'There's a log of Des's work somewhere. An old exercise book. It says who he sold his paintings to and how much he got for them.' She's going through the contents of an old pine trunk now. Heaps of paper that have been chucked in there over the years. It's like excavating an archaeological dig. I'm half expecting her to get out a chisel and brush. 'I know the old fogies could well have snuffed it by now but they might have offspring with a passing interest in art. What was it you called it? Retro kitsch?'

'It was meant to be a compliment, you know. Was Des upset?'

She waves away the thought with a flick of a hand like I'm an annoying bluebottle and she couldn't give two hoots about whether Des was upset or not. She's a woman on a mission. Now her passion – her beloved wine – is in jeopardy, she will raise the funds to save it, come what may. All talk of money being vulgar has been buried.

'Where is Des, anyway?'

'Painting,' she says. When she notices the look of concern on my face she says: 'Don't worry. He's working on his commission, not his own stuff. There'll be time for that after he's done this painting.'

I feel bad for Des now. I really hope he'll still have the urge to follow his passion.

A LITTLE WHILE later, as I'm sorting out the laundry – so many smalls! – there's a knock at the door. A half-hearted woof from Luther and my heart goes; it might be Nathan. I don't know why I think it might be Nathan. Or why I'm so worried. But anyway, it's not. It's a woman.

'I'm looking for my son,' she says.

'You must be Barney's mum?'

'Is he here?'

And like her son, she doesn't appear to be one for small talk either because, when I ask her inside for a cup of tea, she declines and says she'll wait in her car. I watch her stride away towards a hulk of a four-wheel drive. It's actually acceptable to own one of those here, where there's potentially the need to go off-road – unlike in London, where I used to get so annoyed at the Chelsea tractors. This Land Rover is genuinely scruffy. As is Barney's mum. It looks like she's dressed herself in the dark, having rummaged around in the contents of a lost-property bin, but hey, that's the country way. I've let my own standards slip and have been gadding about in one of Eve's old Laura Ashley skirts from the eighties, paired with a Fair Isle jumper cast-off from Des, which more than amply covers my bottom.

'Retro,' Scarlet always says.

Which is good enough for me.

'I'll go and fetch him for you,' I call out after her, but she's shut her door and has the radio on at full blast – Beethoven's Symphony No. 5? – so I doubt she can even hear me.

When I glance over again, I'm pretty sure there's something familiar about this woman. I know her from somewhere.

FIVE MINUTES LATER, and I have no idea where either Barney or my daughter are. Ruby's bedroom is abandoned, the only evidence of them having been there a pack of playing cards spread across the carpet.

They're not in the living room either.

I check the study. Eve says she hasn't seen them for a while.

Then the studio. Des says: 'Who's Barney?'

Finally, I have to ask Melina. She's in her bedroom on her laptop.

'I haven't seen,' she says. 'Maybe you call police?'

'The *police*?'

'He could be drug dealer.'

'Barney?'

'They use children these days. As drug donkeys.'

'Barney isn't a drugs *mule*. He plays the trombone, for goodness' sake.'

She shrugs. Then she smiles. 'I stick you into a bottle,' she says before laughing out loud.

'You what?'

'I pull your leg,' she translates. 'They went for a walk. To see Nathan.'

'Nathan?'

'Yes. Nathan. About an hour ago. I told her to be back for dinner. I make her favourite: sausages, peas and *plaki*.'

Ruby does like *plaki*. Greasy fried-potato pancakes that Melina swears by for a hangover cure – more effective than Eve's (green hemlock in your socks). But why am I comparing hangover cures when Ruby and Barney are next door? What am I going to tell Barney's mother? There is no time to decide; I have to hurry up and find the pair of them.

Back in the yard, Beethoven's Symphony No. 5 is reaching its rousing climax. I knock on the window of the Land Rover and Barney's mother – seemingly lost in a trance – screams with surprise.

She winds down the window, switches off the stereo, glares at me. 'Where is he?' she asks again.

'Next door with Ruby,' I tell her.

'The big house?'

'Yes.'

'What on earth are they doing at the big house?' she barks. Before waiting for an answer she follows up with an order: 'Get in. I'll drive there. He's got choir practice.'

'He sings?'

'Of course he sings,' she says, as if it's common knowledge. Or I'm a total no-brain. 'Soprano.'

'Oh.' I try to be gracious. 'How lovely.'

'Till his balls break.' She shrieks with laughter.

I think she might have a screw loose.

'Right.' What else can I say to this?

I scramble into the passenger seat as she revs the engine, trying to find a space for my feet amongst the scrunched-up crisp packets, parking-ticket stubs, stray banana skins and other detritus.

She skids out of the yard, almost giving me whiplash, and shunts into the lane with barely a glance to see if there's oncoming traffic, despite it being dusk. What have I let myself in for?

'Why are they up at the house anyway?' she asks.

'They went to see Nathan, the owner. He's a... family friend.'

'Family friend?' she asks as if she doesn't 'do' such a thing.

'Sort of,' I add.

A few minutes later and we've swerved through the gates and past the lodge, racing up the long tree-lined drive that leads to the big house, past oak and beech trees, ornamental shrubberies and rhododendrons. The grounds are vast; we head through acres of parkland with views of grazing meadows to the east, towards the formal gardens, which are bordered by woodland to the west that slopes along the river valley towards the distant sea.

'It's been ages since I've been here,' I announce, for something to say and because my memory has been stirred. 'We used to come to the Christmas fair and carol concert here when I was a kid. When Old Joe's wife was still alive.'

'I used to come to hunt balls back in the day,' she says.

'You hunted?'

'Of course I hunted,' she says. 'Not any more. I haven't the time.'

'Do you work?'

'Of course I bloody work! I run an online company selling baby equipment.'

I try not to snigger at the incongruity of this filthy, rude woman having a job that revolves around babies, but I manage to keep it in. 'Lovely.'

She practically does a handbrake turn on the gravel of the carriage driveway in front of a monumental fountain.

And there it is, looming above us. Just as I remember it. A fine country house in the Gothic Revival style, designed by none other than John Nash. Soft Portland stone, like London Bridge. Castellated parapets and turrets with clusters of chimneypots so the place has the feel of a castle.

Breathtaking.

I can't quite believe it belongs to Nathan these days. Or that Ruby is inside it with this crazy woman's son.

Dusk is falling fast now, and lights have been switched on within. Barney's mum – Jacqueline, it turns out she's called – is already out of the vehicle and striding towards the pillared coach gate – or *porte cochère*, as it feels more appropriate to call it.

Jacqueline's about to knock when the door opens and out rush Barney and Ruby in a state of great agitation. What has Nathan done?

Ruby spots me as I emerge from the tip of the Land Rover and rushes over.

'We've had such a brilliant time, Mum.' She's flushed with excitement. The sort of excitement that often ends in tears. 'Nathan showed us around and it's the biggest place you've ever seen. There are ten toilets and a swimming pool. He says we can come whenever we want.'

Does he now.

I want to interrogate Ruby as to why she has apparently got over his lengthy absence from her life so quickly. But now is not the time. Later will have to do. 'Where *is* Nathan?' I ask.

'He said to come in for a glass of wine. And Barney's mum. We saw you come up the drive from the library upstairs. You should see the amount of books he's got

– more than our new school and old school put together.'

At the mention of wine, Jacqueline has visibly brightened, all thoughts of choir practice banished, and is already making her way towards the door.

'Come on!' she shouts back at me, like we're best friends all of a sudden.

And so this is how I find myself inside the circular hall and being ushered into the drawing room, where an enormous fire rages beneath an imposing marble mantelpiece – with Nathan shoving a glass of champagne into my hand, having already seen to Jacqueline. Ruby and Barney have disappeared again. Maybe to use one of the ten loos.

'This could be your fizz we're drinking in a couple of years' time,' the lord of the manor says. 'Forget champagne! English sparkling wine is smashing all the awards right now.'

'You should stop comparing it to champagne,' I remonstrate. 'English wine should be about its individuality. Its very Englishness.'

'I love a glass or two of Moët,' Jacqueline says. 'Not sure about British wine. Isn't it all vinegary and bitter?'

'*British* wine is actually imported grape juice made into wine. *English* wine – and Welsh – is made from grapes grown here, in this country, in vineyards like ours down the road.' I'm becoming quite a wine buff, even if I say so myself. 'We're thinking about doing sparkling wine, but we've had some problems.'

'I've tried your mother's wine,' Jacqueline says, knocking back the rest of her glass and putting an end to this conversation with a look that says, *You're living a pipe dream*. 'Shame I can't stay for another tipple, Nathan,' she adds, fiddling with her wiry salt-and-pepper hair that doesn't look as though it's seen a hairdresser since the eighties. 'I've got to chauffeur Barney to choir practice before his balls drop.'

I do wish she'd stop referencing her son's downstairs bits. It really isn't appropriate. What kind of mother is she?

'How about you, Chrissie?' Nathan asks, all sweetness and light, knowing full well I'm getting worked up, having already gulped down my drink. 'Time for another?'

'Must get back,' I tell him. 'Though I'd like a chat another time.'

'What about?'

He knows what about so I'm not going to spell it out in front of Jacqueline, who's now prowling the room like a curious cat, examining probably priceless pieces of porcelain.

'Could you get Ruby and Barney please?' I ask him, rather forcefully.

'Of course,' he says, performing a little bow before withdrawing from the room.

I stand in front of the fire and feel the heat of it over my face and right to the roots of my hair so I wish I could plunge into that fountain outside.

'He's a bit of all right,' Jacqueline says, repeating that cackle of hers. 'Got better with age.'

And that's when I remember. This is Jackie. From school. The quiet, shy one with the braces and frizzy hair who played the piano and rode ponies. Whatever's happened to her?

Bedtime. Scarlet is out for the count, having hiked with her group of friends over miles of countryside this afternoon. I've never thought of her as the outdoor type but she's revelling in it here. Her cheeks have a healthy glow and she looks strong and lean – she's taller than me now and I think she's probably grown an inch since Rob left. Ruby's like a child next to her – and right now that child is sprawled on her bed, playing some kind of virtual game against Barney, obviously back from choir practice. What a house he must live in! It turns out he's one of five, which might account for his mother's erratic behaviour, though despite her barking there's something likeable about her. It's probably better to have her as a friend. Keep your enemies closer and all that.

'So, what made you decide to go and see Nathan?' I ask Ruby now.

'I showed Barney Rob's blog and then we got talking about stuff and I mentioned that Rob's not actually biologically my dad even though he's brought me up. And I told him about Nathan and that I haven't spoken to him yet and he said why don't we go and see him. So we did.'

'*Barney* suggested it? Barney, who won't say boo to a goose?'

'He's sort of determined and strong once you get to know him. Don't be fooled.'

'Well, if he's anything like his mother, then I have every reason to believe you.'

'She is a bit scary, isn't she?' Ruby pulls a face. 'She asked me to dinner tomorrow, but I said I have to practise my harp. Then she told me she could do with a harpist for the carol concert and I didn't like to say no.'

'So you said yes?'

'I said yes.'

'Oh, Rube.' I give her a hug.

Then she says: 'Nathan's all right. Sort of funny and cool. And his house is a-maz-ing!'

'It is amazing,' I agree. And then I take the chance to ask more. 'How do you feel now you've had a chance to meet Nathan, you know, after all this time?'

'Do you mean am I angry with him?'

'Not necessarily. Maybe.'

'I thought I'd give him a chance first and then decide if I hate him or not.'

'And so far?'

'I don't hate him. He's actually quite nice. But he's not Rob.'

'No,' I agree. 'He's not Rob.'

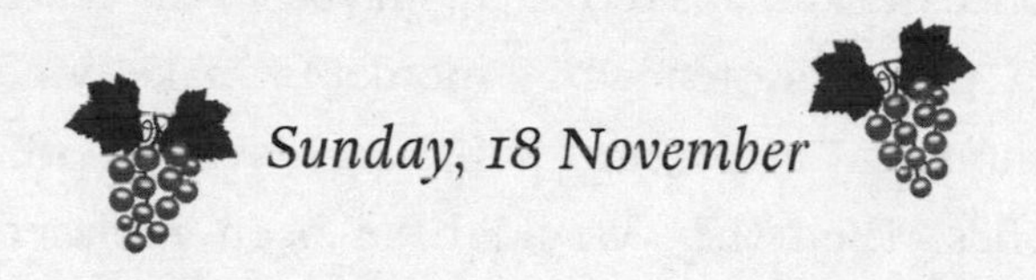

Sunday, 18 November

IT'S A COLD and windy day. When I take Luther out for his morning constitutional, I head up to the vineyard. From the top of the hill the landscape is laid out like a painting. The red fields. The curve of the river down the valley. The barn and the smaller, squatter old milking parlour beyond it. Generations have lived here, eking out a living from the land. Beef cattle. Dairy herds. Crops. Through feast and famine. Invasion and war. From the plague to foot-and-mouth.

It all looks so different from harvest time. Everything is asleep. It's hard to believe we can ever make a go of it with these woody stalks for vines. But I feel a connection with this place. If I shut my eyes, I can picture a prosperous Roman family adjusting to a new life, away from their Tuscan villa with its mosaic floors and a bath house. I imagine the vines that would have been transported here so the family could have their own wine to drink when so far from home. The taste of sun-soaked hills replaced by that of hedgerows and damp earth. And then the vineyards probably went to seed once the Romans retreated. Maybe, as the centuries passed, they were tended by monks to make wine for communion. Until Henry VIII had his way with the Catholics. Then they would have been replaced by arable crops, grazed by cows and sheep. And now, with longer, hotter summers and milder, wetter winters, the conditions are perfect for the renaissance of English wine. I smile at the thought.

We've embraced the champagne of France, the cava of Spain, the Prosecco of Italy, so now is the time – our time – to produce a wine that reflects this island race. A race blended with peoples from all over Europe and across the globe, who have brought with them their winemaking skills and viticultural knowledge. There's no reason why we can't live communally and still express our personality.

I think of Des, the patriarch. He might be an almost-octogenarian but nevertheless he is having his own renaissance. Not only is he painting on commission, he is also doing so for himself, evoking dystopian landscapes in oil.

Then there's Eve. Despite her fall, she is gaining strength from the nature around her while continuing with her yoga lessons and t'ai chi. She's even considering running classes in the barn once it has been renovated.

This barn would make an amazing wedding venue, darling! Eve said last night, all enthusiasm and passion. *We could convert the milking parlour to a winery, too, once we've raised enough money to buy a press and vats.*

She shares my vision, taking it even further, so I need to stay grounded and practical and realistic.

Next up, there's Melina. She is a completely different person from the one I thought I knew in London. She is capable of anything she puts her mind to. She takes up the slack when others fall short, instinctively knowing how to approach problems with a store cupboard of ways passed down from her grandmother. She wants to learn more about the vineyard, the agricultural side of things, and also the winemaking itself – hence the course at Plumpton. I'm happy dealing with the accounts, the business, the events that can grow alongside the wine. But we have to get the wine right. Then and only then will our venture be credible.

And Ruby? Well, Ruby has met Nathan and didn't hate him. Which I know is a good thing, even if I would have quite liked it if she had; I am obviously just worried that she might get let down again. It's clear she misses Rob. She's constantly checking for updates and messages and is counting down the days to the next time she can speak to him. Fortunately, having found a firm friend in Barney, she is keeping up with her harp-playing – even if she's been forced to play in the carol concert.

Which leaves Scarlet, far away from her father but happy with her new friends – so different from those in London, with names like Bogger and Persephone, Morley and Indigo. The city girl who went on marches, now a hiker. Who'd have thought it?

While I'm reflecting on all this, at the top of the hill, my phone beeps. A signal. It might be Rob, I think excitedly. But no, it's Nathan.

He wants to talk.

WE MEET ON neutral territory up at the beacon, the highest point in the area, with views over the moors and downlands to the sea. The River Chud is even clearer from here, snaking its path through the valley.

Nathan points out Home Farm. The rows of vines make a stripy pattern on the patchwork quilt of Devon countryside, slightly grubby-looking in the murky morning.

We let the dogs off their leads and they run about, even Luther who normally only wants to sniff. The spaniels are like happy, enthusiastic toddlers playing with a pensioner.

'So what is it?' I ask him.

'You wanted to talk. About Ruby.'

'I did. I do. I was going to contact you.'

'Does it matter that I contacted you?'

I almost react and tell him yes, of course it matters. But I manage a moment of self-awareness and keep quiet, let him carry on and see what he has to say for himself.

'Firstly, I appreciate you not kicking off yesterday. You had every right to. Secondly, Ruby is brilliant.'

'I know—'

'I'm not expecting to be her father.'

He interrupts my response before I get going.

'I'd just like to be another father figure in her life. And before you say anything, I am different now. I've grown up. Yes, I was annoying when we first saw each other again after all those years, but to be honest, I was embarrassed.'

'Embarrassed?'

'Ashamed.' He's sheepish as he says this, like it's a word he doesn't often utter in connection with himself, but it's a word that he should jolly well own. 'What I did to you and Ruby was terrible,' he stumbles on. 'I should have kept in contact. I should have paid you.'

'You're not getting any argument from me.'

A wry smile. 'And, thirdly, I really should mention that you and Rob have done a great job.'

'Oh. Right.' What else am I supposed to say? Thank you?

'Are you managing all right without him?' he adds, like it's his business, when he should be minding his own.

'I'm managing fine, thank you.'

'Do you miss him?'

'Do I miss him?'

He waits for me to answer.

'Of course I miss him!' I snap. And why do I snap? Not because he's so unbelievably and annoyingly nosy but because, possibly, I have to admit to myself that maybe I don't miss Rob as much as I thought I would. But there's no way I'm telling Nathan that.

Seeing my reaction, he changes tack, moving to safer ground. 'So, how's "Operation Fizz" coming along then? I have to admire you, Chris; it's a great idea. Maybe I could help? You know, as a financial backer or something? It'd be a great investment.'

Maybe I should accept? After all, he has a lot of years to make up for financially. But not a good idea, however in need of money we are. He's involved enough in our lives as it is.

'There's one other thing,' he says. 'It's Charlotte.'

'Charlotte?'

'She's coming to stay. There's nothing between us any more. But she's asked for a few days away and I thought my house is big enough to accommodate her.'

'It's none of my business,' I tell him. I am grateful for the heads-up but I don't need to let him know that.

Luther has now tired of the young spaniels. He sits by my feet, looking up at me expectantly. *Can we go home now?*

'I reckon he's fed up of my two.' Nathan whistles and they're both at his heel within an instant.

I clip on Luther's lead and stroke his ears. 'Come on, old boy.'

As I turn to go, Nathan says, all jokey and matey, 'Old boy? I'm only six months older than you.'

I ignore him, pretend I can't hear in the wind, and head downhill, Luther by my side, back home.

SUNDAY LUNCH IS the one unmoveable feast of the week. Eve and Des might not be entirely traditional, but this is something they never miss. There are always pre-dinner drinks – gin and tonic, or sherry perhaps, sometimes mulled wine on a cold winter's day. Des always carves, with an extravagant sharpening-of-the-knife ritual. The joint of meat is always accompanied by every sort of trimming. And there are always, and obviously, lashings of wine. Now we're down to the last few bottles of white, it's good to know we'll be getting our stocks replenished soon – as long as we can pay the winery the remainder of what we owe.

So there's Eve, Des, Scarlet, Ruby, Melina and me for lunch. Plus Barney, this time happy to stay for food rather than absconding up to the big house. Two of Scarlet's new friends are also here. Also vegan. Morley, who it transpires is Barney's twin, and Indigo. They seem good-natured, enthusiastic and chatty, and I'm so pleased that Scarlet seems to have found her tribe.

After lunch, quite a bit later, once Des has regaled us with anecdotes of the Swinging Sixties and Eve has lectured us on the importance of saving indigenous tribes in Peru, we disperse to various locations around the house – bedrooms, study, studio, living room. We're all on high alert – phones, laptops and computers at our sides – because Eve's auction ends soon. Although she's already reached £3,455, there's a buzz of excitement in the hope that there'll be a last-minute bidding war.

As the countdown approaches, there's much hooting and yelping as bids fly in, and suddenly it's over and Eve is whooping the loudest.

'I'm worth £4,670!' she shrieks.

Everyone swarms back to the kitchen, to witness Des giving his wife a passionate whopper of a kiss on the lips, and a squeeze of her bottom – the man who fell for the young woman on the canvas.

'You're priceless, my love,' he says.

And they share one of those intimate moments that I'd pay a squillion quid for.

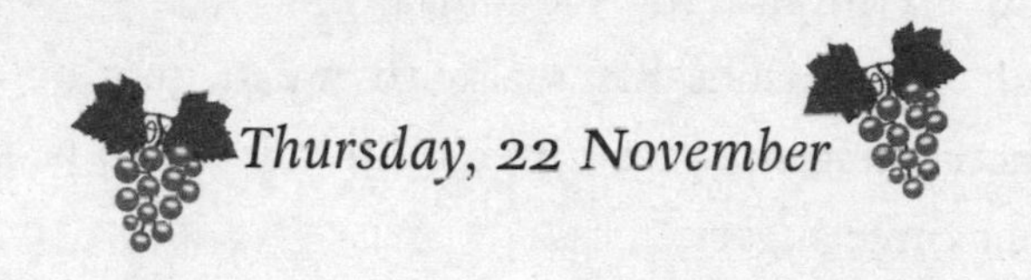

Thursday, 22 November

MALCOLM ARRIVES FOR Ruby's harp lesson. He is charm personified. Des must have given him a thorough talking-to about what is appropriate language to be used in front of Ruby. Well, in front of *anyone*, actually.

Ruby wheels the harp into the kitchen, where it's light and airy and warm enough for her fingers to work properly, and begins her lesson, while I get down to work on my laptop to the dulcet strains of music.

Before I know it, the hour's up and Ruby's disappeared to her room, leaving me to entertain Malcolm.

'Tea?' I ask him.

'Ooh, that'd be lovely – three sugars, please.' As if he's dehydrated. He'd probably hang around for supper if I asked him.

Which maybe I will. He's actually an intelligent, educated man. He's travelled the world with his harp and is always delighted to take on a new pupil because it's not the sort of instrument many children want to learn.

'Ruby was always determined,' I tell him, 'ever since she and Scarlet were bridesmaids at our wedding, drifting up the aisle to "Ave Maria".'

Malcolm finishes his tea with much gulping and satisfaction and so I give him a refill into which he stirs another three sugars.

'Ruby tells me she has another father living next door up at the big house,' he says suddenly, taking me by surprise.

'I wouldn't say "father". Did Ruby say "father"?'

'Not in so many words.'

'Right.' I offer him the biscuit tin.

He rummages around and picks out a ginger nut, dips it into his tea. 'I know Nathan.'

I wait for him to expand on this, though he's temporarily distracted by Luther slobbering at his hand.

'Mm,' he continues. 'I met him at a recital of mine last year. He was there with a young lady.'

'Young lady?'

'Well, I *say* young. Everyone's young in comparison to me. She was probably your age.'

'Right. That would be Charlotte.'

'She was probably very pretty once. Some might even say beautiful. But she had a face like a slapped—'

'Malcolm!' Des appears on cue, stopping the word that was about to escape from his friend's potty mouth. 'Are you staying for supper?'

'No, no, old chap. Too much to do, I'm afraid.' He's on his feet now, producing a silk handkerchief from his jacket pocket and wiping his mouth quite delicately, which is when I notice what long fingers he has.

'Glass of wine?'

'Very kind offer but no.' He's firm on this point. 'Must be going. Same time next week? I've given Ruby the Christmas carols to practise and we'll focus on those from now till the concert.'

'And she's happy about doing the concert?'

'I wouldn't say *happy* exactly. But resigned. It's very hard to say no to Jacqueline.'

'You know Jacqueline, then?'

'Of course,' he says. 'Her husband's my nephew.'

My heart does that thing – sinks a little before popping back up again. I know you're supposed to like that about living in the country. You're supposed to like knowing everyone. But I do sometimes long for the anonymity of London. Where people are happy to ignore you. Where your cousin isn't married to your dentist and you don't shop at the same chemist's as your kid's teacher.

'Let me see you out, Malc,' Des says.

I realize my expression must be pained.

They both disappear into the yard, Luther in their wake.

I'm exhausted; that must be why I'm so jumpy. Niggling thoughts keeping me awake at night: Do I love my husband? Will we ever make good wine? Why doesn't *Nathan* sell up and go and cycle across Africa?

I sigh, remind myself that this has been a good day. I've made some progress with advertising the paintings. They're catalogued and scheduled to go on eBay; there's no point in using an auction house since the sale of *Eve* – this is working perfectly well. We might not be so lucky with the next batch, but it's got to be worth a shot.

When Des returns, I ask him about something else that's been bothering me.

'Do you mind selling your paintings, Des?'

'Not at all,' he says without even considering his answer. 'That's why I painted them all those years ago, to make a living. It's just that they fell out of favour and now we need to make wine while the sun shines, so to speak.'

'I see what you did there,' I tell him with a smile. 'And about that...'

'Yes, my love?'

'Any thoughts on doing up the milking parlour? Just enough so we can possibly think about buying a new press? And a couple of steel vats? We should be looking beyond this year.'

'I realize that, my honeybun,' he says with an enormous sigh that is strong enough to knock over a small child. 'Problem is, neither your mother nor I appreciated just how long a game you have to play with a vineyard. Five years to establish the vines adequately. Another two if you want sparkling wine. And we're only a small concern, aren't we? Just a couple of acres. Two hundred or so vines. We're never going to be a Nyetimber or a Sharpham.'

I smile, pleased these English winery names are familiar. Then, 'But we do *want* a business, don't we, Des?' I check.

'Of course we want a business. It's just that occasionally, when I'm having a senior moment or when I'm a bit glum, I wonder if your mother and I will actually live to see it running to profit. If we'll ever see our bottles on the shelves of the local off-licences or displayed in a crate of hay in a farm shop. Or indeed if anyone other than us will actually *like* the damn stuff.'

Sometimes I doubt if *I* will live to see this day.

Unless we diversify.

'You're thinking about weddings, aren't you?' he asks, reading my mind.

'How do you know that?'

'Call it a hunch. An educated guess. A stab in the dark. Any of those really. Am I right?'

'Yes, you are indeed right,' I respond, reminded of just how well he knows me. 'I *am* thinking about weddings.'

'A shame about you and Nathan,' he adds.

'Me and Nathan?'

'Your marriage. I know it wasn't your fault...'

And I wonder for a moment – a very brief moment – if I *was* partly to blame. I *did* tell him to go, after all. Though he didn't have to take me quite so literally. And I *could* have asked him back. I could have intervened sooner and made it easier for him to see Ruby. But this is what happened. He left. And he didn't come back.

'Are you and Rob, you know, having a time of it?'

'It's not exactly ideal, him in Africa.'

'It's certainly not. Any more news?'

'He's in Botswana now. The Elephant Highway.'

'Sounds exciting.'

'Exciting, yeah. But scary too – for me as well as him. He says there are lions about so it's too dangerous to wild camp. He and his new cycling buddy have no choice but to keep going even though the distance between towns can be up to 100 kilometres. It's sparsely populated and the scenery is so repetitive, like one endless road. I think they're actually suffering from boredom, despite the sight of roaming elephants and the prospect of being eaten alive by big cats. When they reach the interior there should be more farms, more people.'

'So, all being well, if he survives?'

'If?'

'Obviously there's some levity in my question.'

'When he gets back, well, we shall have to see.'

And this is probably the first time I have actually

admitted to myself that there is even a choice in the matter.

'Right.' He claps his hands. 'The sun is so far over the yardarm it really must be time for a double gin. There's no wine left.'

Is it wrong, I wonder, to whoop and holler with joy?

Winter

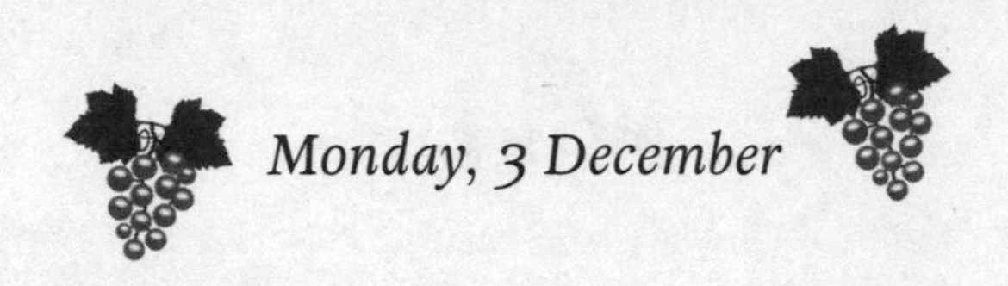

Monday, 3 December

ANOTHER MONDAY MORNING. No need these days to put a sausage casserole in the oven – not with Eve and Melina around. Only Melina isn't here today, as she left yesterday afternoon to drive to Brighton to stay with her cousin in preparation for her wine course at Plumpton College. She should be back late tonight.

It's strange without her. Although she doesn't talk an awful lot, she's normally bustling around, cleaning, cooking, sorting. She's been quieter of late. I asked her a few days ago if she was all right, and it turned out she's just been distracted, studying for the course. She's taking the whole thing very seriously. Which is actually rather brilliant. But I hope this doesn't mean she's definitely going back home, to put this studying to use there. She has every right to do that, of course she does. But, blimey, we'd miss her.

Not just because she has a knack of waking those

girls up. I'm starting to realize that's she become a trusted friend to me, too.

Maybe I should consider that sausage casserole?

BREAKFAST TIME. GIRLS are their usual grumpy morning selves, faces in their cornflakes, but when I mention the word 'party', they both perk up.

'Can I really have a party?' Ruby asks, wide-eyed, a child again.

'Well, you are going to be sixteen, and Scarlet had a party for hers in London so I think one's in order.'

'That seems like ages ago,' Scarlet says, just a little wistfully.

'It was only at the beginning of September,' Ruby adds. 'I never thought I'd be having mine in Devon.'

A moment's silence that I will not allow to bloom.

'How about in the barn?' I suggest. 'Like we did for the pickers.'

'Really?' Ruby shivers dramatically. 'Won't it be too cold?'

'Not if we have a barn dance.'

'A barn dance? Could we be any more yokel?'

'Bit regionist,' says Scarlet, spreading some Marmite on her toast.

Which makes me splutter out my tea. The girl who loved London, now sticking up for Devon. The one I thought would resist, now a firm believer.

'Only problem is we need to find a band. It's a bit short notice.' I'm aware that I seem to be winging it these days. Making it up as I go along. And whereas before that would have caused me anxiety, now I feel all right about it. It's really not so bad.

Ruby gets up from the table, scraping her chair across the flagstones, Luther following her optimistically to the compost bin where she chucks her banana skin. 'Malcolm's in a folk band,' she says.

'Is he?'

'The Chud Valley Stompers.'

Scarlet sniggers.

Ruby gives her evils, suddenly Malcolm's defender. 'I think they do weddings and stuff.'

'Barn dances?' I ask. Maybe this will work out.

'I suppose. But isn't a barn dance completely crap, Mum? I mean, be honest.'

'No, really they're actually great fun. I went to a few when I was your age. Everyone joins in. I promise.'

Ruby remains unconvinced but grudgingly agrees to speak to Malcolm about it.

At this point Des enters the kitchen, ears flapping. 'Did someone mention a party?'

'Mum wants Ruby to have a barn dance for her birthday on Saturday.'

'Splendid!' He does a quick shuffle. 'Gay Gordons and the Barley Reel. To coin one of your girls' phrases, *bring it on!* I found a case lurking in the cellar so . . .'

Ruby's face drops and I suspect this will be a hard one to sell.

By midday, after I've completed various tasks around the house, I list three more of Des's smaller paintings on eBay. All of them doe-eyed, buxom women. Perfect for the walls of hipsters. Depending on the outcome, I might suggest we *do* give the auction houses a go. Just for the larger canvases; he still has around twelve. It's possible we could make more money that way. And then we really might have the cash to turn the milking parlour into a home for a new wine press at some point.

After a quick bite to eat, I turn my attention to Ruby's birthday on Saturday. Usually I'm all prepared by this point of December, what with Christmas coming up and all that means at work and at home. But now, without work, I don't have to think about conferences and events. Just the party.

On cue, Ruby texts me.

Chud Valley Stompers are free Sat. Malcolm plays fiddle and is the caller, whatever that is. x

Probably free because no other bugger would want a barn dance in December.

I've asked swing band friends to come n Scarlets inviting her crowd.

This second text is followed by a smiling-face emoji which makes me smile in turn. Hopefully this won't be an out-and-out catastrophe.

Instead of worrying, and definitely instead of winging it, what I need is a plan: food, decorations, staging. Hay bales. Trestle tables. Strings of fairy lights. Some kind of heating that won't give Des palpitations.

While I'm googling party balloons, Declan phones me. I take him into the understairs cupboard so I don't get disturbed by Eve or Des, who are both lurking.

'What's up, Dec? You sound worried.'

'You'll never believe what's happened,' he says.

I'm thinking the worst. Redundancy. Illness. Accident. 'What is it? You've got me all worried.'

There's a huge intake of breath and then he blurts out: 'Things have been getting serious with Mark.'

'Right.' I let this sink in a moment while relief washes over me. 'And?'

'And he asked me to move in with him while we look for somewhere permanent to live. Together.'

'Right. And you said what exactly?'

'Nothing.'

'Oh, I see. That was the problem.'

'Yes,' he says with a massive sigh. 'That was the problem.'

I can hear the regret in the silence that follows and I know I have to pursue this now. 'Can you see yourself ever settling down?'

'I genuinely never thought I would,' he says. 'Didn't think I was the settling sort. But...'

'But what?'

'Well, now it's over, I can't stop thinking about what I might've given up.'

Declan sounds lost, vulnerable, so different from that confident exterior he puts up. I've seen him waver once or twice before, but he always bounces back. This seems to be different, though. He must really, *really* like Mark, more than he's ever liked anyone.

'Do you love him?'

Without even having to think about this, he replies: 'Yes. I love him.'

'Mark sounds like a great guy. What's the problem?'

'Don't,' he says. 'Just don't. I'm an idiot.'

'Probably, but look, why don't you speak to him? Tell him what you've told me. Be honest. In fact...'

'What?'

'Throw your life into the wind and see what happens?'

'Touché,' he says, followed by a rude word, and then he's back to his usual self and turns his attention to me. 'How are you? Rob? The girls? The vineyard?'

I give him the lowdown and, while I listen to his witty asides, I realize how much I miss this man, my former daily companion. But Rob? Not so much.

'Come down and stay in the new year, won't you?' I ask Declan.

'I wouldn't miss your next party – or should that be vintage? – now, would I?' he jokes.

Who knows if this will pan out? He could be in love with another bloke by then. Or maybe even back with Mark. More likely on an all-inclusive to Puerto de la Cruz.

I finally emerge from the cupboard like a mole blinking into the light.

AFTER SCHOOL, THE girls arrive home tired and hungry as usual. Once they've had their bread and jam and half an hour fiddling about in their rooms, Ruby seeks me out in the study.

'Thanks for throwing this party,' she says. 'It sounds fun.' She gives me a hug and, even though it's just a brief one, it's precious enough that I want to pop it in a drawer for safekeeping.

Only then she drops a Ruby bomb. 'Do you think Nathan would come, you know, if I invited him?'

The question I've been dreading. 'Er...'

Without waiting for a reply, she wanders off, leaving me speechless, leaving me hankering after the old days – the swimming party, the trampoline party, the year we had the magician who made balloon animals and juggled with actual knives. Party bags. Pass the parcel. Fancy dress. Hectic but fun. Controlled chaos. And now?

Does she just have her eyes on the prize? Nathan does have a lot of money. And Nathan does have a lot of birthdays to make up for. But maybe I'm being unfair. Maybe she genuinely wants to share her special day with him. And that's what scares me.

LATER, AFTER WE'VE eaten vegan sausage casserole and Des hasn't even objected to the lack of meat, he and I sit at the table and discuss the future of Home Farm wine.

'There's so much to be done, Des!' I say, fired up by the prospect. 'The dairy parlour. The barn. The press. The paintings. The wine licence applications. Once we're up and running properly we can think about hosting events – parties, weddings.'

'You really are a marvel, Chrissie.' Des is as enthusiastic as he's ever been. A bon viveur. A joy.

Then a beep on my phone just as Eve wanders in with a basket of vegetable-dyed yarn. 'I'm making Melina socks for Christmas,' she informs us. 'She's been hankering after a pair. What are you two up to?'

'Plotting and planning, my love-cherub. Plotting and planning.' Des squeezes my mother's bottom as she passes by his chair.

'I'll leave you to it,' she says. 'After I've made us all cocoa.'

And for ten minutes it's like being a child again. And it's rather nice.

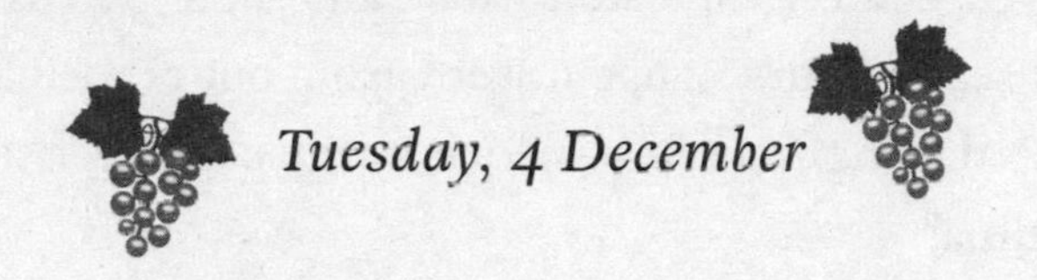

Tuesday, 4 December

I GO DOWNSTAIRS to the kitchen to make a cup of tea and Melina isn't at her normal spot at the sink or bustling around banging cupboard doors. I can't see her bag on the window seat or any evidence of her being here. Did she decide to stay another night in Brighton? I wouldn't blame her. It's a long journey back. Surely she would have texted? But there's nothing on my phone except a video from Declan of a baby panda tumbling down a slide.

Once I've checked the yard and confirmed the car is missing, a surge of panic rises within me.

What if she's been in an accident? I'm good at imagining the worst. No, there are heaps of reasons why she might not be here, I try to convince myself.

I take Luther out for a quick walk. I've got twenty minutes or so before I have to drag the girls from their beds and some fresh air might calm my nerves. Across the yard and up the lane as far as the common. Luther used to sprint across the grass like a greyhound but now he's happier to sniff and trot sedately. I take him as far as the edge of the Chudston Estate and there, across the way, I see Nathan's Range Rover easing out of the gate.

He's driving. There's someone in the passenger seat.

Melina?

I catch her eye and she nods to me, glum. Where's she going? And more to the point, where has she been?

ONCE THE GIRLS have left for school, I get to work on the accounts, trying not to think about that whole car thing.

So: we've paid the winery for pressing our harvest. The next job is to think about the dairy parlour refurb. It's not as big as the barn – never had a large herd here. Stone, with a tiled roof and concrete floor. It's been used for storage over the years we've lived at Home Farm, even in my grandmother's day. A ride-on mower, tools, logs. Rusty pieces of dangerous-looking equipment, the sort you see during the set-up to an episode of *Casualty*. It shouldn't take a huge amount of work to get it up to speed. Then there'll be room for a press – a state-of-the-art bladder press like they have at Chudston Winery – and a couple of steel tanks for fermentation. And further down the line, somewhere to store the bottles so the wine can mature 'on the lees'. Because now I'm determined that we will have sparkling wine: the most expensive, labour-intensive and time-consuming way to make wine, but there you go.

NATHAN CALLS IN just before lunch. 'I need to explain about Melina,' he says.

'It's none of my business,' I tell him.

'What?'

'You and Melina.'

'Me and Melina?'

'She didn't come home last night. Then this morning I saw you both coming out of the estate in your Range Rover.'

'Right.'

'Where did you take her?'

'To the airport.'

'The airport? What have you done?'

'Me?' He does his continental gesture of protest. 'I haven't done anything.'

'Come on! She stays the night with you and now she's gone to the airport?'

'She didn't stay the night with me. I saw her this morning, getting into the car as I drove past your gate. She was in a right state.'

'What?'

'She'd had a phone call from Poland. Her grandma's really ill.'

'Oh, poor Melina. Why didn't she say anything?'

'It was early. She said she left you a note.'

'I haven't seen a note.'

He looks round the kitchen, points to the fridge. 'What's that?'

I get up and have a look, snatch the note from its magnet claws and read it. Oh. Poor Melina.

'I told her to get in my car,' he goes on, 'seeing as she was in no fit state to drive. We only nipped back to the house 'cause I'd forgotten my phone.' He takes it out of his coat pocket as if it's a piece of evidence. 'Then I drove her to Bristol Airport to get the flight to Kraków.'

'That was... nice.'

'She's a nice woman.'

'Do you like her?'

'Of course. As I said, she's a nice woman.'

He's making me work hard here. 'I mean do you *like* her?'

'You mean do I fancy her? No. I don't fancy her. She's lovely. Attractive. But no. I'm off women for a while. The last one led me a merry dance and I stupidly tried to keep up. And the one before, well... I made a mess of that.' He looks at me, unusually coy, before snapping himself out of it. 'Anyway, why are you asking? It's not actually any of your business. Is it?'

'I'm curious, that's all.'

'What about you?'

'I don't fancy her.'

'Ha, ha, Chris. I meant have you heard from Rob, as you well know.'

'I have, actually. There was another blog post this morning.' I check my phone because I can't remember the place names. 'They've crossed the salt flats of the Makgadikgadi Pans National Park and are now in Zimbabwe heading for Victoria Falls.'

'Sounds like he's having a blast.'

'Hmm. Well, it's definitely an adventure.' I skim the post again. 'He says it's been tough getting through Botswana because of the heat and the thunderstorms. And they crossed paths with a bull elephant, so that must have been a bit dicey for a moment there, until they got off its territory.'

'And here you are with this bull elephant.'

'Here I am.'

For a moment I remember. That school disco. The evenings he spent here after school, being fed, doing homework, mucking about to *Top of the Pops*. The A-level revision in our meadow, before it was planted with vines. The promises and the plans. How he was going to meet me in Rome but never showed; he'd got a job and then a place at uni in Leeds. I carried on travelling – I'd had enough of education and wanted to work. Be independent. So I got a job in a bar in Spain and stayed for months.

'Do you remember when we met up again in London, when I got back from travelling?' I ask him. 'I thought that was it. Us for life. And then we had Ruby and somehow it went wrong. Why did it go wrong?'

'Oh. Well. Get straight to the point, why don't you?'

'So?'

'OK. Whatever I say will sound like a pathetic excuse but I reckon I just didn't know how to be a father,' he says. 'All I knew of parenting was learned from your mum and Des.'

'But they were good to you. Don't have a go at them.'

'No, no. I'm not. They made me feel part of your family. I'm just saying I never had that at home. So then when it was you, me and Ruby, I was overwhelmed. I acted like a prick, I know I did. And I don't blame you for chucking me out once you found out about Charlotte.'

'You *were* a prick.'

'I know. And I'm really sorry for that. And so sorry I didn't come back. It's unforgivable and I hate myself for it.' He looks at me. 'Please forgive me?'

I don't answer. I can't. Maybe he takes my non-answer as me considering it. At any rate, he reaches out to me and before I can think, I find myself being hugged and I remember what it used to feel like to be held close by him. So I let him hold me. For a short time. And I feel like I've come home. But then I come to my senses as his phone beeps.

'I've got to go,' he says. 'Sorry. Let's catch up very soon.' And he ruffles my hair. Actually ruffles my hair, so I'm glad when Luther growls at him.

MUCH LATER, AFTER the girls are back from school and we've had tea and updated the guest list, I realise I *could* have invited Nathan to the barn dance. But I'm glad I didn't. If Ruby really wants him to come, she'll have to phone him or visit the big house. I want nothing of it.

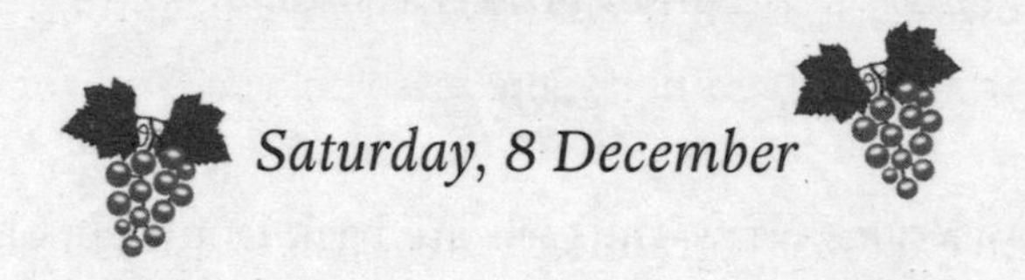

Saturday, 8 December

SATURDAY DAWNS MILD and dry. A clear winter sky, a rare one with a low sun. We might even get through this barn dance without hypothermia – if we wrap up warm and keep moving.

Ruby comes into my room first thing, bringing me a cup of tea and climbing into bed with me.

'Happy birthday, love.' I give her cheek a kiss. It's cold. 'Do you want to open your presents?' I reach down to the floor and pick up a pile of gifts. All tied with ribbon and bows, the way she likes it.

'Let's wait for Scarlet,' she says. 'She's coming in a sec.'

And in Scarlet staggers, her hair like an explosion, dark half-moons under her eyes. 'Happy birthday, Rube.' She yawns and lobs a small package onto the bed, before clambering under the covers on the other side of me.

Ruby unwraps her presents. Like me, she takes extreme care doing this, peeling back the Sellotape and gently unfolding the paper, taking her time. Scarlet and Rob always rip it off, desperate to see what's within. In this respect, at least, it's like parent, like daughter.

Scarlet has given her some joss sticks and an incense burner.

'Don't let your grandfather see that,' I warn them. 'You know how he is about fire. If he gets a hint of a match, he'll be paranoid about the house burning down.'

'Why does he get so worried?' Scarlet asks.

'The thatch. He remembers a bad fire at home when he was a kid. Their house on Dartmoor. They lost everything.'

'How sad,' Ruby says.

I nod in agreement. 'The irony being that they'd lived through the Blitz in Exeter and then once his dad was demobbed, they moved out to Dartmoor for some peace and quiet and a new life. A chimney fire caught the thatch and the house burnt to the ground.'

Silence while we contemplate the enormity of this for poor old Des and his war-weary family. Now would be a good time for another lecture on the evils and dangers of smoking but it's Ruby's birthday so I'll leave that for later.

'Don't worry, Mum. I'll be super careful,' Ruby says angelically and sympathetically. 'Plus Granddad has no sense of smell so he'll never know.' She sniffs the incense packet. 'Ooh, jasmine. Thanks, Scarlet. This is lush.'

'Glad you like it,' Scarlet says. 'Now open the rest. I

can't hang around all day. I'm off hiking in a bit.' She yawns again, barely fit to scramble back to bed, let alone walk in the cold for miles. She really has caught the rambling bug. 'And don't panic, Chrissie. I'll be back in time to help get ready for tonight.'

'I'm not panicking.'

They both laugh at me.

Ruby opens my stash and is very pleased with her perfume, pyjamas, and a silver chain with a cute little ruby set in a heart.

'Oh, Mum,' she says, damp-eyed, throwing her arms around me, which is all the thanks I need.

Before I get the chance to weep, we're called down by Eve who's made a feast of a breakfast for us all, and we sit together in relative harmony while more presents are opened. The socks knitted by Eve go straight onto Ruby's feet. And then there's the most beautiful painting from Des.

'Did you really do that for me, Granddad?' Ruby asks, amazed.

'It's the view from your bedroom window,' he says.

'I'd know that view anywhere.' She smiles at him. 'Thank you.'

'You won't always live here,' he says. 'But if you have that view then you'll always return.'

At this point Ruby becomes a bit tearful but then a phone call cheers her up. Rob hasn't forgotten her.

We're nearly ready for the party. Fruit punch has been made. Birthday cake iced. A plethora of baked potatoes are warming in the Aga and a huge pot of veggie chilli simmers on the hob.

The barn's been decorated with balloons and streamers and there are hay bales aplenty. Now the band are setting up and we're just about to head out there before the teenagers arrive when Ingrid phones, demanding her granddaughter's immediate attention.

'Hello, Granny,' Ruby says, a little impatient and fidgety but trying hard to be polite. She moves away from us, out of our earshot, to hear her better.

I imagine Ingrid telling Ruby she's transferred some money into her bank account, which is what she always does at birthday time.

But she has clearly dropped a bombshell instead; I see it explode in the expression of horror on my daughter's face.

Once Ruby has freed herself from the phone, she tells us what her grandmother said. 'Granny's going to be on her own for Christmas!'

Normally, Ingrid has Christmas dinner at the house of her sister and brother-in-law, who don't 'do' children, which is how we've always got away without spending the actual day with her. But it seems they're off on a cruise this year.

'I asked if there was anyone from church who might invite her round for lunch but she said she couldn't possibly impose on a family at Christmas time.'

'Oh dear.' I'm not in the least surprised no one's offered to take her on. Who on earth would put themselves out for a grumpy, self-righteous old battleaxe like Ingrid?

'Poor Granny,' Ruby says.

'Yes, indeed.' I try to look suitably sad. 'Poor Granny.'

No time to dwell on it now, as I need to rally the troops and get this party started.

THIRTY MINUTES LATER, and the party is well and truly started. The band is playing, Malcolm is calling, and nearly everyone is dancing. Des hands me a flute of sparkling white made from the grapes of Chudston vineyard. It's rather delicious, reminiscent of rhubarb crumble and English roses. Not champagne. But something just as quaffable. Something altogether more British and un-continental.

'This bottle of fizzy delight only cost me £20, with mates' rates.' He takes a sip, his head flung far back as his nose is too big for the glass. 'Worth every penny.' And another sip. 'This country is rather good at sparkling wine. We have the right soils with the right acidity and with long-ripening grapes.' And another sip, draining the glass. 'A fresh yet elegant taste.' He gives a satisfied sigh followed by a full-throttled belch before going for the refill. 'Bottoms up, my dear girl.' He downs this second glass then puts his arm around my waist. 'Come and have a dance. It's about time you let your hair down.'

THE CHUD VALLEY Stompers are well into their stride. Malcolm, it turns out, is a spectacular caller. Loud and clear. Funny and charming. He is also on his best behaviour. In fact, he goes above and beyond. He quickly puts us at our ease and soon we're all flinging ourselves around the dance floor. Reels and squares. Circles and couples. Dips and spin-outs. Casting off and promenading. Do-si-dos and figures of eight.

Ruby's well into it, dancing alongside Barney and their fellow band members. Maybe Ruby too is finding her tribe.

I smile, think back to the day we brought her home from the hospital, Nathan cracking open the champers and some elderflower fizz for me, making me feel special. Like we had something to celebrate. Which we did, our Ruby. But then there came the disturbed nights, the breastfeeding. I couldn't so much as sniff a wine gum without feeling paranoia. The other mothers in my group all seemed so much more laid-back than me. Less panicky about routines. Maybe I *was* over the top. Maybe I *did* push Nathan away. Three years later, it had all gone wrong and he left. New Zealand. As far away as he could possibly go.

Now, as if the memories have conjured him up, the man himself arrives with an armful of presents for the birthday girl. I watch her smiling at him. Happy. A look I haven't seen in a long time, and I wonder what all this means.

Scarlet watches as Ruby opens her presents, one for each birthday he's missed. Ten in all. This includes a Pandora charm bracelet with sixteen charms.

'Thanks, Nathan,' Ruby says, trying not to smile too much, a little overwhelmed.

And then I catch sight of Scarlet's face. Like thunder. Trouble ahead, I suspect.

Next time I check, she's disappeared with her friends. Probably smoking or maybe drinking illicit cider and I feel jealous for a second that I'm not that age again when everything was either brilliant or hideous.

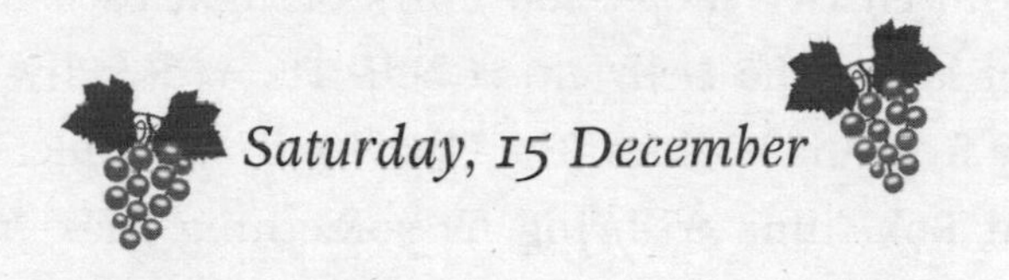

Saturday, 15 December

We are hurtling towards Christmas, so today is all about emergency planning and action. This is the first time since I was a teenager that I'll have spent the whole Christmas season at Home Farm. And the first Christmas spent without Rob in a long time. I want to make it as good as possible.

Not long before evening draws in at only half past three, Scarlet returns fresh-faced from another of her rambles, and she and Ruby set about decorating the tree I bought today from the forest park a few miles up the road. It is now standing upright in its very own copper coal scuttle, thanks to Des, in the large bay window of the sitting room, its lights reflecting in the old dimpled glass.

The girls unpack the boxes of tinsel, the biscuit tins of tissue-wrapped glass baubles, and the shoeboxes of plastic elves and glittery snowmen, nostalgia for their childhood illuminating their faces. Each item brings back a memory, reminds us of Christmases past – decorations school-made by infant hands, treasures found in charity shops, souvenirs brought back from distant lands. The Delft china bell. The red-and-white moose from the Rockies. The Nativity from Bethlehem. Would Rob think to bring us something back from Africa for next year's tree? I shut my eyes and try to visualize this. A Masai beaded star. An Egyptian cat. A banana-leaf manger.

But I can't. Not now. He's too far away, in every sense. Besides, we have to be at church in an hour for choir practice and, in the meantime, Barney has magically appeared in the house with his trombone like a heralding angel.

'Nice tree,' he says, which is high praise indeed from this boy of few words.

Eve has followed him in and she too compliments the tree. 'Don't forget the star,' she adds before rummaging around in one of the boxes and holding up the wonky, tinselly, pipe-cleaner excuse for the holy star which has always gone on top of the tree. 'Who's going to do the honours?'

'You do it, Ruby,' says Scarlet.

'But I'm not tall enough,' Ruby says.

'Jump on my back.' Scarlet turns around, gets down on her knees and after just a moment's hesitation Ruby climbs on. Very carefully, Scarlet stands up and makes her wobbly way closer to the tree. With her arm outstretched, Ruby reaches the top branch and attaches the star, and Scarlet releases her. They stand back and admire their efforts. It's hard not to think of this as Rob's job but, to be honest, the girls have done it pretty damn well all by themselves.

Eve claps her hands in delight, then takes Barney, Ruby and Scarlet off to the kitchen to fill them up with crumpets and tea, with me following behind. For such a small young man, Barney can't half pack away the carbs.

'These are the best crumpets I've ever had,' he says.

Which makes Eve smile. And I wonder what on earth Jackie does to her crumpets.

REHEARSAL TIME AT St Mary Magdalene, an un-fancy Norman church with a rustic vibe. The walls are whitewashed, adorned with only a few of the standard brass and marble plaques; honours to former estate owners, a roll call of the war dead. The pews are plain and sturdy and there's a baptismal font at the front, though goodness knows when a baby was last christened here. Then there's a simple wooden pulpit. A brass eagled lectern with an old leather Bible opened to the last reading. The board with the last hymn numbers to be sung. And up three steps, an altar laid with a white cloth, a pair of brass candlesticks and a cross.

I remember from my childhood the way that on a bright day light cascades through the beautiful stained-glass windows, illuminating the shepherds, lambs and green pastures. Tonight it is black outside. But within these stone walls, the church is breathtaking. Candles bathe the scene in a heavenly glow. The choristers sit beatifically in the stalls while musicians file into the north and south transepts. Two harps sit one either side of the crossing. One is Malcolm's thirty-six-string Celtic harp, the other Ruby's pedal harp. I feel a flutter of hopeless nerves on her behalf.

We're the first to arrive, followed in dribs and drabs by more band members, and then a sudden influx of young people, parents and instruments in tow. Flutes, clarinets, saxophones. Violins and cellos. A drum kit. A keyboard.

I watch on as Malcolm helps Ruby tune up and, after everyone is brought to a hush and parents have been dismissed by the scary-looking conductor and choir mistress, there's a flutter of music sheets and coughing and before we know it we're outside in the drizzle.

As parents from further afield drift back to their cars, I head towards home, but the lychgate with its twinkly coloured lights stops me in my tracks, a festive spirit taking over, and I invite everyone back for a drink. Not one person declines the offer, and so we all huddle together against the weather, walking along the lane and into the yard of Home Farm.

Inside, in the cosy kitchen with its smell of cinnamon and nutmeg, a pan of mulled wine is brewing on the Aga. Eve and Des, in their absolute element, welcome the community into their home. They both fuss about, relieving guests of their coats and scarves, then dishing out booze, coffee and nibbles.

I sit on the window seat and look out over the shadows in the yard, thinking back to last year's carol concert in London – a very different affair, in the girls' school hall. Rob, Scarlet and I watched Ruby plucking her strings with gusto through twelve carols and then we went for pizza in Blackheath. Scarlet was in a mood because after the concert, while we were having mulled wine and mince pies in the school cafeteria, she'd had an argument with her geography teacher over the tax on sanitary products. By the time we got to the restaurant and ordered our food, Ruby was exhausted and practically falling asleep over her *quattro formaggio.*

Back in the sitting room now, everyone's relaxed, chatting, milling about. Des offers a guided tour of the studio for some while Eve takes a group out to the barn to talk about our future plans for the winery. Our guests are entranced by the idea of an artist at large, and even more so by the vineyard, standing dormant on the hill behind us, waiting until spring to spurt back into life.

It's almost time to return to church to collect the musicians. I'm putting on my coat in preparation when

I feel my phone vibrate. I excuse myself and retreat into the understairs cupboard. Melina's name is flashing at me.

'Hey, Melina. How's it going?'

'Is very bad,' she says. Her voice sounds distant, younger, with a vulnerability I've never heard before. 'Babcia is very sick. She is in hospital. Very good hospital with excellent doctors but she is old and she has pneumonia.'

I can hear her sniffing so it's clear she's been crying. She never cries. Not even when Jason chucked her out back in September. Not so much as a tear or a raised voice. But now.

'I think she must die soon,' she says. 'She has give up. She is happy to go. But I am very sad.'

'Of course you are.' A wave of sympathy washes over me. 'I wish there was something I could do to help.'

'I must put up a good face for a bad game,' she says, enigmatically – one of her Polish phrases that has lost a little in translation.

'Do you have anyone with you?'

'I have Tomasz.'

'Tomasz? Tomasz who was over here?'

'Yes, same Tomasz. He lives close by in Poland but now he stays with us on farm because his bad girlfriend has found another lover for herself and he has no home. He sleeps in our barn which is not like your barn. Is very modern and clean.'

Melina is not impressed by thatched roofs or cob buildings. She doesn't appreciate the concept of historical or architectural significance. She'd have everything bulldozed and rebuilt from scratch if necessary. *People are more important than buildings*, she always says. And though she has a point, I think I'd still rather have such beauties as St Mary Magdalene.

'I must go,' she says suddenly – and that's it, she's gone. Back to her grandmother's bedside. Maybe her last vigil. Maybe next All Saints' Night she will be lighting a candle for Babcia.

I sit in the cupboard for a while, thinking of this old woman who I have never met and never will meet now, but am somehow brought close to thanks to her granddaughter. I listen to the voices and footsteps of the guests on the other side of the door; they must be gathering to walk back to the church to collect their offspring and drive them home. I sigh. I just need five minutes' peace for contemplation. I only wish there was some wine left, which is something I never thought I'd think about Eve and Des's vintage.

Then I hear another voice, loud and booming, calling my name.

Bloody Nathan.

Last time I saw him alone, in the farm kitchen before Ruby's party, I was being held in those toned arms of his before we were saved by his phone and his sudden departure.

'Chrissie!' he shouts now. 'Chrissie! Where are you?'

I feel embarrassed. I'll have to ignore him. And anyway, I'm not at his beck and call.

'Chrissie!'

Maybe there's actually a slight edge, an urgency to his calls? Is he in trouble? Has something happened? Is it Ruby? I only left her an hour ago. She's been with safe people in a safe environment, what on earth could've gone wrong?

I'm deciding whether to step outside when the door is yanked open and there he is, backlit by the hall light.

'Why are you hiding in the dark? Is this a game of sardines?'

'I was having a moment. What is it?'

'It's your daughter.'

'Ruby?'

'The other one. Scarlet.'

'What's wrong with Scarlet? Where is she?'

'In the kitchen.' Now that I can actually see his face, I recognize a touch of anger there. Or is it fear? 'I found her wandering about on the estate with a couple of her friends.'

'Is that it? I thought something terrible had happened. Were they smoking or something? I'll have a word—'

'No, you don't understand. Give me a chance to explain.'

'All right. Explain. What were they doing?'

'I'm not entirely sure,' he says, frustratingly. 'Scarlet insists they were just out walking. I suspect there was some smoking and drinking involved. I'm not judging, I know what we were like at that age.' A brief flashback to summer nights on the moors, wild camping and bottles of Merrydown. 'I got angry with them for trespassing when it's dangerous out there, but they wouldn't come inside so I had a bit of a go at Scarlet.'

'Dangerous? Why would it be dangerous?'

'There's a trained marksman after a fox,' he goes on. 'And I don't want any accidents.'

I must look horrified, because he says, 'Don't worry, it's over and done with very quickly and much better than being torn apart by hounds.'

For a second I must look even more horrified before I realize he's talking about the fox, not Scarlet, and I'm just so relieved he's brought her home. She's safe. Alive.

'Where are her friends now?

'Waiting in my car so I can take them home.'

I rush to the kitchen. There she is, sitting at the table, arms folded, the old look of fire in her eyes. I am so pleased to see it, I bend down and give her a huge hug and don't say a word. After a moment of this she hugs me back and whispers into my ear, 'Nathan's a jerk.' And I love her all the more for these words of wisdom and clarity.

'He is,' I agree. 'He really is.'

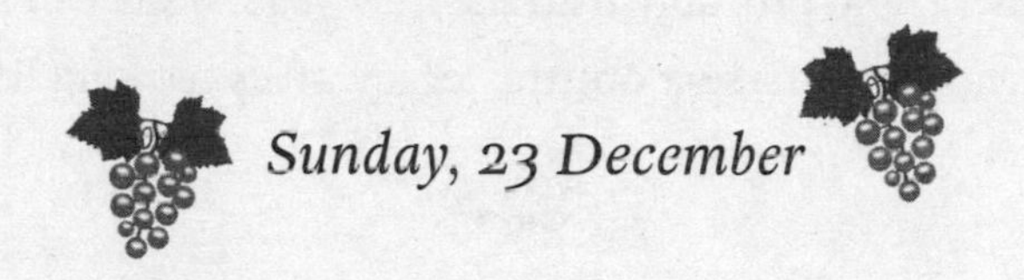

Sunday, 23 December

TONIGHT IS THE big one, 'Carols by Candlelight' at St Mary Magdalene. To add to the festive excitement, it's also a Christingle service. Alongside the singing of 'Hark the Herald Angels' and 'We Three Kings', there will be small children holding candles precariously aloft, stabbing their fingers with cocktail sticks and spitting out dolly mixtures. There will be weeping and wailing and half-hearted, awkward parental singing, phlegmy coughs and little noses bubbling with snot. Rob and Melina don't know what they're missing.

My husband has reached Victoria Falls, according to his blog, where he and his Doncaster mate, Jumbo, have been spending the last couple of days resting and recuperating. Though I hardly think a bungee jump over the Zambezi River can be either restful or recuperative. Still, tomorrow they cross the border into Zambia and he will be one country closer to home.

Melina, by contrast, is in mourning – her beloved

grandmother passed away earlier today, in the bed she was born in, surrounded by her family. Melina will stay on for the funeral and probably into the new year so she can help her uncle and aunt sort out the legacy of a very long life.

AFTER NATHAN'S ANGER at Scarlet and her friends the other night, I finally manage to grab a word with her in a spare moment following another of her hikes. I drag her to the cupboard, where we're surrounded by the seventies wallpaper and the musty smell of home. We sit cross-legged, knee-to-knee, like we're about to sing 'Row, Row, Row Your Boat'. The old Scarlet would never enclose herself in such a confined space with me, or with anyone who wasn't an immediate friend. So this is progress. But still. I have to ask her the question.

'Why the moonlight walks on someone else's property?'

She opens her mouth as though to tell me in no uncertain terms *exactly* why, but then she changes her mind, containing her temper, obviously weighing up how to answer. There's no *I have every right to walk wherever I damn well please!* or, *The rich just get richer while the poor get poorer!* or anything that the old Scarlet would have preached about – which, though idealistic, would have made perfect sense to me. Instead, she doesn't lecture me. She keeps quiet.

'There could've been a terrible accident,' I tell her, her

calmness rubbing off on me.

'Shooting is not accidental,' she replies, calmness evaporating. 'You have to *intend* to shoot a target.'

'That's true.'

'Unless you're one of those American toddlers who kill their siblings by mistake.'

'Also true,' I agree. 'We should be thankful the worst you ever did to Ruby was shut her finger in the car door.'

'That was an *accident*!'

'I know! I'm not accusing you. Anyway, we're getting off track. Why were you there, on the estate?'

'It's beautiful land,' she says. 'We wanted to explore it.'

'In the dark?'

'We'd get caught in the day.'

Logic at its finest. 'You only have to ask Nathan,' I remind her. 'I'm sure he'd be more than happy to let you walk there.'

'I'm not so sure.' There's an enigmatic set to her mouth.

'What do you mean?' I prod her knee with my knee, jokey, keeping it light.

'I told you,' she says. 'He's a jerk.'

'I know that but why do *you* think he's a jerk?'

She waits a second and then she says: 'Because of what he did to you and Rube, of course.'

'Well, yes, there is that.' The evidence of his jerkiness is very hard to dispute.

'And he shoots animals,' she adds, firing up now. 'I'm

not talking about the foxes; I can *sort of* understand him shooting foxes even if I don't agree with it, because they do kill poultry – though maybe they shouldn't actually keep poultry, because if they were vegans they wouldn't need to eat eggs.' A deep breath. 'I know it's better to cull foxes with a trained marksman at night than to tear them apart with hounds by day, but why does Nathan have to let idiots kill defenceless birds for pleasure?'

'I don't know, love,' I tell her while she takes another pause for breath, most of the oxygen in the cupboard having been sucked away. 'I don't like shooting either. I don't like field sports. But it's not going to change.'

'We'll see about that,' she says with a grim determination, and my stomach feels like it has a pebble in it.

RUBY HAS ALREADY been at St Mary Magdalene for a couple of hours for a final run-through by the time I arrive, shepherding Eve, Des and Scarlet. We sit midway down the nave, which is already filling up, near the table in the aisle that is crammed with Christingle oranges, candles waiting to be lit. There's a wonderful smell in the cool air of spices and citrus which will no doubt be upstaged by the pong of singed fringes further down the line. I've already noticed the strategically placed buckets of sand and fire extinguishers.

It's a joyous occasion, and we're surrounded by a hum

of expectation and anticipation. The choir sing that one from *Home Alone*, 'O Holy Night', and people hush and listen, fidget gently in their seats, getting coughs out of the way, sweets from pockets, tissues from handbags.

We're welcomed by Isabella, the rector, dressed resplendently in her purple Advent robes. She's in charge of several rural churches but always has the Christingle service here as it's the prettiest and most central location with a connection to the Chudston Estate. I've seen her around in the village, in town, up at the school. She's hands-on and involved in the community – and receives great praise for this from Eve. Quite different from the old parson back in the day, who used to give me the creeps and sing the mass in Latin.

The orchestra and choir fire up with a jazzy version of 'Once in Royal David's City' and we're off. Ruby is a picture of concentration, her hands moving fast over the strings and her foot on the pedal. She shadows Malcolm and I remind myself to thank him later for his efforts over recent weeks to keep Ruby on board.

After all the usual suspects, with the lighting of the Christingle candles accompanied by 'Away in a Manger', Isabella delivers a brief Christmas message. The relevance of Jesus's birth today. How he was born in an animal feeding trough. In an occupied land. How he became a refugee. How the God of Love is on the side of the vulnerable and powerless.

While Scarlet is listening intently, focusing on this woman of the cloth and the message she's delivering so succinctly, one of the church wardens passing down the aisle offers her an orange. She accepts it with a coy smile, her eyes sparkling with childlike joy.

As he lights the candle for her with a taper he says, 'You're never too old for one of these.'

Then he pats Des on the back, obviously a friend or acquaintance of his, and I wonder at all these people and where they've come from to get to this point, here and now, in this little piece of the West Country.

The children – including Scarlet – are entranced by the flames they are allowed to hold so close to them, going against all the warnings they have ever heard about playing with fire. The glow of the candles, the beauty of the music and the incense and orangey smell make me realize with a rush that Christmas Eve is tomorrow and Rob is still away. I think there was a small part of me that thought he might have given up by now. That he'd have come home with his tail between his legs, rather than his bike. But no. He has persevered and I can't help but feel quite in awe of him. Impressed that his usual butterfly brain has stayed focused for all these weeks. Whether he can keep it up, though, is another matter.

But now the service is ending. We are dismissed with a blessing and a prayer, and as the band put away their instruments and music, and the parents chivvy out their kids, it's time to go home.

'My dear?' An arm slips around my waist and it's not Des's, though it could be.

'Malcolm? Everything all right?'

'Everything is joyous. Marvellous. Peace and goodwill to all men and women and even to young musicians.'

'Is that a reference to Ruby? Is she getting on all right? She seemed to be enjoying the playing. Actually more than I've seen her before.'

'I believe she has talent. And that she could perform rather well if she gave herself the chance.' He beams at me.

I'm not entirely sure what he means or how she would give herself the chance to do this.

'How does she do that?' I ask him.

'By channelling her wayward teenage emotions into the music.'

'Wayward teenage emotions?'

'She has a fire within.'

'She does?'

'Don't look so worried, my dear. An internal fire is a very good thing. She can use it to fuel her harp-playing.'

'Right. Have you been talking to Des, by any chance?'

'Only about the state of his grapes. Talking of which' – he checks his watch – 'it must be time to get back home for a tipple. It's nearly Christmas, after all.' He gives me another of his beaming smiles and I wonder if anyone other than his students receives this grin.

His wife died many years ago, Des told me. He has no children...

'What are you actually doing on Christmas Day, Malcolm? Anything nice?'

'Very nice, thank you,' he says. 'I shall be dining with the best company.'

'Oh really? Who's that?'

'Myself, of course.' A cheekier grin this time.

'You'll be alone?'

'You're never alone if you enjoy your own company.'

'I suppose. But still. Christmas.' And before I can stop myself, I ask: 'Would you like to spend it with us?'

'With you?' He sounds bewildered. So bewildered that I wonder if spending Christmas Day with us is that horrific a prospect. But no. 'How very kind,' he says graciously. 'And thoughtful.'

'Well?'

'I should be delighted to accept your invitation.' He gives a little bow.

'Eve and Des will be very happy.'

'Not so Ruby?'

'I'm sure she'll be very happy too. Inside. Deep down. Hopefully.'

He has a chuckle. 'We'll get that fire stoked by hook or by crook. Or failing that, good old hard cash.'

'Pardon?'

'You leave it to me, my dear. You leave it to me.'

Christmas Eve

WHEN I WAS a child, Christmas Eve was my favourite day of the year. It was all to do with excitement and anticipation. By the day after Boxing Day, the house would be in disarray, the tree wonky and half-bald, paper chains hanging limp in the draughts. Half a dozen baking trays encrusted with burnt offerings would be rusting outside in the yard alongside a crate of empty wine bottles.

As an adult in London, things were different. I was organized, for a start. Well in advance. Though by the time the girls woke us up early on Christmas morning I'd be shattered from the previous weeks' run-up of school concerts, work events, parties, presents and preparations. In they'd creep, dragging their bulging pillowcases, heaving themselves up onto our bed with cold hands and feet and noses, with big smiles and bright eyes, while Rob and I fought to wake up. And then in the dark days between Christmas and New Year

I'd have a plan of activities ranging from the panto to ice skating. A new diary. A list of resolutions. A clear-out for the charity shops.

This year, I've decided to let go of stress. What will be will be. There are no traditions that need to be upheld, except that the girls are still demanding pillowcases. Even the prospect of Malcolm combined with sprouts and booze is not going to faze me.

BUT THERE WILL always be surprises. Shocks, even.

At twelve o'clock, as I'm at the sink peeling the carrots for the next day, a taxi pulls into the yard. We're not expecting anyone so I have no idea who it could be.

I wipe my hands on Eve's Mother Christmas apron, the one she's insisted all week that I wear, hand-made by a women's cooperative in Nepal, and go to the door to see who it is.

Ingrid?

Why the hell is my mother-in-law standing in the middle of our farmyard in her polished court shoes, twinset and pearls and *Mad Men*-style coat?

And not only that. Why the hell is *Declan* standing beside her in his best Paul Smith?

'What on earth are you two doing here?' My heart's all a-flutter. 'Has something bad happened?'

'On the contrary,' Ingrid says. 'We've come to stay for Christmas.' And she looks most put out by the lack of a fanfare.

THEY MET AT the railway station, apparently. Somehow discovered they were coming to the same place and so shared a ride. Declan tells me this. In the cupboard. Where he's followed me after I tried to retreat with a bottle of Harvey's Bristol Cream while Eve deals with Ingrid.

'Tell me again why you're here, Dec? On Christmas Eve? With Ingrid?'

'Like I said, I didn't plan it. I spotted her waiting for a taxi and we got talking. It took her a while to recognize me, but then she remembered seeing me at one of your barbecues. Apparently my appearance made quite an impression! Did you know she hates your barbecues – thinks they're nonsense! – but accepts every invitation just to get to see her granddaughter?' He looks incredulous and then immediately sheepish.

'Soz,' he says. 'Did I say too much?'

I ignore his apology. After all, it's not Dec's fault Ingrid's so snobby. 'She thinks our barbecues are "nonsense"?'

'Er... Yes.'

'Why the bloody hell is she here? Did she tell you?'

'She did. It's Christmas Eve and she always sees you on Christmas Eve. She was quite firm about that.'

'But that's when we're in London. That's when Rob's here. I thought we'd get away with it under the circumstances. I sent her an amaryllis *and* a Christmas card. Isn't that enough?'

'Evidently not.'

'And did you see all those bags?'

'I did. She's brought John Lewis with her.'

My heart sinks. 'Poor John Lewis. What did he do to deserve that?'

Declan chuckles, tops up my drink, then reaches for the hip flask in his jacket pocket like a cowboy going for his gun.

I'm so glad he's here, even if it is a few days earlier than expected. But... 'Why on earth are you wearing a suit anyway? This is Devon.'

'You never can tell who you might meet on a train journey,' he says with a wink. 'Though if I'd known it would be your mother-in-law, I wouldn't have gone to such trouble.' He pulls his cuffs down and straightens his tie. 'Though there's always a chance I might meet a hot farmer. Do you know any hot farmers?'

'No, I don't.'

'Shame.' He juts out his bottom lip in mock sadness. A mock sadness that is no doubt covering over some genuine sadness.

'Maybe it's time you had a break from men?' I suggest.

'Maybe.'

'Have you heard from Mark?'

He shakes his head. 'Not a thing.'

'I'm sorry.'

'Me too.' He takes another swig from his hip flask and hands it to me because I've drained my own glass.

Brandy. Hot. Shocking. Delicious.

'ROBERT IS DOING ever so well with his epic journey,' Ingrid tells Des a little later, during a late and hurriedly assembled lunch. Des nods in all the right places, uncharacteristically quiet. 'He's raising money for elephants.'

'Elephants?'

'Elephant conservation.'

'Marvellous,' Des says.

'Good for Dad,' Scarlet chips in. 'He didn't tell us that.'

'He phones me every week for an update.'

'Every week?'

'Without fail,' Ingrid says smugly. 'He's a very dutiful son.'

Not such a dutiful father or husband is what I want to say, but I keep these thoughts to myself as I don't want to upset Scarlet. 'Please may I have the chutney?' I ask Eve, so that I can do something with my hands other than strangulation.

Eve smiles, sympathetic, and passes me the jar of home-made piccalilli, giving my arm a gentle pat as she does so. I feel unusually warm and fuzzy towards my mother, who is like the Madonna in comparison to the battleaxe at her table.

'Piccalilli?' Ingrid looks appalled.

'Home-made,' Eve confirms. 'My mother's recipe.'

'How quaint.' Ingrid smiles. At least, I think it's a smile, but you can never quite tell as her lips are so thrifty.

Declan tops up my glass with cava. 'Chin-chin-bottoms-up-cheers-m'dear,' he whispers into my ear.

I'm very aware of Ingrid staring at us, disapproving of such shared intimacy. Surely she realizes Dec is gay and not cosying up to me? Maybe she is homophobic? I certainly wouldn't put it past her. She comes from a traditional family who believe in clearly defined gender roles, a marriage between a man and a woman that should last a lifetime, however much misery that entails for either one or both of the spouses.

Declan nudges me. 'You'll shatter that glass if you squeeze it any harder,' he whispers again.

THE REST OF the day drags. I assign Scarlet the task of discovering just how long Ingrid plans to stay, and when she reports back that it could be until the new year, another pebble plops into my stomach.

Horror of horrors.

Must make sure the telephone cupboard is restocked with wine.

I've hardly had a chance to think about the wine lately. It'll be ready to try next month – our first opportunity to see if a new press has made all the difference. Then we need to think about buying our own. Converting the dairy parlour. Doing up the barn. Getting licences! I haven't even started the paperwork for those. I feel a panic coming on. There's such a lot to do to make this into a real business but each day is taking my energies in other directions. And now Ingrid. Thank God for Declan acting as a human shield.

As I GET ready for bed, pillowcases filled and left outside the girls' bedrooms, I feel a shiver. It must be the cold. Though the fire has been going all day, the heating working to the max, and it's quite mild as Christmas Eves go.

My grandmother would have said someone was walking over my grave. I think of Rob. He messaged yesterday to say they'd crossed the Zambezi into Zambia and are now cycling through what westerners imagine is the real Africa. The roads are poor, mainly dirt tracks, but the people are the friendliest he has met. They're living off maize flour dumplings and filtering water, as there's nowhere to buy bottled. He's praying the bike will hold out through this country. It's already been repaired a few times but they've been warned there's nowhere in Zambia to do this. And there are long distances to travel between pit stops. 'It's a simple life on the road,' he says. 'We just make sure we have enough food and water for a couple of days and find somewhere to pitch the tent before it gets dark.'

I think of him lying in his tent in the dark. Lying near Jumbo from Doncaster. Does Jumbo snore? Does it keep Rob awake? Or is he more concerned with the prospect of lions and elephants? I hope his cycling chum will come to his rescue and not leave him for dead.

Whatever the obstacles, finding some Internet is the least of their troubles. It looks like we might not get a Christmas phone call after all.

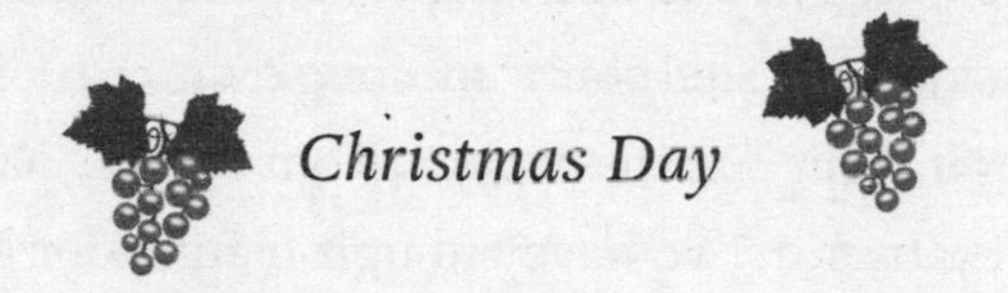

Christmas Day

DAWN IS DARK and gloomy. It's hard to know if the sun has actually risen, but my phone tells me it's eight o'clock. And we have a turkey the weight of a toddler to go in the Aga. I venture downstairs to check Eve has done this. She was setting her alarm for four.

It's freezing this morning. I don't know how Ingrid will survive. There's no meat on her bones and she feels the cold like no other person in the whole world or in the history of humankind. I can't believe she's actually here. I haven't even got her a present – other than the dratted amaryllis – as she was the last person I was expecting to appear yesterday. I was so ecstatic to see Declan and so shocked to see her standing next to him in the yard.

Swings and roundabouts.

You win some, you lose some.

I shiver and tiptoe into the kitchen, where I find Eve sitting at the table in the dim morning light, nursing a china cup of what smells like witch's brew. Oh, if only she could whip up a magic potion to pull me through today.

'Come and join me, Christabel,' she says, patting the chair beside her. She pours me my own cup of tea or whatever it is she has in that pot. 'Don't worry about the present for Ingrid; I've wrapped up a blanket for her, one of the ones I've just finished making for the homeless shelter in town.'

'Aren't they more deserving and in need than my mother-in-law?' I ask.

'Charity begins at home, Christabel,' she replies, tutting.

I've never agreed with this philosophy and am surprised that Eve would spout such nonsense, but it saves some embarrassment, so I try to sound gracious.

'Well, thanks very much,' I say.

My hot drink smells distinctly of booze.

'The alcohol preserves the tincture,' Eve says, all innocent.

'Tincture? You're sure that's all it is? Tincture? It has the same kick as Tomasz's *wódka*.'

'Just a little cup of Christmas cheer. I'll slip a wee dram into Ingrid's morning coffee and that should help ease things.' She winks and I realize that Ingrid is as much a pain to my mother as she is to me. 'Happy Christmas, Christabel,' she says.

'Happy Christmas, Eve.'

An hour later and Des has the log fire going in the living room. The girls and I sit amongst randomly strewn wrapping paper and ribbon – Ruby's, obviously, folded up neatly. Ingrid is having her morning constitutional around the village. She offered to take Luther, half-heartedly, and Luther feigned exhaustion, so she has gone alone. Eve and Des are having Buck's Fizz while cooking up a breakfast that will allow us to keep going until a late lunch at three. Ingrid thinks this highly bohemian as she is used to lunch at one, every day of the year, no let-up even for the celebration of the birth of Christ. But today she will have to keep step with everyone else. Which means Buck's Fizz for breakfast, party hats by midday, and a Christmas luncheon that will go on until teatime, when everything becomes a little hazy. Suddenly, I can't wait.

I'm just reaching my bedroom to get showered when my phone beeps in my dressing-gown pocket. I feel a tug in my stomach in the brief moment before checking who it is calling me on Christmas morning, when all my family are here except for one person. My husband. So when I see Rob's face on the screen that I'm gripping in my hand, I feel a moment of profound relief – a highly underrated emotion. Rob hasn't forgotten us. He's found some Wi-Fi. He's gone out of his way to contact us.

I must have screamed, because the girls have thundered up the stairs to see what's the matter. When I show them the phone with Rob smiling at us, tinsel wrapped around his helmet, they both laugh out loud and their own relief is clear on their faces too.

It turns out that Rob and Jumbo have reached Lusaka and are now having a few days' R & R on the island of Zanzibar, which sounds incredibly exotic.

Eve is impressed. 'Freddie Mercury was from Zanzibar,' she says, a big fan of Queen if ever there was one – pretty much the soundtrack to my days growing up at Home Farm. Fat-bottomed girls, bicycles and Flash Gordon.

Rob and I manage a minute or so of private conversation before the connection fractures. I catch the words *Happy Christmas... I miss you*, but before I get the chance to reply, the line goes dead.

Lunchtime. A packed table: Eve, Des, Scarlet, Ruby, Declan, Ingrid, Malcolm, me. Also... Nathan. Yes, Nathan. Des bumped into him as he was giving Luther a quick walk down the lane to lure him away from the overwhelmingly tempting smell of giblets. Nathan was walking his springers and Des discovered he was home alone.

'No one should be alone at Christmas,' Des says.

And I don't know if Nathan put up a fight, but he did at least have the decency to return his spaniels and swap them for several bottles of fizz and claret from his cellar.

I've been dreading this lunch, but even more so now that Ingrid is sitting next to my ex-husband.

'Happy Christmas, Ingrid. It's nice to meet you,' Nathan says graciously when I introduce them, beaming my mother-in-law one of his winning smiles.

'And the same to you,' she says stiffly in response, giving me a look that suggests I am a wayward woman.

She's always disliked me for marrying her son: the divorcée, who came with a daughter in tow and a failed marriage behind her. It didn't matter that Rob had a child too – he was a widower. And now he's miles away in Africa and she's here at my mother's table being charmed by my ex.

Des, ever my saviour, brings the table to order by proposing a toast with the champagne Nathan has brought.

'Here's to absent intrepid travellers and present new adventurers,' he says, raising his glass. Candlelight gleams through it, turning the blush a deeper shade of perfect pink, the bubbles shooting like little stars. 'To family and friends. Merry Christmas.'

We all join in the toast and pull crackers. Hats arc put on and jokes read. Food is piled onto plates. Glasses are filled. All is going well. Declan is entertaining Ruby and Scarlet with slightly edgy tales of the city. Nathan continues to charm Ingrid. Eve, meanwhile, is in clover, listening to her family around her while Des and Malcolm revisit the old days. I try to be the same; happy to be here, now, alive and well. And spare a thought for Rob, so far away. Has he even managed a Christmas dinner of any sort?

As plates are cleared from the table by two unusually helpful teens, talk turns towards the vineyard. We bring Ingrid up to speed on what has happened in previous years, and on Melina's breakthrough with the wine press. Des talks about his paintings. His artistic reputation's rise and fall and possible resurrection. I squirm when I hear Ingrid's praise. I know exactly what she thinks of Des's paintings, but now that they are increasing in popularity and value she seems less disapproving. I steer him towards the plans for the barn and dairy parlour. I want my mother-in-law to know that I am fully committed to this project and that my parents are not quite the feckless bohemians she believes them to be. If nothing else, she *knows* I am good at my job, having been to events I have organized. And I know that Declan will have been bigging me up to her because he has my back.

'And also, Ingrid, in the new year I shall be applying for a licence to sell alcohol. And further down the track, once we've renovated the barn, a licence for weddings, too,' I tell her proudly.

'Weddings?' she asks, as if I am living in cloud cuckoo land. 'In a barn?'

'Yes. People can have the ceremony in St Mary Magdalene if they like and then have their reception here. Or if they don't want a church wedding, they can do the ceremony here, too. Laws are much more lenient these days.'

'And society is going to hell in a handcart!' Ingrid blurts out.

'Oh no, Ingrid, that's not true. But Christabel is right: couples really do have so many more choices these days. Register offices, churches, hotels. Barns. Blessings, hand-fasting, tree-planting ceremonies. Barn dances.'

Thank God for my mother, yet again coming to my aid in a moment of crisis.

Ingrid sits still, listening but not hearing, blatantly dismissing my mother's ideas.

I want to tell her I'm losing the will to live and no longer care what Ingrid thinks of us. She made up her mind about *us* a very long time ago. It isn't going to change. She clearly believes me to be the spawn of Satan and en route to opening a den of debauchery to rival Caligula's palace.

But I don't have to say anything, because Eve puts Ingrid in her place with some words of scripture that I didn't know she had in her repertoire.

'"Honour the Lord with your wealth",' she says. '"Then your barns will be filled with plenty, and your vats will be bursting with wine".'

Ingrid squints at her, suspicious.

'Proverbs 3, verses 9 to 10,' Eve continues. Then she empties her glass and lifts it aloft for someone to refill.

Declan comes to her aid, opening another bottle of pink fizz, one he brought with him from London. The pop of the mushroom cork, that explosion of joy, is one of the most glorious sounds you can hear, at once reassuring and full of promise. I could kiss each and every one of us at the table. Except for a red-faced Ingrid. And Nathan, of course.

Nathan, who has gone very quiet as he looks askance at the screen of his flashing phone. I can't make out the name of the caller from here but he answers abruptly, almost snappily, before disappearing into the other room without so much as an apology.

Rude.

Meanwhile, I notice, Ingrid doesn't put out her hand to stop Des refilling her flute. In fact, she makes a point of saying how champagne is the best drink in the world and that no English wine could ever compete.

Then she pulls her own quote out of the hat. 'In the

words of Napoleon Bonaparte,' she says, '"in victory, you deserve champagne. In defeat you need it."'

Which is passive-aggressive, to say the least.

But Des trumps her Bonaparte with his Churchill. 'Champagne is the wine of civilization,' he quotes. 'And the oil of government.'

I'm not entirely sure this works as an argument but the sentiment is clear. We underdogs will fight with all our heart and bodies to make a decent sparkling wine.

'Chin-chin-bottoms-up-cheers-m'dears,' Declan says in his campest voice. Just to annoy Ingrid, I'm sure, as she fumes silently into her cups.

PEACE RETURNS ONCE the Christmas pudding is set alight and dished out with a choice of brandy butter, clotted cream or custard as accompaniment. Everyone eats in silence; this is perfect comfort food and there's nothing to say.

By the time I've served teas and coffees, with mince pies for those who still have space, Nathan is back. He's been gone a good forty minutes – not that I'm timing him or anything.

'Important call?' I ask him, wondering who it was. His parents are no longer alive – not that they gave two hoots about him when they were – and he's an only child. No other relatives I know of. So it was either something to do with the estate. Or a woman.

He doesn't answer my question but nods in thanks at the cup of tea and mince pie I hand him.

And now another interruption. A furious knock at the door which sets Luther off in a frenzy, teeth bared and hackles rising, terrifying Ingrid. I have an image of Miss Gulch in *The Wizard of Oz*, demanding Luther's execution, and I have always wondered what happened to Toto at the end when Dorothy wakes up from her dream.

But that's fantasy and this is real. There is a strange woman standing in my mother's kitchen. She is tall, thin and pale with long dark hair and those slug-like eyebrows. And yes, it's fair to say she is quite beautiful. Nathan stands a few feet away from her, looking as though he's unsure what to do.

'Well,' Des says. 'Aren't you going to introduce us, Nathan?'

He coughs an embarrassed cough. 'This is... er, this is...'

But he can't do it. He can't say her name.

'Go on, Nathan. Introduce me,' the woman says, hands on hips.

'This is Charlotte,' Nathan mumbles.

'Charlotte?!' I exclaim. 'As in *Charlotte* Charlotte?'

'Yes,' he confirms.

I've only ever known her as a name. A figure I could jab pins into. But here she is, in the flesh, standing in my parents' kitchen on Christmas Day, my family gathered around the table, all watching the tableau unfold. The woman who stole my husband.

'I've come to see Nathan,' she says. 'He put the phone down on me,' she adds, addressing the rest of us.

'I didn't realize you were outside,' he says, annoyed, embarrassed, awkward. 'If you were outside why didn't you just come in?'

'I didn't want to impose.'

'You're imposing now.'

'I didn't want to spoil this family's Christmas with what I've got to say.'

She's certainly *not* going to spoil this family's Christmas if I have anything to do with it, even though we'd probably all like to hear what she's got to say.

I stand up, scraping my chair rather loudly across the flags to add fanfare to my forthcoming command: 'Nathan, I think you'd better take this outside.'

Charlotte looks at me with those bright-blue eyes of hers. A quick scan of me, up and down. A brief nod of the head and a half-smile. Nathan steers her out of the kitchen before any more can be said.

Happy Christmas to the pair of them.

WE DON'T SEE Nathan for the rest of the day. Stepping into his shoes, Malcolm man-marks Ingrid, which is beyond kind seeing as he could be enjoying his own best company in his own boozy home instead of pandering to this battleaxe's every whim. Though I do soften a little – just a little – when I catch her later checking her phone, hopeful for a message from the dutiful yet very absent son. I realize that she is lonely. And, though she has no one but herself to blame, it's still sad that a life should come to this, its emptiness all the more hollow on this sacred day that should be stuffed full of love. Though love is an emotion I'm battling with right now. Why would Charlotte come into my home, even if she had just had a tiff with her boyfriend? What sort of woman is she?

EVENING COMES AND I get a phone call from Melina wishing us all *Wesołych Świąt*. 'Unfortunately is not really happy Christmas for me or my family. Babcia is gone.'

'Oh, Melina. I'm so sorry,' I tell her, knowing words are useless but having to say something. I feel such sadness for her.

'We do not keep calm and carry on,' Melina continues. 'It is not our culture to smile and tell jokes of the dead.'

'Of course,' I say, not quite sure where this is going but knowing she just needs me to listen.

'Babcia, she downstairs in coffin. We cover mirrors and stop clocks. Her *gromnica* candle will light her way to afterlife. We pray – all of us – say rosary around her. Is very sad, Chrissie, very sad.'

I hear her choke back tears and my heart aches for her.

'In three days we bury her,' she continues, between sniffs. 'Next to my grandfather. He is waiting very long time for her.'

'Oh, Melina. Have you got help with all this?' I ask her, as if she's planning a corporate awayday, not a final farewell to the most important person in her life.

'My uncle is not very good at help but my aunt is excellent and strong. And I have Tomasz.'

'Tomasz?'

'Yes. Tomasz is still here,' she says, a gentleness to her voice as she speaks his name.

Before I have a chance to think about Tomasz and how important a person he seems to be in Melina's life, she asks: 'And what about Nathan? Is he still sniffing you?'

'*Sniffing* me?'

'Around you?'

'Oh. Nathan. No. He's been sniffing someone else.' I tell her about the appearance of the blue-eyed Charlotte.

'She should stuff herself with hay,' Melina quips.

I have no idea what this means though it sounds rather violent so I don't pursue it.

And as I listen to her talk, about her home, her grandmother, her extended family, I feel my heart melt for Melina. And I remind myself to give Eve and Des an extra hug before this day is out. Our loved ones are precious.

'We shall raise a glass to your *babcia* tonight.'

'Thank you, Chrissie.'

THIS DAY IS far from over. Once the kitchen is cleared up, we retire to the sitting room to lounge by the fire and open more presents.

Des pushes in the drinks trolley where there is a veritable cornucopia of bottles and shakers on display. 'Anyone for a snowball and gin?'

I have no idea where Des gets his cocktail recipes from or whether he just pulls them out of his brain, but they invariably work out just fine. Lethal, but fine. Though I'm giving the 'Home Farmarama' a miss as it'll knock me out cold till Epiphany. I'm more than happy with a glass of wine.

While I have a sip of warming Merlot, I make a silent toast to Babcia – silent because I don't want to spoil the day any more than it already has been by passing on this sad news. That can wait till tomorrow. Meanwhile, I just need to get through the next couple of hours and then I can tell myself I've survived a Christmas without Rob, if not a Christmas without drama.

'Please can I have a snowball and gin?' Ruby asks her grandfather innocently.

'And me?' Scarlet adds, not wanting to miss out.

The pair of them sit on cushions by the log burner, their new gifts spread around them – fluffy socks and fancy stationery and sparkly bracelets – and it's so nice seeing them content and getting on with each other that I nearly agree.

But I'm forgetting the voice of the authoritarian in the corner. 'Don't be ridiculous,' Ingrid says. 'I didn't have my first sip of alcohol until I was twenty-one.'

The irony of watching their party pooper grandmother slug back a glass of Home Farmarama does not go unnoticed by Scarlet or Ruby. Nor does the surreptitious wink from Granddad Des, which puts a smile back on their faces. They can always rely on him to break the rules.

Oh, give me strength.

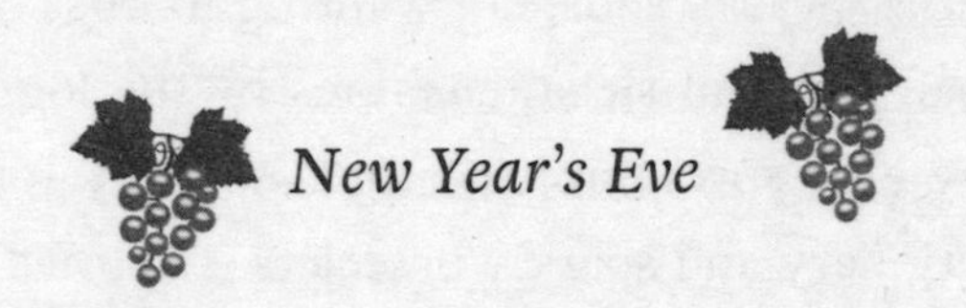

New Year's Eve

I WAKE UP with a hopefulness in my heart because the girls and I have made it to the last day of December and Rob's return 'next year' suddenly doesn't seem so far off. I can't help my feeling of doubt about this, though. Doubt in Rob? In me? Or in us? I'm not sure which.

I also have an anxious feeling gurgling away in my stomach. Tonight we have been invited up to the big house for drinks.

'I wondered if you'd all like to come over on New Year's Eve?' Nathan had asked me when he returned to Home Farm on Boxing Day to apologize for the showdown the day before. 'Charlotte's invited some of her London crowd here for a party,' he explained, looking sheepish.

'So are you two back together?'

'No, we most certainly are not back together.'

'So why is she bringing her friends? And why would I want to go?'

'I thought it might be nice. I thought it might help atone for the mess on Christmas Day.'

'But *Charlotte*?'

'I know, I know.' He sighed, cross with himself. 'It was all over long ago but I still feel some responsibility for her.'

'It's clearly not over for her.'

He shook his head, not a no, but a gesture of helplessness. 'I just feel sorry for her.'

'You feel sorry for her?'

'It's stupid, I know. Look, I shouldn't have asked.'

I hesitated. Maybe a party would be good. Might be preferable to staying in with Ingrid. But still. Charlotte?

As he turned to leave, I thought of Ingrid, the way she judged me all those years ago without knowing me, and sighed, and agreed to go to the party – not wanting to be like my mother in-law. Not wanting to judge. After all, I thought, if Ruby wants to get to know Nathan, despite what he says, Charlotte could well be part of the package.

I'd do it for Ruby.

So it's decided. At seven o'clock on New Year's Eve we all head next door in our semi-glad rags, which means me in a corduroy dress that's supposed to be vintage but just looks second-hand. Des drives Eve and Ingrid while Declan, Scarlet, Ruby and I walk. We will stay for a couple of hours, sample the good bits of the evening like the bubbly and canapés, the buffet and the band, but leave before it gets too boozy.

The air is fresh but still and after a few minutes we warm up and stop complaining about the cold. It's actually a relief to be away from Ingrid for a while and just be with my daughters and dear Declan, who they adore.

After a while, as we turn into the entrance to the Chudston Estate and begin the hike up the driveway, the girls steam on ahead, deep in conversation. It's so lovely to see them communicating with each other in words rather than grunts and complaints.

'What are they in cahoots about?' Declan asks.

'I don't know and I'm not going to pry. I'm just happy they're not getting steamed up in each other's company.'

Though when I catch the name 'Nathan', my heart freezes for a moment. Maybe Scarlet is quizzing Ruby over him, or Ruby defending him? Maybe I'm overthinking this? Maybe I should stop fretting and be grateful they're not tearing each other's hair out.

THE FIRST PERSON we meet at the grand front door, welcoming us in as if she owns the place, is Charlotte. Bloody Charlotte. I give her the once-over, which she reciprocates. She is attractive, yes, but close up I can tell she has had Botox. And lip-fillers. And possibly teeth veneers. And definitely eyebrow tattoos.

'Come in, come in,' she says, all cheery though her smile doesn't reach her eyes, possibly because her face can't actually move. 'I'm Charlotte. Who have we here, then?' As if she's never met any of us, when she knows damn well she barged into our kitchen during Christmas lunch. When she knows damn well she ripped my family apart once upon a time. Has she whitewashed that from memory?

Politeness takes hold and we introduce ourselves all round before Charlotte makes sure we each have a drink and our coats are taken care of. Then she disappears into the throng in the grand hall, other partygoers spilling out into the rooms offstage.

I have to admit the hall does looks fabulous. A humongous tree dotted with hundreds of fairy lights, and decked out with glittering chandelier-like glass droplets, takes pride of place at the foot of the magnificent staircase, the banisters of which are adorned with woodland garlands. A fire blazes in the huge stone fireplace, its mantelpiece swathed with greenery. A handful of smartly dressed waitresses move effortlessly, silver trays brimming with Buck's Fizz and mulled wine. Scarlet actually stands with her mouth open in awe. 'I never knew it would be as fancy as this inside,' she whispers eventually, once her sister has poked her in the arm.

They disappear soon after, the girls upstairs, Declan hunting down the bar, and I'm suddenly Billy No Mates, so I do the only thing to be done – start enjoying.

By nine o'clock, I have eaten my way through mini sandwiches, cocktail sausages, an assortment of cheeses and a sea of smoked salmon. I have mingled. Chatted. Made small talk. And now I'm knackered and wanting to go home, though my feet are aching at the prospect of the hike back. But just as I'm thinking about finding the others to see if they're ready to leave – which I know is a long shot as there's still so much free food and wine – in walks a familiar person.

'Chrissie! What the hell are you wearing?' she exclaims, taking in my shabby-chic appearance.

'Hello, Jackie. You look nice too.'

She snorts in derision.

'I've seen that son of yours somewhere with my daughter,' I tell her, sweetly, calmly, her jagged edges smoothed by my wine-induced fuzziness.

'Which one?' she asks.

'Ruby.'

'I mean which son?'

'Is there another one here?'

'There should be at least two of them here. And a couple of daughters. I'd better round them up to check they're all still alive but quite frankly I need a drink. What are you having?' She nods at my glass. 'As if I didn't know. Sampling the opposition?'

'The opposition?'

'Champagne, of course. Still planning on making sparkling wine? Are you off your trolley?'

'Excuse me?'

'It'll never work.'

'Have you ever *tried* English sparkling wine?'

'No, I jolly well haven't,' she says, as if I've asked if she's ever licked an elephant's bottom.

Nathan joins us and hails a waitress the way he hails cabs.

Such a show-off, I think.

Catching her eye, the waitress weaves in and out of the party people until she's standing smiling at Jackie, proffering a tray filled with flutes of champagne.

'Don't mind if I do,' Jackie says. She takes one. Then she takes another one in the other hand. 'For your mother,' she says to me.

But before she hightails it, Nathan stops her.

'Guess where this wine's from, Jackie?'

'Don't tell me it's from England.'

'No, it isn't.'

'I thought not. Spain?'

'Nope.'

'Italy then.'

'No.'

'New Zealand? South Africa? America?'

'No, no and no.'

'Where, then?'

'Wales.'

'*Wales?*'

'Yes. Wales.'

She sniffs it, the wine. Puts the glass to her lips and tilts her head back. Takes a sip. Then another. '*Iechyd da*,' she says.

I'm not sure if she's swearing at Nathan but I don't get the chance to ask because there's a sudden rumpus in the middle of the ballroom nearby. We all turn to look at Declan, who's been holding court with a group of WI members. He's just let out a piercing scream of joy and is currently staring adoringly at a tall dark-haired stranger, who looks as though he has just come in from the cold.

It seems that Mark, 'the only man that I have ever genuinely loved', as Declan told me, has decided to visit.

'HOW ON EARTH did you find me?' Declan asks Mark a few minutes later, once we've moved away from the main crowd and are sitting in the great hall by the fireplace, with Ruby and Scarlet, too.

'I got a cab to Home Farm and was told you'd be here,' Mark says. He looks around him in awe. 'I didn't realize you were keeping such high society.'

Declan shrugs, like this is the sort of place where he always hangs out. 'Who told you that?' he asks. 'We're all here, everyone from Home Farm, so it wasn't one of us.'

'An old bloke was driving past,' Mark says. 'He stopped me as I was getting out of the cab. Said I'd find no one at your place as you were all up at "the big house".'

'Weird,' Declan says. 'Who could that be?'

'He was a bit weird,' Mark says. 'Eccentric-looking. Funny smell, like he'd been rolling in cow pats.'

'Malcolm,' the four of us say in unison.

Ruby explains who Malcolm is. Mark is impressed she can play the harp. He can play the piano. They talk music. A foreign language.

'And who is that?' Mark has stopped thinking about treble clefs and nods at Nathan, who has just walked in.

He still scrubs up well, I'll give him that. A crisp white shirt and faded jeans. He's giving the locals his I'm-the-down-to-earth-lord-of-the-manor act, doling out more booze like there's no tomorrow. Which there probably will be. With headaches.

'Where to begin...' I say.

Declan sits back and pretends to eat popcorn. 'Now *this* is a story,' he whispers loudly to Mark, nudging him in the ribs.

By the time we've brought Mark up to speed, Nathan has made his way over to us and is introducing himself.

He ruffles Ruby's hair. 'Happy New Year, Ruby,' he says. 'Here's to exciting adventures in 2019.'

He squeezes his arms around her shoulders and I don't fail to see a look of pride and longing and whatever else this man I used to know so well is feeling right now. He probably doesn't even know himself. I'm sure I don't. How must Ruby feel? I mean, *really* feel? It's hard enough for young people to untangle their emotions, let alone in this situation. The squire with his heir. And what about Scarlet?

And then, as if he can read my mind, Nathan says: 'Happy New Year to you all. May we have a great year ahead getting to know each other.' He raises his glass.

Ruby is smiling at him with genuine admiration. I feel that pebble in my stomach again. It's really quite uncomfortable despite the possibility this could be a good thing, Ruby forging a relationship with her birth father, especially as Rob is away for so long.

Rob. Will he ever return? And do I truly *want* him to?

Pushing my doubts aside, I go in search of my parents to see if they've had enough carousing for this year. I presume not. I'm sure they'll want to stay put for the chimes and the 'Auld Lang Syne's, but I'm heading home. I'm done in. I don't have the energy to deal with all these people. I might be good at *organizing* events but

I'm rubbish at being a guest at them, especially when they're filled with snooty, husband-stealing types like Charlotte.

Time to go.

I make my excuses to Nathan and head off to search for Eve and Des, eventually finding them in the library. With Jackie. And a bottle of home brew.

'Blackberry wine,' Des says, answering a question I haven't even asked. 'Not a bad little tipple.' He holds up the glass. The muted lighting makes the purple liquid gleam like amethyst. He's lost for a moment, then notices I've got my coat on. 'Are you off, honeybun?'

'We are.' Oddly to me, the girls haven't made a fuss about leaving early; as far as adults go, Declan and Mark are highly entertaining and so they're happy to see the new year in with them. So we're leaving en masse. 'Have you seen Ingrid?' I ask my parents, as a guilty afterthought.

'She was with Major Carter,' Eve says. 'They were dancing to T. Rex.'

'Ingrid was dancing with Major Carter to T. Rex?'

'Don't look so horrified, Christabel,' she says. 'Us old people like to let our hair down from time to time, too.'

'But *Ingrid*?'

Eve knocks back the rest of her wine, suppressing a smile.

Then Jackie, slightly the worse for wear, her lips stained blue, pipes up. 'Can you take Barney with you? And possibly Morley? They get on with your girls, apparently – and don't worry about shenanigans. They're good boys. I'll pick them up tomorrow. Probably not early. Let's say midday. Ish.' She hiccups, then starts belting out 'Solid Gold Easy Action' in a very good approximation of Marc Bolan.

Much as I want to stand and stare, I do as I'm told and hunt everyone down so there's quite a crowd of us leaving – just in the nick of time, judging by the noise level; I sense a party on the edge of degeneracy.

Outside, light from the windows tumbles onto the gravel, and there's a cold, sharp chill in the still air. January is on its way.

I pull my coat around me and put my head down, the others chatting and shivering, fumbling with buttons and zips, pulling on gloves. We're a few yards from the fountain where Charlotte and a friend of hers are sitting on the wall, smoking. They're drunk. Possibly worse. Rowdy and vulgar, the way only the London rich can manage. Scarlet hurls scornful looks their way so I try to herd the young people past them, quick-sharp.

'You off?' Charlotte calls out. She might sound chummy and friendly but I can see right through her. 'You'll miss the fireworks.'

'Fireworks?' Scarlet says, shooting daggers with her glare. 'Our dog *hates* fireworks.' She turns her back and strides off, muttering under her breath, but I can hear the words 'selfish pigs' clearly enough.

'I couldn't agree more, love – poor old Luther,' I tell Scarlet once I've caught up with her. And Morley, who is shadowing her closely. 'Des won't be happy with fireworks either.'

'Nor am I,' Scarlet says grimly.

'I can see that. We'll sit with Luther in the living room, curtains drawn and fire lit. He'll be OK.'

Ruby and Barney are skipping along ahead of us like kids, chucking twigs at each other and singing songs, oblivious to the class war going on in front of their eyes. I'm so relieved they've found each other and I reckon any 'shenanigans' between them seem unlikely – or would be pretty innocent, anyway, maybe just the odd sip of illicit cider. Morley and Scarlet, on the other hand, are a tad close for comfort, talking intently, intensely, but too quietly for me to catch a word. I shall have to keep an eye. I don't believe for one minute Jackie's insistence that he's 'a good boy' when it comes to sex; Jackie's clearly deluded – he's a sixteen-year-old lad, for goodness' sake! Entranced by a beautiful, intelligent young woman, for whom I'm responsible. To whom I am stepmother and *in loco parentis*.

I turn around to check on the others and see Declan and Mark lingering behind us, hand in hand in the light of the moon.

At five minutes to midnight, I am sitting in the living room in front of a roaring log burner looking at the faded empty pink patch on the wall above, where Eve used to recline in all her glory. I have my girls with me, one on each side, on the sofa. Luther lies across us, a jumble of long limbs. Barney and Morley are sprawled on cushions on the threadbare Persian carpet that as a child I used to pretend was magic and could whisk me away to far-off places.

And thinking of magic, Declan and Mark are squished up together on Des's big armchair, looking so loved-up you can almost hear the cherubs singing. I've never seen Declan like this and I really hope it means they have worked out their issues.

And now, as the chimes ring out for midnight, we watch Big Ben and the fireworks over the Thames. All that money going up in smoke, as Eve likes to say. And then we hear the other fireworks. Real live ones being set off next door. Rockets and bangers. Scarlet pulls Luther closer to her as he begins to tremble.

'Nathan is such a jerk,' she growls on the dog's behalf.

'Don't say that.' Ruby is suddenly protective. Which is a shock. She gets up and goes to the window, pokes her head under the faded velvet curtains that have hung there all my life. Barney joins her. They kneel down, mesmerized.

The fireworks go on for ten minutes or so and I think of Des, somewhere outside and doubtless fire-watching. Finally the booms and cracks stop and there is a blissful silence.

'Look!' Ruby exclaims to Barney. 'There's one of those Chinese lanterns.'

'And another,' Barney says.

'There's a whole load of them.'

Ruby and Barney start counting.

'Pull back the curtains,' Declan says. 'So we can all see.'

We get up and watch and gasp at the pretty lights floating in the clear night sky, like the candles on All Saints' Night in the graveyard.

Only Scarlet refuses to be impressed. 'They're an environmental nightmare,' she says. 'They fall back to earth as litter. They cause damage to wildlife. Lots of countries ban them. But then, I shouldn't be surprised at anything Nathan allows on his land.'

'It might not be him, to be fair,' says Morley.

'It wasn't,' says Barney. 'I heard that woman with the eyebrows telling her mates she had a load.'

'You never said!' berates Scarlet.

'I didn't know they were dangerous.'

'Honestly!' She shakes her head, as if Barney – who is actually only a few months younger than her – is a silly little boy. 'Nathan could've put a stop to it. It's his land.'

We stand and watch, and I wonder where the burning lanterns will fall. Miles away, most probably. But one hovers overhead, floating slowly downwards. Towards Home Farm. Towards the barn.

The barn.

With its thatched roof.

Des would be having kittens if he were here.

But he isn't. There's just us.

'We should—'

But before I can say what we should do, Scarlet has legged it from the room, barking orders for us all to follow.

By the time we've caught up with her outside in the yard, she's screaming: 'CALL THE FIRE BRIGADE!'

For, there above us, sparks fly across the thatched roof. Sparks that catch alight.

Suddenly there's chaos. The flames are taking hold. Ruby's calling 999.

'What shall we do?' Scarlet shouts.

'Keep back,' I yell at her, waving my arms frantically.

'The fire brigade are on their way,' Ruby says. 'Reckon they'll be ten minutes yet.'

'Ten minutes! Oh my God! What are we going to do?' Scarlet repeats, her teen bravado faltering.

'Go and check on Luther,' Ruby urges her.

'Stand right back!' Mark orders. He's brandishing a fire extinguisher.

Of course, a fire extinguisher. Why didn't I think of that?

Declan looks on in wonder as Mark confidently aims the nozzle at the roof, but as the jet of water falls short of its target, panics. 'It won't reach!' he yells.

'Get the garden hose over there,' Mark shouts back.

'That won't reach either.'

'I know that! But we need to contain the fire. Drench everything you can.'

'I'll do it.' Morley springs into action while the rest of us grab the buckets stacked beside the water butts and take turns to fill them.

But the flames are still spreading.

The smell of it. The sound. The gut-wrenching horror of our dreams burning before our eyes – Oh my God! My parents! All Des's fears are coming true!

Just as I'm losing my grip on the situation, here they are, Des and Eve, with Nathan in tow.

'The river!' Eve's shouting, moving determinedly at speed towards it, gesticulating like a commander in battle. 'We need to use the river!'

So we follow, all of us, running back and forth, fetching water, chucking as much as we can on the walls of the barn. On the ground. Anywhere. Everywhere. Anything to save what we can of the barn. Anything to protect the house.

And then the wonderful noise of the fire siren. The

wonderful sight of the truck pulling into the yard, and the firefighters leaping into action.

MUCH, MUCH LATER, with dawn cracking, while the teens sprawl, comatose, on sofas in the living room, and while the rest of us – Eve, Des, Ingrid, Mark, Declan and me – wait, exhausted, in the kitchen – the chief officer knocks on the door and I let him in.

He looks tired and dirty but there's a faint smile playing around his dry lips.

'It's out,' he says.

And the relief is palpable. From all of us.

'Thank God,' Eve says.

'We'll assess the damage once it's light,' he goes on.

I'm about to ask some more questions, when Nathan turns up.

'Charlotte's mortified,' he announces, looking somewhat contrite himself.

'So she should be,' Des says hotly. 'To think I was almost prepared to give her a chance!' He shakes his head wearily.

Eve hugs him.

'My great thanks to you, Mark,' he says. 'You made a terrible situation slightly better. Hopefully it's just the roof that's gone.' He turns then to the fire officer. 'And you and your colleagues, sir, you've done a sterling job.

I can never thank you enough.'

Poor old Des has tears in his eyes and it's impossible to tell if this is from the smoke or relief or memories of the house fire in his childhood. I give him a kiss and Eve takes him to bed.

A few minutes later, as everyone troops off to a well-deserved sleep, just Nathan and I remain, sitting opposite each other at the table.

He rubs his face. 'I should've stopped her.'

'Where were you?'

'Helping Jackie. She was so pissed, I couldn't leave her. Your mum and Des were there too. It took three of us to get her home. We missed all the fireworks and by the time we left her house, we realized something was wrong – we could see the smoke. We could smell it. For a moment there I thought it was the house and God, I was relieved when I saw you all fannying about in the yard.'

'Excuse me? "Fannying about"?'

'Well, you're hardly firefighter material, are you? Apart from Mark. He's a bit of a hero, isn't he? And not just in Declan's eyes, either...'

He's smiling that smile that used to work its charm on me, so glad the fire's out that he's resorted to teasing. And I can't help but smile back. Until I think of Charlotte and the anger bubbles back up.

'Where's Charlotte now?'

'Still at the house. She'd like a word before she heads back to London.'

'A word?'

'She wants to apologize for cocking up.'

'For cocking up our marriage?

He sighs. 'Look, I know that was down to me as much as her. And I *have* tried apologizing. And I'll keep *on* trying until you accept I mean it.'

I don't say anything. I'm going to make him work for every morsel.

'So can she?' he asks again. 'Can she have a word with you?'

'She can try.'

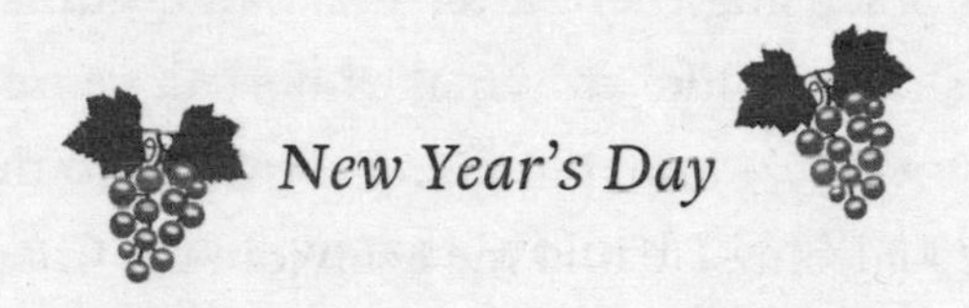

New Year's Day

Today is a late start. I sleep till eleven and by the time I make it downstairs to the kitchen, the place is abuzz with activity.

'They've checked the barn and given us the all-clear, darling, so it's all hands on deck,' Eve tells me, on noticing my entrance. She hands over a broom so I can join in with the clear-up.

'How *could* they just release a bunch of those lanterns like that?' I rant to Des outside in the yard, assessing the damage. 'I know we were lucky it was just the barn. And that we managed to hold it back until the fire crew arrived – but only thanks to all of us pitching in – and the weather! What would have happened if it had been summer?'

'It's really only the roof, Chrissie,' he says, always one to be positive. 'And poor Ruby's harp, of course. Nobody was hurt.'

'No, I know that.' I turn to look at my daughter,

sweeping nearby. 'Hey, Ruby? Why was your harp in the barn anyway?'

'I was practising there after I had an argument with Scarlet,' she says, like this makes perfect sense to her. 'But don't worry, Mum. I'm going to switch to the Celtic harp like Malcolm. He told me I can join the Chud Valley Stompers, Barney too. We'll get paid!'

I have had only a moment to reflect on how readily my daughter has accepted the loss of her beloved instrument when Charlotte turns up.

'I'LL PAY FOR the new roof,' Charlotte announces, once I've taken her aside, back into the kitchen away from everyone, fearful of giving her a right old ear-bashing in front of Ruby and Scarlet. 'Whatever it takes to put this right,' she adds, looking genuinely remorseful.

And while I know she's referring to the fire, she might as well be talking about my life, but quite frankly, I don't have the energy to revisit the past right at this moment. I want to get this mess sorted. So I resist the urge to say *stuff your money* and focus on Eve's thoughts about gift horses.

'Thank you, Charlotte,' I manage to say.

She has tears in her eyes and I feel like slapping her when *I* should be the one with tears in my eyes, but I will more than happily take her money. That way we don't have to make it an insurance job; our premiums won't go up and a whole lot of paperwork can be passed over.

Though first thing tomorrow I'll have to inform the local building officer. Ironically, I have an appointment booked for tomorrow anyway at the council offices to discuss the licence application and so I'll also ask the building officer about the possibility of using the barn in the future – once the repairs are donc. I will not let this set us back any more than can be helped.

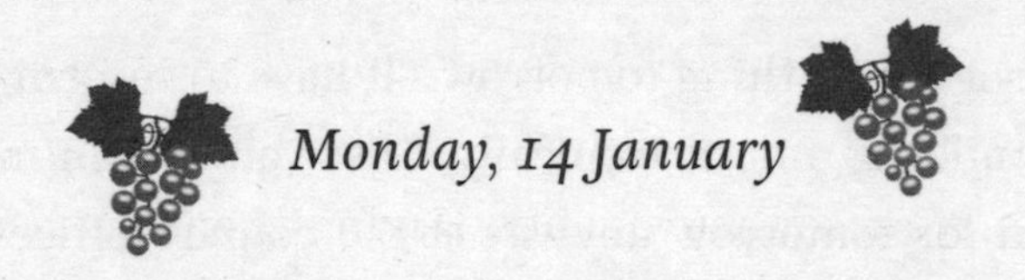

Monday, 14 January

ROB HAS FALLEN in love with Tanzania, which he's now criss-crossing because he can't bear to miss any of it. According to his blog. Which means this trip is getting longer by the day. Zanzibar. The Masai Steppe. The Ngorogoro Crater. Arusha. The foothills of Kilimanjaro. Then on to Kenya.

I sigh. It all sounds like quite a contrast to damp, dark January in Devon with its relentless dull-grey skies. I sigh again, try to push aside my husband's adventures, focus my thoughts on all we have to do: declare our wine production plans to the Food Standards Agency, complete the licence applications, calculate our finances, recover from the shock of the fire. Two weeks later and I'm still reeling from it. No one was hurt, I remind myself. I must focus on the here and now.

THERE'S ALSO MUCH work to be done in the vineyard. The vines have been in hibernation since December. The sap has descended into the root systems and now is the time for winter pruning to limit the growth of the plant and the quantity of grapes produced, whilst also improving their quality. Having been delayed by the fire and also by lack of help, we now need to crack on. It's a lengthy job, pruning each vine, clearing out the old wood and then carefully bending the new fruiting canes to encourage the sap to flow before the budburst of spring.

Some viniculturists say pruning's an art form, that good pruners know each vine as an individual. To me, the vines look sad and bare right now, lengths of naked wire waiting for the branches to spurt into life and stretch along them.

So we wait. We prune. And we wait some more.

Snowdrops are cropping up in the garden and down in the churchyard amongst the gravestones. Early signs of life pushing through the hardened earth of bleak midwinter. We're still a long way from safe. Listening to the forecast, I hear there's a threat of frost this coming weekend. Frost right now is all right. It will kill off the bugs. But as soon as those buds appear, a frost can see them drop off. A frost can wipe out an entire crop. It is the winegrowers' greatest fear.

After another day's hard toil, we all troop into the kitchen, fuelled with excitement that Melina's due to return tonight. Declan and Mark will miss this reunion because they are long gone, reluctantly, home to London, very much loved-up and with promises to return soon, although they did have a chaperone for the journey in the form of my mother-in-law, the passion-killer.

It's late in the evening before we hear a taxi pull into the yard – Luther alerting us with a deep bark.

Scarlet and Ruby are in bed, exhausted from school; Des is back in the studio working on his landscapes. 'You really must return to your own work, darling, now that the commission is done,' I heard Eve say to him earlier. He did not argue. He's making the most of it because there could well be more paid work in the pipeline; it makes me smile to think that he and Eve have discovered for themselves that social media is not always a bad thing.

So Melina has to make do tonight with a two-woman welcoming committee consisting of my mother and me.

'Welcome home,' Eve says, enveloping our Polish friend in one of her voluminous hugs.

Of course this is Melina's home too, and again the dual life of an immigrant is revealed to me. It's hard enough, the flip from London to Devon, let alone Poland to Britain. And how must Rob be feeling in a continent where he's largely known as a *mzungu*?

'Your barn looks very sad,' Melina announces once she's been made camomile tea by Eve and baked beans on toast by me. 'You must knock it down. Start again.'

'We can't,' I try to explain, patiently. 'It's a listed building. We'd get in trouble. Besides, like I said before, Brits like old stuff. They think it's romantic.'

She tuts. Does that laugh of derision she is so good at, and it hits me how much I've missed her.

'It's good to have you back, Melina.'

'I am happy to be back but I am very sleepy. I have spent many hours at my wine course today.'

'You've been there today?' I ask, surprised.

'It is Monday. I come to England yesterday and stay with my friend. I have paid much money for this course and do not want to miss it. Babcia would never forgive me.'

'What did you learn about today?' Eve asks, the same way she used to ask me after school, the same way I ask Scarlet and Ruby. The normal response to such a question is 'nothing', but Melina gives a straight answer.

'Polyphenolic profile, terpene and volatile compound content,' she says.

She might as well be talking Polish for all I understand of that. Though I do realize she's talking about the wine itself and not the terroir.

'I thought you were interested in the vineyard side of things, not the winemaking?' I say.

'I am interested in both,' she replies. 'Vine to wine.' She smiles at this rhyme, though in her accent the words sound the same, so what it loses in sense it gains in comedic effect. Though I really shouldn't laugh at her pronunciation. I know only a handful of words from her mother tongue.

'How is wine?' she asks, nudging me because I seem to have drifted off into a semi-trance. 'Have you tried?'

'The wine? No, actually. Not yet. But they've said we can go along this week. How are you fixed for tomorrow?'

'I can be fixed for tomorrow. Is good for me.'

'Great.'

'Also, I have surprise.' She shows us her left hand. Waggles the ring finger, showing off a ruby the colour of shiraz.

'Babcia's,' she says.

'For a moment there I thought you were going to say you're engaged!' I laugh at my mistake, then stop abruptly when she gives me that stare and I know what she is going to say.

'I *am* engaged.'

'You *are*?'

She nods, almost coyly, aware that we have no clue that she even had a boyfriend, and there's a moment while we wait for her to fill us in until Eve can take it no longer. 'Such marvellous news,' she says warmly. 'But to whom, my dear?'

'To Tomasz,' Melina says, as if it's obvious.

'You dark horse. I thought you were just friends.' I beam, surprised but happy for her. So happy.

Eve is still rather confused. 'Tomasz?' she asks, searching in her memory for a potential candidate. And then it clicks. 'The picker Tomasz?'

'Yes, Tomasz,' Melina says. 'Doctor of Philosophy Tomasz.'

Eve's eyes widen, burning as brightly and mischievously as ever. She's never able to hide a thing.

'They are the same and the one,' Melina confirms.

'One and the same.' I don't mean to be pedantic, but some things I can't let go.

'Yes,' Melina says, somehow managing to keep impatience at bay. 'The same and the one.'

'Right,' Eve says. 'And where is your Dr Tomasz now?' She looks around as if he might be hiding under the table. 'We must celebrate.'

'He is next door. He stays with two other friends in Nathan's castle. Nathan says he has work for them. But first I think they must help with pruning.'

'Ah. Yes. The pruning.' Eve shakes her head. 'We've been making very slow progress with that. You've returned at the perfect time.'

'Yes,' Melina agrees. 'Perfect time.' And she twiddles that ruby ring of hers.

LYING IN BED that night, I'm thankful for the return of my friend safe and sound: sad for her loss, but happy for her engagement. A little jealous too, perhaps, at the obvious signs of her being in love. I close my eyes and try to remember that feeling, but it was such a long time ago. And now, with my eyes shut, instead of my loving husband, all I can visualize are the flames licking the roof of the barn.

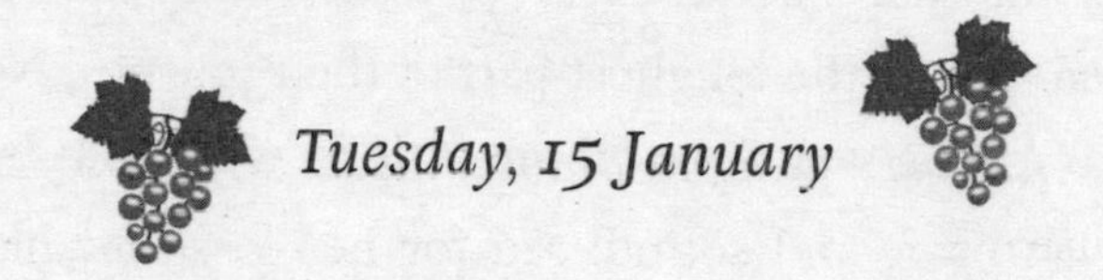

Tuesday, 15 January

LUCKILY, WHEN YOU taste wine properly, unlike when on a drinking bender, you don't imbibe it, so we can't be accused of getting drunk on a school day.

Des, Eve, Melina and myself head up the valley to Chudston Winery. It's a much bigger concern than ours. Not as pretty a place, more commercial. Not that I see 'commercial' as a filthy word in the way that Eve does – though it has to be said, ever since her portrait sold so well on eBay, she's been much more interested in things of a financial nature. Maybe a leopard *can* change her spots? I don't think I'll ever see her and Des move into a bungalow, but now I'm living at Home Farm and the girls are settled and doing so well, I can see us staying here for the longer term, and so there's no need for them to downsize.

There, I've said it. To myself at least. I wouldn't mind staying. Which of course means I wouldn't mind giving up my London life.

But where does that leave Rob?

Right now, in Kenya, somewhere between the Tanzanian border and Nairobi, in the lead-up to what they have been warned will be the toughest part of their journey, North Kenya. A long way from home. A long way from being my husband.

WHIZZING ALONG THE Devon B-roads in Des's old Capri, everywhere looking dirty from recent rain, reddish-brown rivulets running down the gullies of the lanes into the high hedges on either side. A glimpse of a pink-stained sheep or two. A horse in a blanket looking over a gate. The River Chud full and flowing on the nearside of the car.

We almost overshoot the turn-off to the vineyard but, as we swerve into the entrance, there before us are the southerly slopes with row upon regimented row of spindly vines.

We park in front of the family-run winery – a very modern, clean, shiny barn. It's right up Melina's street and she's already out of the car, wellies on, before Des has turned the engine off, striding ahead to see for herself the hive of industry within.

Eve and I head with Des to the cafe so he can show us his commissioned painting of the vineyard in situ. The place has a young, fresh vibe to it – industrial chic, copper pipes and bare Edison light bulbs.

'It'll look lovely when it's finished,' Eve says, not a hint of irony.

The painting, however, looks fantastic, we're all agreed on that. It hangs above a long refectory-style table on the far wall, almost as if it's a window. Des is recognized straight away by one of the staff and we're whisked off for a tour and then to sit down for the tasting. This takes place informally, in the family kitchen, around a table with a white linen cloth. Plenty of wine glasses, a water jug and tumblers, a spittoon, napkins. The owner's mother is called Ruth. She's the old friend of Des's and is the one who'll be looking after us. She is a fine wine connoisseur and we feel confident in her care.

Ruth is no fool. She has a selection of Chudston's wine for us to try; she knows we have no stocks of our own yet and need to build up our reserves so we can use them for blends in the future – not every harvest will be good. We also need some bottles now and for the intervening years.

What else are we supposed to drink, after all? And how else can we market our vineyard without wine?

'Try this,' Ruth says, bringing me back with a jolt to the here and now.

A frisson of excitement bubbles up around the table.

'It's your Pinot Noir,' she explains.

We try our Pinot Noir.

'I can smell raspberries. And strawberries,' I say, feeling a little naive and childlike in my observations.

'And on the palate, a touch of incense,' Eve adds, impressively.

'Sensuous and fragrant,' Des says, breathing deeply and then glugging.

'This will add backbone and body to your wine,' Ruth says, clearly impressed with our response. 'Now your Chardonnay.'

We try our Chardonnay. I remember the white grapes so clearly, hanging in big succulent bunches on the vine. And here it is as wine. Flowery. Lemony. Nutty, even. More of a delicate fragrance.

'This will be slower to develop,' Ruth says. 'But it ages very well.'

'Like us, eh, Ruth?' Des teases.

'Just like us, Des,' she agrees with a chuckle. 'What do you think, then?'

'I'm blown away,' I say without thinking. It's quite an emotional response. Remembering those grapes, Rob ferrying them from the vineyard to the barn. The blisters from the secateurs. The volunteers. The pickers. The appearance and discovery of Nathan. It seems so long ago, despite only being a few months. Rob's been gone all this time, having adventures, following his passion, and what I thought was going to be a terrible year has turned out to be an adventure of our own.

'Try our Pinot Meunier,' Ruth urges gently. 'It's an overlooked blending grape.'

'Ruth's a big advocate of Meunier,' Des tells us, sniffing deeply from the massive glass.

'It can make lovely wines in its own right,' Ruth says. 'It's not without its challenges. It's not the easiest to grow. The leaf is furry, velvety, looks like it's been dredged in flour,' she continues. 'It's known as the miller's grape.'

Ruth's a veritable bundle of knowledge. Maybe I should be taking notes.

'Unlike Chardonnay,' she goes on, 'which has very straight shoots, Meunier is more bushy, which means there's a lot of canopy work. But the buds appear a little later and so it's less prone to frost. And even if it does get caught out by the frost, it can go on to produce a good secondary crop. You'd never get that with Chardonnay. Try it.'

We try her Pinot Meunier. Another black grape. It's aromatic. Fruity. A little smoky. Earthy. Acidic.

Melina is missing out on all this. Where is she? Has she fallen into a vat?

'As well as adding richness to your sparkling wine, the Pinot Meunier will help it age more quickly.'

'Well, that's sorted then, as my granddaughters might say.' Des laughs out loud, pleased with himself, then becomes a little more serious. 'Good wine is worth waiting for but I don't know how many more years I have on this planet.'

Serious but not morbid. He's never worried about his own mortality, not when he has so much to enjoy in the here and now.

So it is agreed. We will work with the winemaker here to make a vintage blend, the cuvée, with a combination of our Pinot Noir and Chardonnay and their 2018 Pinot Meunier.

But there is a niggle. Quite a big niggle, actually. And I just have to bring this niggle to the table. 'You don't think we're competing, do you?' I ask Ruth.

'Competing? My dear girl, no. Not at all. We are lovers of wine – your family and my family. We want to spread the joy. Share the love. There's a big enough thirst for many more vineyards on this island. The people of this country will never tire of drinking wine. And what we do the best is sparkling wine. The way forward is collaboration.'

Eve nods vigorously in agreement. She is oddly quiet this afternoon. I think she's also somewhat blown away at the prospect and at the realization of having produced decent wine.

'As we divide from the rest of Europe,' Ruth goes on, 'we need to find ways to tie us together. We can be a part of an international wine community. But we can also be neighbours who make wine together and alongside each other. Like so many do in France.'

'I can almost hear the "Anthem of Europe",' Des jokes.

'Ah,' Ruth says. 'Beethoven's "Ode to Joy". What a cracker.'

They share a dreamy look.

'"She gave us kisses and the fruit of the vine",' Eve adds and a rueful sigh whooshes around the table.

I need to bring this meeting back on track. 'Have you ever considered doing weddings here, Ruth? Like I said, I don't want us to pit ourselves against you because I don't think we'd come out of it too well.'

'Nonsense, my dear. From what your parents tell me, you'll make a wonderful job of it. And Home Farm will be the perfect setting. Once you get your new roof. Besides, we don't want to go down that route. We want to concentrate on the winery, the tours, and the cafe – probably a decent restaurant. We may do some events – corporate, mainly – but not weddings. And there might well be some work for you here too, Chrissie.' She smiles. 'There's no competition, just collaboration.'

'Really? Well, that's good then, I suppose. I mean, it's really good.'

And before I make a fool of myself by being mushy in my thanks, in rushes Melina, almost falling through the kitchen door in excitement.

'The wine is very good,' she says. 'My *babcia* would approve.'

LATER, FALLING ASLEEP, I realize my mind is less cluttered, that things are coming together. I feel less pressure, as if my life has slowed down to a particular rhythm. A rhythm that's much easier to keep time to. A country rhythm in tune with the seasons and all those who went before us. You don't get the constant rumbling of traffic out here – but you do get all sorts of other noises. At first I couldn't get used to it. Now I sleep through most of them.

Tonight, however, something wakes me in the small hours. Something I don't usually hear. A click. A dull thud. Like a door closing. I lie there, imagining burglars. Imagining all sorts. So I get up, panicky, to check there isn't a murderer on the loose.

Every step is creaky. This is a very old house – hundreds of years old, I remind myself. A click or a thud could be anything.

With a raised heart rate, I use the torch on my phone to make my way downstairs in the proper country darkness. I check the study, living room and studio. All clear. So on to the kitchen. Silence. I hold my breath as I switch on the light, not sure now whether I really expect to see an intruder. There's no one. Not even Luther, who must have snuck upstairs to sleep with Scarlet.

The back door is locked, and after I've checked the boot room, laundry and pantry too, I head back to my room, heart rate lowered considerably. My feet are freezing and I can't wait to climb back into bed and curl up; I've got used to sleeping on my own. Those sultry nights of tangled sheets with Rob seem very far away now.

I put my head round Ruby's door. Fast asleep. Deep breathing and very still. The creases that have marred her forehead of late smooth again. Maybe she's come through the worst.

Don't divide the skin while it's still on the bear. I can hear Melina whisper this in my ear and I actually physically shake my head to get rid of the nag. I won't count my chickens, thank you very much. Actually I have just checked on one of my chicks. So better do the other one.

Scarlet is all tucked up, her head almost covered by her duvet. She looks snuggly. Especially spooned next to Luther, the big lump. He lifts his head, dares me to move him. When he knows he'll get away with it, he drops his head back onto the bed – the pillow, I ask you – and sighs. Then in a blink he's fast asleep and snoring.

I'm an idiot. If a burglar was creeping round our house, Luther most certainly would've mentioned it.

I am a worryguts.

Sometimes you need to listen to your guts. But right now, I'm looking forward to blissful sleep.

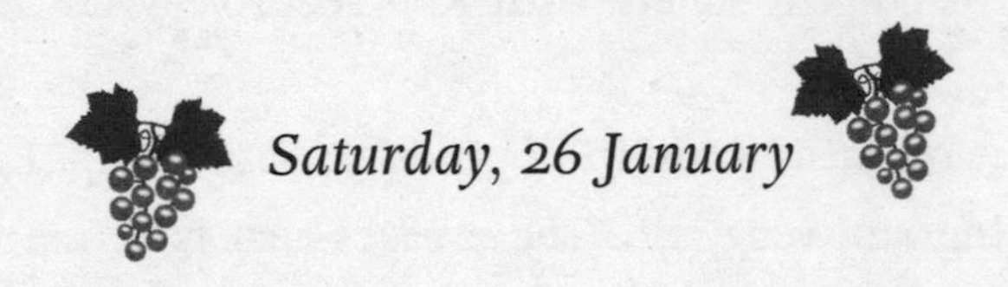

Saturday, 26 January

CRACK! CRACK!

Gunfire. This is probably the last shoot, because it's almost the end of the pheasant season so hopefully Scarlet can then relax a bit.

Bang. Bang. Bang.

Time to get up, then.

EVE IS ON her own at the kitchen table by the time I'm showered and dressed.

'Morning, Christabel. Sleep well? You look refreshed. Your bags have shrunk.'

'My bags?'

'Under your eyes.'

'I wasn't aware I had bags under my eyes.'

'Well, it's hardly surprising given the last few months. But not to worry. Sleep seems to have sorted them out, so don't fret about it.'

I wasn't fretting until she mentioned it, but now of course I am considering how many bottles of sparkling wine will pay for cosmetic surgery.

'There's tea in the pot. Builder's. Just how you like it.' Eve is oblivious to my new plight. 'Can you manage some eggs and bacon?'

'Yes, please.' I'm six years old again, waiting for Eve to rustle up some Saturday morning magic, wishing I could watch *Saturday Superstore* like everyone else in my class, but we didn't have a telly. 'I should check on the girls first though.'

'Let them sleep,' Eve says. 'It's Saturday. They've had a busy week.'

She puts my mug of tea on the table and nods at me to sit down, so I do as I'm told because sometimes it's easier.

'I'll let them have another hour.'

BUT IN LESS than an hour, Scarlet is standing in the kitchen, fully clothed in black trousers and fleece, hair stuffed into a bobble hat, army boots shedding mud over the flags. The only colour is a streak of blood running down her face. It appears to be coming from a cut above one eye.

'Scarlet! What's happened? I thought you were in bed.'

'Those bastards,' she seethes.

'What happened? Who did this to you?'

She doesn't answer because in comes Ruby, also dressed in black, as if the pair of them have been to some bizarre funeral.

'It was one of the hunters,' Ruby says. 'On the shoot.'

'You've been on the shoot?'

'Yes. Well, no. Not actually *on* it,' she says.

Scarlet hasn't said another word. Her mouth is set in a grim line. Her hands are shaking with rage. Eve moves her to the window seat and dispenses a dose of Rescue Remedy. Asks calmly what happened. Far more calmly than I am capable of being.

'What on earth has been going on?' Both girls look at me warily and I realize my voice sounds a little high-pitched.

Eve takes control. 'Why don't you get Ruby cleaned up in the bathroom,' she suggests, quite firmly. 'She's covered in mud. And is that a scratch on her cheek?'

'I'm fine,' says Ruby, touching her cheek to see if it hurts.

I take a closer look at her face. It is dirty and sweaty but I can't see any blood. Why is Eve fussing over Ruby when Scarlet's the injured one— Oh. I catch a mother-to-mother movement of Eve's eyes. I take her point and reluctantly leave them to it, taking Ruby with me to the bathroom so we can talk without upsetting her sister any further. So I can get to the bottom of this. Because if anyone will tell me, it's Ruby – the little grass.

'It was Scarlet's idea,' is Ruby's opening gambit.

'What?

'Sabotaging the shoot.'

'What?!'

'Morley was in on it too. Then Barney and I said we'd help out. Scarlet's spent ages on the planning.'

It hits me now. I've been an idiot. I thought Scarlet had caught the rambling bug. But all the time she's been 'hiking', she's actually been on recces, working out ways to disrupt the pheasant shoot. I don't know whether to be angry or proud. A bit of both, if I'm honest.

'And what happened? Why's she bleeding?'

'One of the blokes got all shirty. He threw a stone at us and it hit Scarlet above the eye. Then Nathan was there, ordering everyone around. He punched the bloke. Then the police were called.'

'The police? Who called the police?'

'Dunno. All of a sudden a car was there and two rozzers were questioning everyone. Then they just told us to go home and so Jackie brought us back.'

'Jackie?'

'She was on the shoot—'

'For God's sake! What is wrong with that woman?'

'Well, she has first-aid training and she looked at Scarlet's cut and said it always bleeds a lot there, above the eye, and it looks worse than it actually is.'

'But I thought she'd given up hunting?'

'Only foxes. She's moved on to birds, because you can't eat foxes. She makes pheasant stew. Only Scarlet said that most of the pheasants don't even get eaten. Butchers won't have them because of the lead shot. And some of the birds just get wounded and die a horrible, painful, slow death.'

I know someone else who might suffer a horrible, painful, slow death when I get my hands on him.

'Don't be angry, Mum. You look really angry. Jackie's all right. A bit weird. But she dropped us home, said she'll be back after she's dropped Barney off and had a word with him. He's in trouble. Am I in trouble?'

'I'm not sure, Ruby. Do you think you should be in trouble?'

'The police just told us off and said it could have been a nasty accident. Someone could've got shot.'

The thought of one of my girls felled by a gun is too much. The bathroom floor slides and I have to sit on the edge of the bath where Ruby has chucked her muddy socks so that she can wash her feet in the bidet. From here I can see across the vineyard to the row of trees behind, the estate boundary, and I feel the anger bubbling inside.

'Tell me again what happened, Ruby.'

It turns out that last night, Scarlet and Ruby crept out

of the house while everyone was asleep, taking Luther so he wouldn't wake us up with barking, and because they are both afraid of the dark. Which accounts for the thud waking me up, which was them returning from moving the pheasant feeders Scarlet had located on previous recces. The feeders were at the top of a hill in a line, so they moved them as far as they could to draw the birds away from the shoot.

'We left an aniseed trail,' she says.

'Aniseed?'

'Yeah, aniseed essential oil mixed with white spirit and spraycd with onc of Dcs's watcr things. Phcasants will follow an aniseed trail and then stay put if you've left enough food.'

'Whcrc did you gct it from?

'What?'

'The aniseed oil.'

'Nana Eve.'

'Nana Eve knew about this?'

'No,' Ruby says, sticking up for her grandmother. 'She gave it to Scarlet for a cough.'

'Scarlet doesn't have a cough.'

'I know.'

I go over this in my head, taking out the plaits from Ruby's hair and brushing away the mud as I do.

'But why were you there today, if you'd already moved the feeders overnight?'

'Scarlet was worried that wouldn't be enough to shut down the shoot. So we went next door and...'

'And...?'

'Waited for the beaters and shooters to get in position... and then... and then... we...' She trails off.

'Then you what, Ruby? Tell me. You didn't...'

'We stood in front of the shooters to stop them.'

Before I can respond, we hear shouting coming from the kitchen: Scarlet's gruff voice and a much lower booming one. We rush back to see what the commotion is all about – though I'm pretty sure I can guess.

Nathan. In the kitchen. Pacing up and down. Ranting.

'I knew something like this was going to happen,' he's saying, running his hands through his hair like he's going to tear it out. 'I've been patrolling the boundary walls of the estate for weeks. Most evenings. I've never caught anyone, seen anyone – until that day you were there, Scarlet. You and your mates.'

He doesn't seem to notice my appearance, or Ruby's for that matter. He's too busy fuming at Scarlet, who is pointedly looking out of the window, twitching her leg, that nervous habit of hers reserved for times when she is trying desperately not to go off on one.

'I innocently thought you were just walking,' he goes on, his voice quieter now. 'I should've known you were up to no good.'

That's it now. I'm not having this. 'No good? Have you

seen her face?' I jump in.

'Yes, I've seen her face. Things got out of hand. That's why I'm here. To check she's OK. To give the pair of them a rollicking. They could've been shot!'

'And where are the police now? Why didn't they do anything?' I ask.

'They left pretty quickly. It's the last shoot of the season and so they're hoping tensions will die down naturally.'

'Probably given a brace of pheasants for their trouble,' Scarlet mutters.

Eve puts her hand on Scarlet's arm.

'Well, I've a good mind to talk to them about an assault on a minor!' I'm livid. 'A grown man threw a stone at her.'

'I don't think he meant it to actually hit her. He was just upset,' Ruby says, suddenly an arbitrator.

'Upset? I'll give him upset.'

'Not a good idea, Christabel.' Eve is the picture of serenity. Her complexion glows. Her hair shines. She could have a hippy halo above her and I wouldn't be surprised. But she's a tough one and you ignore her at your peril. 'Scarlet and Ruby could get in trouble. They *were* trespassing, after all.'

I point at Ruby. 'It's *her* father's property.'

There. I've said it before I knew I even had those words in that order in my brain.

Her father.

Everything in the room slows down, almost stops for a little while. The words hang heavy, heard by everyone, felt by everyone, and I can't take them back. I can't make them be unheard, or unfelt.

Her father.

Rob's her father.

But Rob's not here.

And Nathan is.

Right. Yet again I'm going to have to deal with this single-handedly. I've got to halt this extreme behaviour. Who knows where it could have led? I could be phoning Rob to tell him that Scarlet is badly injured. Or in custody. And what's next in store? Building tree houses? Digging tunnels? Gluing her hands to the windows of governmental buildings? Who knows what she'll get up to in the next few months?

'That's it,' I tell Scarlet. 'I'm calling your father. It's time he came back.'

But when I do, an unfamiliar voice answers the phone.

Spring

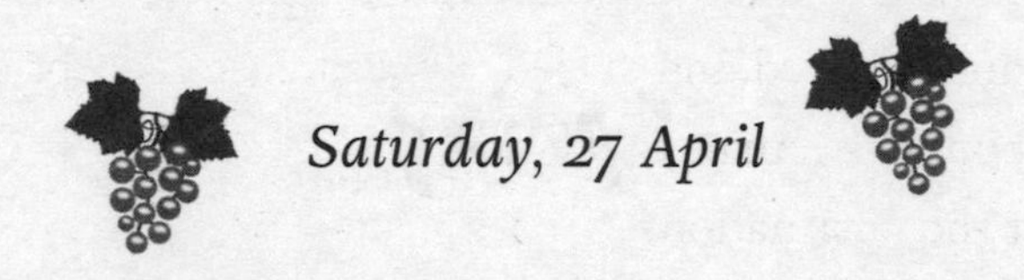

Saturday, 27 April

THREE MONTHS HAVE passed since I asked my husband to come home. Three more months without him while he's been lying in a hospital bed in Nairobi recovering from malaria. Though we've had more contact with him in recent weeks, since he's been feeling better. It turns out his biggest struggle over the time he's been away hasn't been the malaria, the flies, the corrugated roads, the relentless heat. It wasn't even the face-off with that bull elephant. It was missing his daughters. Both Scarlet *and* Ruby.

'And I miss *you*, Chrissie,' he said.

So I told him I missed him too.

'Come to Cairo,' he said. 'I've only got Ethiopia and Sudan to get through before I'm in Egypt. Then, depending on recovery and fitness, we thought we'd come home via Europe.'

'Europe? But didn't you book a return flight from Egypt?'

'No. I wasn't sure how far I'd make it, to be honest. I've surprised myself. Most people complete the ride in a few months and it's taken me much longer. I've slowed down and stopped and stared. I've learnt to accept that life's about the journey—'

'Not the destination.'

'Exactly.'

A bit like wine. We're on a journey. Though obviously I'm looking forward to the day when we taste our first bottle of Home Farm Fizz.

In the meantime I'll have to make do with whatever Bargain Booze has on offer.

A WEEK SINCE Easter. The chocolate eggs are long gone and thankfully we were spared a visitation from Ingrid because her sister and brother-in-law, a.k.a. the Child Catchers, insisted she spend it with them so they could show her the PowerPoint from the cruise they went on at Christmas. Mark and Declan have not been back either, their lives full-on with work and each other, but they want to come down for a weekend soon. So it's just been us: Eve, Des, Melina, the girls and me.

As for the vineyard, it looks totally different now it's spring. A few weeks ago, the sap rose up from the roots and tears appeared on the exposed wood of the vines where they'd been pruned. Now, with the brighter days and warmer temperatures, the vine buds have swollen and burst out of their protective husks, producing new shoots. Budburst has arrived. Everywhere you look, there are tiny fluffy leaves unfurling on the vines, bringing life and colour to the hill at Home Farm, giving us an idea as to the critical dates of flowering and harvest.

But there is a huge potential problem – something that every vineyard owner dreads. Right now the vines are at their most vulnerable. Eve's always said, 'Beware the blackthorn winter' – when the hedgerows are awash with (confusingly) white blackthorn blossom in springtime, the ground can still be whitened with frost, and a late frost can devastate the vines. She calls it the 'witch-tree', and she should know. Not that I'm calling her a witch; she just understands the country ways. Though she has been known to weave a few protection spells and use incantations in time of need.

We are on frost watch as a result, Des and Melina studying the weather forecasts daily, having installed sensors in the vineyard that will alert them if the temperature heads towards the danger zone so they can head out to cover the vines. Melina knows the country ways too, like Eve, plus she has Babcia's magic tricks up her sleeve. She's already planted rose bushes at the end of the rows of vines to act as a warning against mildew, because roses show it on their leaves before vines so we can counter-attack with sulphur spray if need be. But more importantly, she has weapons to fight off the dreaded Ice Saints – as rural folk call them – if they attack next month. There are a couple of days when frost is a real possibility. And frost at budburst can herald disaster.

Budburst is also an opportunity for vineyards to offer up their new wines to try, and although we haven't reached that stage just yet, we're saved by a visit from Ruth, bringing with her a few cases of our collaborative bottles.

Eve, Des, Melina and I set to work with her around the kitchen table.

'Well?' Ruth asks after we've all had a taste, because all we've said so far is *mmm* and *wowzer* and *gosh*. 'Could you be more specific?'

'The wine is immediately recognizable as being from the local terroir,' Des says, not a hint of pretentiousness, just worldly wisdom.

'Eve?' Ruth turns to my mother, a questioning look on her eager face.

'It smells of the earth,' she responds, eyes closed, meditatively. 'With an underlying mineral taste of stones.'

'Good,' Ruth says. 'I can taste that too.'

'It is also grassy,' Melina says. 'Maybe woodsmoke.'

Ruth claps her hands, excited. 'Yes,' she says. 'I get that too, Melina.'

'And zingy,' I add in triumph. 'With an apple blossom finish.'

I'm quite proud of my comment, but then I lose confidence and wonder if I'm blagging it. 'I could be wildly wrong,' I say, looking uncertainly at Ruth.

'There's no such thing as right and wrong, Chrissie,' she reassures me.

I want to point out my parents' attempts in previous years, when everyone was right that it was wrong. But this is too confusing.

We've drunk (not spat out) quite a bit now.

Des has reached the point of quoting from literature he can only remember when he's been oiled. '"Pour out the wine without restraint or stay",' he says in his Richard Burton voice. '"Pour not by cups, but by the bellyful".' He hiccups, before adding: '"Epi-thal-amion"...' He struggles somewhat with the word, but then who wouldn't? '... 250, by Edmund Spenser,' he finishes, proud to have remembered his source.

Then it's Ruth's turn. Her glasses have gone skew-whiff and flecks of orange lipstick mark her front teeth. '"There is not the hundredth part of the wine consumed in this kingdom that there ought to be. Our foggy climate wants help." Jane Austen.'

We chink glasses, very pleased with ourselves.

Now it's Eve. '"A good wife who can find it?"' Whoops of laughter and bawdy comments. '"She considers a field and buys it; with the fruit of her hands she plants a vineyard." Proverbs 31.'

'Very good, my love.' Des gives my mother a whopper of a kiss on her lips. 'What about you, Melina? Do you have a Polish quote about wine?'

Of course she does. Melina has a Polish proverb for every occasion.

'"*Więcej ludzi utonęło w kieliszku niż w morzu*",' she says. 'Wine has drowned more than the sea.'

This stops the laughter for a moment but I soon get them going again, even if unintentionally, singing the French champagne line from 'Livin' La Vida Loca'. 'Ricky Martin,' I clarify.

Once they've recovered themselves and my blushes have faded a little, Melina says, straight-faced as ever, 'Stupid song. Champagne is always French.'

Babcia would be proud of her granddaughter's wisdom, that I know for sure.

By the time Ruth's son, who dropped her off earlier, arrives to pick her up, we are all, apart from the girls, sloshed. It turns out that the wine is good. In fact it is very, very good.

I love my life and everyone in it, I think. Even Nathan... How it felt to be in his arms, smooching to 'Nothing Compares 2 U' at youth club...

I snap out of my daydreaming, remembering the events of the shoot. But he *was* remorseful – he'd just been frightened for Scarlet and, since then, he really has tried his best to make amends, promising never to have a shoot on his estate again. And he and Ruby seem finally to be forging some kind of relationship that isn't based on what presents he can bestow on her. He's even made progress with Scarlet, paying her to do the social media for the estate and being genuinely appreciative and encouraging of her work.

Meanwhile, Ruby and Barney have been initiated into the Chud Valley Stompers and have had their first gig at a silver wedding anniversary party in the British Legion in Chudston, to great critical acclaim and a shish kebab from Ali Baba's takeaway – which suggests Ruby's vegetarianism has definitely been put on hold.

And then there's Tomasz and his great love for Melina. He visits every evening for supper, welcomed warmly into the bosom of Home Farm – just like Nathan, all those years ago, when we were growing up.

I pause at this realization. Maybe it's true what they say? That everyone comes into your life for a reason. Though I still need to find one for Ingrid...

And just as I am contemplating the meaning of all this big stuff, my phone goes. It is Rob, calling from Addis Ababa.

'How are you?' I ask him, panicking. 'Are you sure you're well enough to be cycling through Ethiopia?'

'I'm OK,' he says.

And I can't make out if he actually is OK or is simply putting on a brave face.

'We're just going to take it slow and do our best. Though we've had a few moments...' he confesses. 'The riding's been a challenge and it's going to get harder. We somehow got through the lava rock desert back in Kenya, and the herds of cattle and camels. Jeez, talk about a hint of what was to come! But we made it through – even saw ostriches at the Rift Lakes National Park.'

'And where are you now?'

'The Sheraton. We just had a buffet breakfast that was as close to heaven as I'll ever get. Honestly, Chrissie, this city is amazing – it's surrounded by forests of eucalyptus trees.'

He talks excitedly. Next they will cycle through the Central Ethiopian Plateau and then the Blue Nile Gorge, which he says is supposed to both terrify and amaze. Then on to the Ethiopian Highlands, Lake Tana, the source of the Blue Nile, and then the most difficult trek up to Gondar where there are ancient castles. Then they'll cross the border and head north through the bread basket of Sudan to Khartoum.

I feel a little excitement on his behalf but it's so hard to picture him there. Even when I've googled and trawled the Internet for information, it's still too weird to think of him cycling every day. Just cycling. And us here in Devon, getting on with life, with school and work, family and friends. I've never felt further apart from my husband than I do right now.

'And how are things with you?' he asks.

I note the worry in his voice and the relief when I tell him all has been well since the shooting incident.

'Have you been reading my blog posts?' he asks, keen for us to know what he's going through.

I just have time to reassure him that we check for updates every day, before he loses his connection and so any questions we might have remain unasked and unanswered. There was no mention of me coming to Cairo from either of us.

It *is* a triumph of human nature, to do what he is doing, but what about the people he's left behind in order to follow his dream? I'm finding it harder and harder to square the circle in my head.

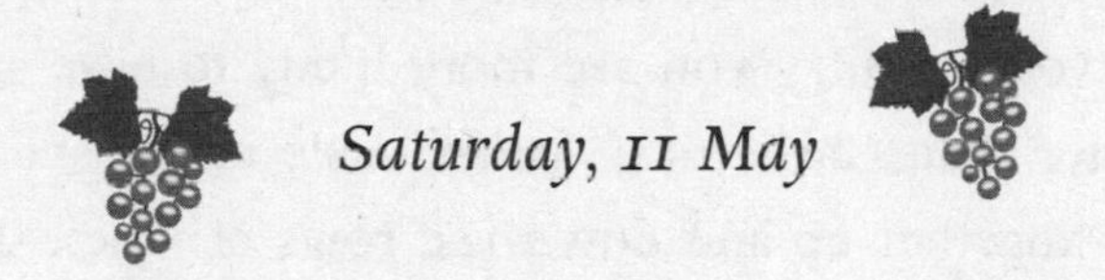

Saturday, 11 May

THIS IS AN important weekend. Declan and Mark have finally come down to visit for a few days. They arrived full of the woes of London and the traffic on the A303, but have gone off this morning with Ruby, Scarlet and Luther for a hike that doesn't involve animal rights. It's a joy to see them again. A joy to know that things are working out so well for them. There's talk of Declan moving in with Mark very soon. They're spending all their time together as it is, but I know this is a big step for my old friend. And a good one.

We're also on high alert about the prospect of a late frost – the coming of the Ice Saints Melina warned us about. She calls these days the *zimni ogrodnicy* – the cold gardeners. The buds are at risk, so we have to do everything humanly possible to stop the frost getting to them.

In days gone by, farmers and winegrowers burned wet wood, green twigs and soil, the smoke rising to form a thick fog over the valleys. This was supposed to help protect any new growth and blossoms from the frost. Fire and ice don't like each other.

'In your country you are more likely to have snow at Easter than Christmas,' Melina tells me as she and I walk together up and down the rows of vines. 'Your gardeners and farmers wait till mid-May has passed before planting seedlings. But we cannot do this for vines. They bloom when they bloom and we have to protect them. So we do what they do in old days. We burn green wood and it will hang in valley and keep away frost.'

I can't fault her logic.

From the top of the vineyard, the valley is spread out before us and the river sparkles in the morning sun. I'm awestruck at this sight. This is our terroir. These are all the ingredients that will make our wine specific to this very location.

'They use bougies up the road in the winery,' I tell her, wondering if this might be easier for us.

She gives me a blank stare.

'They're paraffin candles which give off enough heat to create air movement so frost pockets can't form, hopefully.'

'I know how this works. I am not idiot. But we do not need bougies. I saved vineyard stems from pruning. They are in cow shed. So we use them for fuel. We light stems in bins. Tomasz has gave us bins.'

'Oh, has he? That's nice. Very creative.'

'He takes from Nathan. Nathan does not have the one clue of rubbish he keeps. But some rubbish is very good. We recycle. It's better, no?'

'Yes. Much better.' I have no idea if it's better or not but I'm happy to go along with Melina. She tends to be right about most things and I trust her implicitly. As do Eve and Des.

We head back down the hill towards the milking parlour so that Melina can show me the stems that we'll use tonight if the forecast is right with its prediction of sub-zero temperatures.

'We must protect Chardonnay especially,' she goes on. 'It is more innocent.'

'Innocent? Oh, do you mean *vulnerable*?'

'Yes, I mean *vulnerable*. We concentrate on vines further down hill' – she points them out to me, the specific ones she's concerned about – 'the ones closest to valley, where cold air gathers. We put bins here and there, enough to rise temperature by two maybe three degrees. The smoke also stops morning sun burning buds that are covered in frost. Like all those big trees on Nathan's land. And all the thick hedges that you people of Devon like so much.'

I think maybe Melina also likes the thick hedges of Devon, the big trees next door, the landscape she is getting to know so well. The river that cuts through this valley towards the English Channel. The rambling cob farmhouse with its thatched roof. The sloping vineyard. Would she bulldoze the outbuildings given half a chance? Maybe. But she understands that we are very attached to them and that they are part of the heritage of this area, along with the red earth and soft rain. I think she's coming round to life here.

Once inside the milking parlour, I spot the store of vine cuttings. It's a great idea to use what we have already. And this building has such potential I can almost see how a press and tanks would fit in here. We'd have to consider where to store the bottles after, so they can age. It's not like we have the natural caves of Champagne.

As if Melina can read my mind, she says, matter-of-factly, 'Babcia left me money. She would want me to use money for something good. I want to put money into your business. I could buy new press so we can make wine here, on site. Good wine.'

'I don't know what to say, Melina,' I gush. And I start blubbing and hugging her.

'Maybe just say *yes*?' She laughs out loud, a burst of joy.

'Yes, Melina. Yes! Let's do this!'

MELINA AND I have a hastily convened meeting with Des and Eve around the kitchen table over a sandwich and a cuppa. Melina repeats her proposal and it is grabbed lustily by their very open arms. By the time the rest of the crew return, having walked six miles and nearly seen off the dog, and Declan for that matter, we have great plans ahead of us. Though our weekend's mission to keep this year's crop as safe as we possibly can is foremost in our minds.

'Chrissie!' Scarlet hisses, shaking me awake. 'You've got to get up and help us. The Ice Saints have come.'

It is dark and feels like the middle of the night but her words have shocked me into action. I hastily scramble out of bed and reach for the folded jumper I'd left on my grandmother's cocktail chair, ready for this moment. I'm already wearing my thermals, jogging bottoms and socks so all I have to do is slip the jumper over my pyjama top and go downstairs to add my coat, hat and boots.

Des and Eve are already out there with Melina and Tomasz. Ruby, Scarlet, Declan and I rush to join them, alert for instructions from our self-appointed leader. Melina tells us which fires to light, what to fetch and do, and we rush around in the half-dark to beat these Ice Saints into submission.

Poor Des is conflicted by the need to create fire for our task while also keeping said fire under control.

Thankfully, we seem to tread this tightrope of risk and safety just fine – and it looks like the frost has largely kept off anyway. By the time the sun rises and warms up, we are in the clear.

'Who wants a Buck's Fizz to celebrate?' Declan suggests.

'Now that's what I call magic,' Des says, giving Melina a hug. 'Tomasz, you have a very fine woman there,' he says to her beau.

If Des wasn't Des, then he would be getting a Polish clip round the ear, if not from Tomasz, then definitely from Melina. But instead she smiles sweetly and agrees with him.

'I am lucky woman,' she says, 'to have Tomasz to be my husband. And we wonder, Tomasz and I...' – she appears shy for a moment, a most un-Melina-like state, looks to Eve, to Des and to me – '... we ask if we can use barn for wedding in summer maybe?'

'This summer?!' I exclaim, caught by surprise. 'Aren't you forgetting something, Melina? We have no roof!'

'Yes, but, Chrissie, we *will* have roof because Nathan, Tomasz, Aleksy, Julia and Piotr will make roof.'

The council finally approved our application – hurrah! – for holding weddings in our barn, provided we use roof tiles in place of thatch.

'Oh my gosh, it'll be amazing for you two to marry here!' I exclaim.

How romantic; in the place where they met and fell in love. This wonderful place. And yes, all right, it might not have a roof yet and the inside has an awful lot of work to do but if we pull together we can make it happen. We have got ten weeks, after all.

Summer

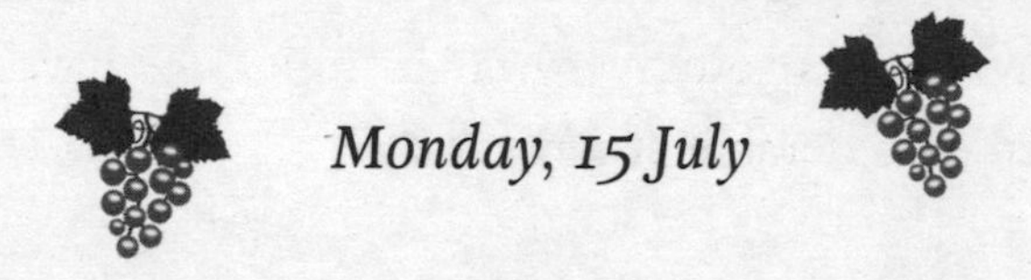

Monday, 15 July

We have survived fire and we have survived ice. We have seen rapid shoot growth and then an early flowering, over before Wimbledon even began.

It's hard to believe that we've lived here for nine months. Before we know it, harvest time will be upon us and that is supposed to bring the return of Rob. He survived Ethiopia. In fact he was completely moved by it. 'The first humans came from the Rift Valley here,' he told me in one of our less and less frequent phone calls, 'and it's one of only two African countries not to be colonized. Plus the coffee is off the scale. And cycling is very popular in Addis.'

He's been all the way through Sudan and Egypt, passing through the lands of the Pharaohs to the Valleys of the Kings and Queens at Luxor and heading north along the coastal route of the Red Sea, through the Eastern Desert to Cairo and the Pyramids and the enigmatic, aloof, solitary Sphinx of Giza.

And now Europe.

A world away from our journey here at Home Farm. But although these last three months might not have involved us going very far in miles, we have also achieved considerable progress.

Today is St Swithin's Day and if it rains then it will be set to rain for the next forty days. But if it is fine, then we are in for forty days of good weather.

I leap out of bed on waking and open the curtains in order to inspect the world outside my window. One of those early-morning mists rises from the river, the kind that typically burn off by midday, leaving behind clear blue skies. We should be in for a scorcher! And if the legend of St Swithin's Day holds true, then the weather could hold for Saturday – and Melina and Tomasz's wedding.

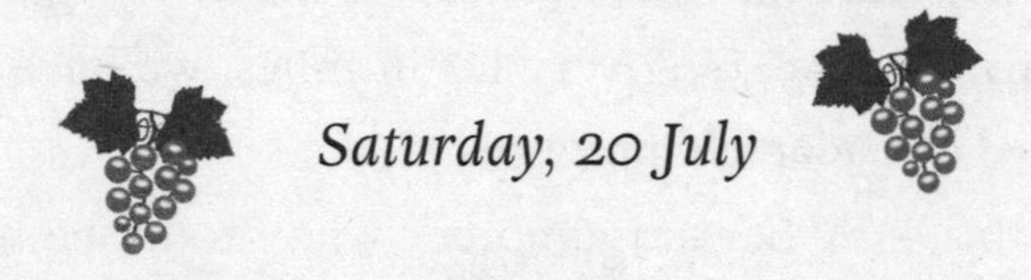

Saturday, 20 July

St Swithin doesn't let us down, because Saturday dawns bright and sunny. By eleven o'clock, Melina is ready. She is in her room – what used to be my room – and she has the women of the house helping her, though for the most part we've just chatted and sipped Buck's Fizz. She has done her own hair – long curly tresses piled up on her head and threaded with violets so she resembles a princess in a fairy tale. She has also done her own make-up, a little heavy on the kohl under the eyes which gives her the doleful look of Princess Diana, but stunning all the same, her Slavic cheekbones highlighted with peach blusher. Her talents know no limits as she stands in the dress she made herself – simple, satin, cut on the bias in the style of a star of the silver screen.

I have a sudden jolt of realization that this woman, this incredible woman who has so many sides to her and such a lot to offer, and who I have known casually for so long, has become over the past nine months something like a best friend to me. I choke back the tears that threaten to spill.

'Let me help you with the veil,' Eve suggests, catching my emotional response.

There's a moment when tears prick Melina's eyes, too, as she thinks of her grandmother who should be here, attending to her, of her own mother who she can barely remember.

But Eve gently steps in, delicately and lovingly helping her with her veil – Babcia's, of course – securing it in place with a wreath of greenery and more fragrant violets.

'They're close enough to blue,' she tells a confused Melina.

'Blue?'

'"Something old, something new, something borrowed, something blue, and a silver sixpence in her shoe". You have an old veil, a new dress, blue flowers. Here's a silver sixpence...' She removes the small coin from her handbag and holds it up to the light. Wherever did she find that? I wonder. 'You just need something borrowed.'

Melina reaches down to put the coin in her unbelievably high heels.

'Oh, I have something borrowed,' she says, remembering. 'Chrissie lent me her push-up bra.'

'Perfect,' Eve says, while the girls snigger. 'Are you ready, my dear?'

By contrast with the English wedding tradition, Melina and Tomasz meet before the service, here in our kitchen. Tomasz's eyes light up like a child's when he sees her. He kisses his bride-to-be in front of the Aga, whose idiosyncrasies Melina has finally mastered. He looks handsome, in a royal-blue suit that shows off his broad chest and wide shoulders.

In front of his parents and Melina's uncle and aunt, all of whom have come over to England especially for this momentous occasion, Tomasz hands Melina her *gromnica*, last lit at her confirmation. In return, she puts a spray of violets into his buttonhole.

Melina and Tomasz are to be driven to the Catholic church in Chudston by Nathan, the rest of us following in my seven-seater. As we drive through the lanes, hedgerows high and trees thick with their summer show, the locals are out in force, waving at us and shouting good wishes.

I've never been to a Catholic wedding, though I've heard the services go on for a while. As dictated by another Polish tradition, one I particularly like, the couple to be married walk together down the aisle. We watch wise, beautiful Melina, her serious face hidden behind Babcia's veil, hand in hand with her beefy-armed Tomasz, as they make their way to the altar, accompanied by Malcolm's rendition of 'Ave Maria' on the organ. Not that Malcolm is the slightest bit Polish. I believe he is Anglo-Saxon through and through and hails from Banbury.

Melina's uncle and aunt sit solemnly in the front row, clearly wishing that Babcia was here, so much so that they leave a space for her. Tomasz's parents, Maria and Izaak, sit alongside them, with two of the groom's younger brothers, Jakub and Daniel.

The church is quite different from St Mary Magdalene. There are candles and incense, statues of Mary and other saints. The priest is very jolly in his bright garments and high cheek colour and the altar boys look angelic in their gear, nudging one another and giggling when the priest's back is turned.

As the ceremony goes ahead I think about how important, how sacred a time this is in the lives of these two people. From this moment onwards, Melina and Tomasz will be a couple. I feel a touch of jealousy, seeing how in love they are, how he looks at her with joy in his eyes. I remember my weddings; the church ceremony with Nathan feels like a lifetime ago. Another life entirely. And then in London, Rob and me with the girls at the register office in Camberwell. And now I might just as well be single.

Eve hands me a verbena-drenched handkerchief.

'Weddings always make me cry too, Christabel,' she whispers. 'All those vows and promises and the hope of love.'

I don't tell her I'm crying for myself.

Afterwards, there is a special blessing at St Mary Magdalene church, offered by its rector, Isabella. Melina and Tomasz were touched by the gesture, seeing it as a step towards being properly a part of this community and less like newcomers. And me? I somehow find it cathartic. As the happy couple make their way down the aisle, past a full congregation, my precious Ruby accompanies them with her harp rendition of Chopin's Nocturne in E-flat major opus 9, no. 2 – the one that's played in all the films.

THEN BACK TO the barn for the reception. It looks beautifully rustic, with garlands and bowers of greenery and flowers made by Eve and Scarlet. The table decorations are simple jam jars holding tea lights, and glass pots of delicate violets, which will no doubt later wilt in the heat. The party will go on. And on. Until tomorrow morning, I've been warned.

The barn is all ready to receive the sixty or so guests – some of their family and friends who have been able to come, all the pickers, the locals, even Ingrid and Major Carter and Jackie and her brood.

The Chud Valley Stompers and some members of the school swing band are set up on pallets and hay bales and have learnt the Polish wedding polka, which they are starting up now. The latest recruits join in with gusto, Ruby strumming Malcolm's Celtic harp, Barney on his trombone that's nearly as big as him.

And as the newlyweds enter, the wedding guests, primed by Melina's aunt, throw coins in their pathway.

'Why are we doing this?' Scarlet asks.

'It's for their honeymoon, apparently,' I tell her.

'Are they having a honeymoon?'

'A few days in Wales. On a vineyard.'

Scarlet grins. She looks stunning today. In a red dress, though still with her trademark Docs. Morley is here as her guest, helping Melina's aunt collect the coins for safekeeping.

'What are the aunt and uncle doing now?' Scarlet asks.

We watch on, as they give the bride and groom some bread sprinkled with salt, and a glass of wine.

'The bread is so they never go hungry, the salt to remind them that there will be tough times and they must stick at it.'

'And the wine?'

'I don't know. Just because?'

She laughs but a swear word is released when Melina and Tomasz drain their glasses before lobbing them to the floor where they smash for good luck.

Then Eve and I, along with the aunt and mother-in-law, help unveil Melina so she can show she is now a married woman. And, more to the point, so that she can eat and drink.

Now the feast will begin!

Along the three long rows of trestle tables, we all sit down on benches to eat the first of many dishes and courses. I have my girls, one on each side of me, and opposite me, Eve and Des. I look around and see such happy faces, it makes me smile inside. Relief. Accomplishment. Contentment. Even seeing Nathan across the room isn't enough to stir any bad feeling.

In between, there is much traditional dancing, the amalgamated band doing a proper job. We even have games such as Mr and Mrs and the throwing of the bouquet (which Declan catches) and the throwing of Tomasz's tie (which Mark catches, to the whoops of the crowd).

Several hours in, and I'm feeling extremely full. The food has mostly been stodgy and fatty – stews and potatoes and dumplings. Even a pig – a whole pig, head and all – is on full display

'That's disgusting,' Scarlet said, when she saw it earlier. 'Whose idea was that?'

Nathan happened to be passing with a pint of cider in hand. 'It's a Polish tradition,' he said. 'My wedding gift to Melina and Tomasz. I wanted to make them feel at home.'

'It's still disgusting.'

'It was free-range,' he added, a cheeky grin on his face. Then he made a swift getaway, trying not to spill his pint, winking over his shoulder so that even Scarlet had to laugh.

'I'll get you back,' she shouted, and when he pretended to hide under a table I thought, maybe it's not as bad as I thought it would be, having him as a next-door neighbour. And when I looked at Ruby, she was laughing and it confirmed that Nathan could maybc find a part to play in her life. And Scarlet's too.

EVENING HAS COME and the candles are lit. And the food is still coming. The advantage of all this stodge is that it helps absorb the vodka which the Polish men have lavishly supplied, adding to Declan and Mark's contribution of kegs of cider and beer. There is also sparkling wine courtesy of Ruth at Chudston Winery, who is sitting with Malcolm at the table, laughing and smiling while he's on a break from calling and playing the fiddle.

So although the guests are looking somewhat dishevelled, fascinators askew, ties undone, hair messed up and make-up smeared, the barn looks beautiful. But most importantly, Melina is radiant.

And then there's the other star of the show. Our very own wine. Everyone has enjoyed a glass or two but now Melina has something to say. She is standing on the stage, microphone in hand.

'I give toast,' she says, nodding at the glass in her hand, the one that has a gold band on its ring finger. '"The feeling of friendship is like that of being comfortably filled with roast beef; love, like being enlivened with champagne".' She raises her glass. 'That is from your Samuel Johnson and here's to our very own sparkling wine in the future. For now, *sto lat!* To you English, this means one hundred years. May I love my Tomasz for one hundred years.'

'*Sto lat*.' Tomasz leaps up on the stage and chinks her glass with his own and reaches for the microphone. 'May I love you forever, Melina.'

She grabs the microphone back and says: '*Człowiek nie wielbłąd, pić musi!* Man is not camel, he must drink!'

Then Tomasz shouts something to his father in Polish and in a trice he is handed two vodka shots. He gives one to his wife and keeps the other before they down them together to much cheering and clapping.

And yet again I find myself with tears in my eye, but this time, I think, for the right reasons. Eve notices and puts her arms around me, bringing me in for a hug, her arms wrapped around me so I'm enveloped in jasmine and love.

'None of this would have happened without you,' she says. 'I'm so very proud of you. You're the best thing I've ever done.'

My heart is filled with bubbles of joy and this moment is as glorious as the best wine in the world.

The party is in full swing. Raucous, riotous, rural. A true country wedding where everyone has contributed. Even Ingrid seems to have shed some of her burden of misery. Not only has she given Melina and Tomasz a set of bed linen, but she has also paid for the waiting staff Eve has hired – basically the other four of Jackie's children. I can't for the life of me understand this sudden generosity, but I'm accepting it with two open arms of gratefulness, just as Eve has urged me to do. I think it might have something to do with Major Carter who is whisking Ingrid around the barn in a dervish polka, and I suspect that the rumours I have heard, that he has been meeting her at his club in Piccadilly, are in fact true.

Just as I'm emerging from the trailer toilets that have been installed behind the barn, I bump into Nathan.

'You've done a great job,' he says.

'It's been fun. Hard work, but worth it seeing everyone celebrate so joyously.'

'Those boys know how to party,' he says.

'And those girls.'

'You've done a great job,' he says again, unexpectedly.

'The wine tastes fantastic and you're a wedding planner extraordinaire.'

'A wedding planner who seems to have lost her own husband somewhere in transit in the vineyards of Europe.'

'Right. Where is he now?'

'Italy, when I last spoke to him. He's making his way to Champagne for the harvest next month.'

'And then home?'

'Home?'

'Wherever home is?'

'Wherever home is.'

'With you?'

I don't have a chance to answer this question, though I've spent every spare moment thinking about it over the last few weeks. Ruby is here shouting at us to come inside.

'Quick,' she orders. 'They're about to open Granddad Des's present.'

We rush inside, both knowing what the surprise is and excited to see Melina's face when she opens it.

Inside the barn there is a rare moment of quiet and calm. Des stands by something tall that's covered in a big sheet. The wedding guests are gathered around, some standing on chairs so they can see.

'Take a corner each,' Des tells Melina and Tomasz. 'After three... one, two, three!'

They yank the sheet to unveil what's underneath.

And underneath is a wonderful portrait of a woman Des has brought to life with miraculous colour and energetic brushstrokes.

Babcia.

Melina hugs Des so hard he stumbles sideways a bit – though that could be the vodka the Polish boys have been giving him at regular intervals. Then she hugs her husband and he kisses the tears from her cheeks and looks at her in a way that speaks volumes of his love for her. A love that I believe will last for way more than a hundred years and into eternity, forever and ever.

A love I know I've never quite had, and maybe now this is something I should want, instead of settling for second best.

LATER, I NEED some fresh air so I head up the hill to the top of the vineyard and sit down between two rows of vines heavy with grapes. I've brought a bottle of wine with me. I should be sitting here sharing this with someone. But I don't even know if that someone is Rob, because he hasn't been here all year. It's been me and the girls. My parents. My friends. Even Nathan's played his part. A much bigger part than I would ever have anticipated.

On cue, as if I've conjured up his presence, Nathan appears.

'I've been searching everywhere for you,' he says. 'What are you doing out here?'

'Looking at the stars, wondering what they look like from Italy.'

'Starlike, I expect.'

And for once, Nathan fails to annoy me and I laugh. I really, really laugh at his very naff attempt at a joke and he sits on the ground next to me, grabbing the bottle of wine out of my hand to have a slug, which he nearly shoots out of his mouth when he too starts laughing, that boom bouncing across the valley, the pair of us sixteen and carefree once again. Until something shifts and he spoils it by getting all serious.

'Are you staying?' he asks.

When I don't say anything he carries on.

'Because I've got used to having you next door. I love seeing Ruby. And Scarlet. Your two girls are growing into two amazing young women.'

'I know. They are amazing.' I take the bottle back off him. Gulp. Wipe my mouth with my sleeve. 'Though they do have their moments.'

And oh, what moments.

'I've got used to seeing you too,' he says. 'You don't seem to hate me quite so much now.'

'I'm not sure I ever managed to hate you. Despised, maybe. Loathed. Really, really didn't like.'

'All right. I take your point. Your very well-made point.'

And then, to shut him up, I kiss him. A full-blown snog, and I try to let it feel nice. I try to go with it. But it just feels wrong. He knows it too. We lie back, side by side, hand in hand, as the sun slips down behind the hill.

Autumn

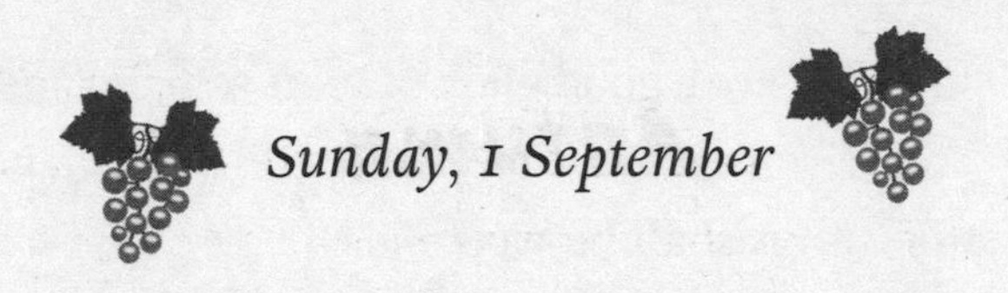

Sunday, 1 September

THE DOG DAYS of summer are moving into the next season. The blackthorn blossom has been replaced with sloes. And the grapes are almost ready to be picked. We've been nearly a year at Home Farm.

Rob was supposed to be back by now so that we could have a family meeting. Decide on our future. But things don't always turn out the way you plan. Sometimes you have to throw your life up in the air and see which way the wind blows.

When I get low, I think of Melina's words to me as she left with Tomasz to go on their honeymoon. 'Don't be sad, Chrissie. Remember to enjoy each day and every moment.' Then she smiled a smile that lit up her face in a way I'd never seen, and I so wanted to smile like that.

And now, as I wait in the vineyard, looking down the valley towards the sea, I wait for Rob to come back. And I don't quite know how I will feel until I see him in the flesh. And that's all right. I don't have to know everything. I can go with the flow. I've finally learnt to stop worrying about the destination and to enjoy the journey.

As long as I have a good glass of wine to hand and my family and friends around me, all shall be well, and all manner of things shall be well.